PRAISE FOR LIZ TOLSMA

"Liz Tolsma has done it again. Following [...] *Bonnet* and *The Green Dress*, *The Gold Digg[...]* will keep you turning pages and staying up late. With characters that you'll love and love to hate, Tolsma keeps you guessing until the very end. A can't-miss read!"

–Jennifer Crosswhite, author of the Hometown Heroes series,
The Route Home series, and *Eat the Elephant:
How to Write (and Finish!) Your Novel One Bite at a Time*

"Liz Tolsma's novel is a delicious combination of mystery and romance, with a rich historical setting and fascinating details. The twists kept me turning the pages well into the night, a series of exciting surprises revealing themselves at every turn. It's the kind of story that will linger in my mind for a good long while."

–Dana Mentink, *Publisher's Weekly* bestselling author

"I'm always up for a true crime read. . . . It's difficult to believe such villainous stories grace our history books, and Tolsma does a wonderful job in bringing them to fictional form."

–Jaime Jo Wright, author of *Echoes among the Stones* and
Christy-Award winning, *The House on Foster Hill*

the

GOLD
DIGGER

LIZ TOLSMA

BARBOUR BOOKS
An Imprint of Barbour Publishing, Inc.

© 2020 by Liz Tolsma

Print ISBN 978-1-64352-712-3

eBook Editions:
Adobe Digital Edition (.epub) 978-1-64352-714-7
Kindle and MobiPocket Edition (.prc) 978-1-64352-713-0

All scripture quotations are taken from the King James Version of the Bible.

Cover Photograph: © Drunaa / Trevillion Images

Published by Barbour Books, an imprint of Barbour Publishing, Inc., 1810 Barbour Drive, Uhrichsville, Ohio 44683, www.barbourbooks.com

Our mission is to inspire the world with the life-changing message of the Bible.

Member of the
Evangelical Christian
Publishers Association

Printed in the United States of America.

Dedication

*To my niece, Rebecca, a talented author in her own right.
Keep working hard and striving for the stars.
Dreams do come true. I love you!*

Chapter One

Where are you taking me?" Ingrid Storset held tight to her sister Belle's hand. If only Belle hadn't made her put on this ridiculous blindfold. By the noise of the people around her, the clomp of the sidewalk under her shoes, and the yeasty odor of bread from the bakery, it was obvious they were somewhere in the middle of town.

Behind her, Belle's two daughters, Myrtle and Lucy, chatted and giggled the way eleven- and nine-year-olds do. Phillip most likely ran ahead of the group, a typical five-year-old boy. Jennie, Belle's foster daughter, had stayed home today. Almost a grown woman, she likely wanted to steal a little time with Emil, the farmhand and her beau.

"You're going to love this." Judging by where Lucy's voice came from, sometimes ahead of Ingrid and sometimes behind, she must be skipping around. So like her.

"Yeah, you're going to be shocked."

Ingrid chuckled at Myrtle's pronouncement. "I'm glad you are learning new Norwegian words. English is very hard for me to speak." Though she had been in the country for five years, since she was just eighteen, Ingrid struggled from time to time with the strange new language.

"Mostly I speak English, but right now, I want you to know what is happening. Because it's a huge, huge surprise." Myrtle grasped Ingrid's other hand.

"I can't wait until I can find out what it is."

"Now, now. You must be patient." Belle pulled Ingrid along. "Soon you will see why I am making this such a surprise. I'm very excited to show you. We're almost there."

They continued to weave around what Ingrid assumed was the crowd, sweet perfume and musky cologne filling the air, until Belle pulled her to a halt. Myrtle squeezed her hand.

"Are you ready?" Even her usually somber sister's voice held more cheer.

"More than ready." Ingrid couldn't help but raise herself on her tiptoes.

Belle fiddled with the knot on the blindfold, pulling at Ingrid's Gibson Girl hairstyle as she did so. If her sister was going to mess up her coif, this had better be worth it. She sucked in a breath and held it.

"All right, children, on the count of three. One. Two. Three." Belle yanked away the blindfold, and Ingrid blinked in the bright light.

She stood in front of an empty brick building, the glass of the storefront window rather dirty, the blue paint on the door peeling. What could this be? How was this a surprise? She passed this place almost every week when she came into town from Belle's farm to shop. "I don't understand." With a furrowed brow, she turned to her sister.

"This is for you, silly." Belle's work-worn face almost glowed. "Your dream."

Lucy danced around Ingrid. "Mama said that ever since you were little, you loved sweets. Now you can have your own shop and sell as many candies as you want. I love the treats you make us."

A little while went by before Lucy's words sank into Ingrid's brain. "This building is mine?"

Belle nodded. "All yours. Actually, I own it, but here is where I want you to start your business. You can pay rent once you are up and running. I saved to buy this for you, and I know you've been hoarding your money, so you should be able to purchase the equipment you need to get started. If you don't follow your dream now, you'll never achieve it."

Ingrid opened her mouth, but the words that hung on the end of her tongue refused to come out. What did you say when given such a spectacular gift? A gift you weren't sure you wanted? Yes, she loved to concoct delicious treats and candies, but owning a shop would mean she would have to interact with the public.

Just the thought of having to do so sent a tingle to her hands. Her mouth went dry at the idea of speaking to people. Strangers. How would she ever do it?

A confectionary was Belle's dream, one she had already had in Chicago. The shop had burned down not long before Belle's first husband died, and she relocated to LaPorte.

What took Ingrid's breath away was photography. Since she had come to the States, she had been taking pictures, hoping to get one published in a magazine or a newspaper. So far, no luck, but maybe someday.

She glanced at her sister, a smile wreathing her face like Ingrid hadn't seen in many years. She couldn't disappoint the one family member she had in this country. The one who had been so generous and had taken her in when she'd arrived on these shores. For Belle's sake, for Belle's happiness, she couldn't reject the gift.

"I. . .I. . . Oh, Belle." She wrapped her sister in a tight embrace, a few tears dripping down her cheeks, some from joy, most from sheer terror. "This is the most wonderful, most amazing, most. . . Thank you. There aren't enough words, in either Norwegian or English."

"Sweet sister, you don't have to thank me. I'm happy to do this for you."

"Who would have imagined, when we were growing up in Norway, so poor, so many of us, that we would be standing here today. You have your farm, and now I have my own shop. It's almost too much to take in."

It *was* too much to take in.

From her pocket, Belle produced an iron key and handed it to Ingrid. "Go inside and check it out."

"I'll go, I'll go." Lucy grabbed the key from Ingrid and sprinted to the door.

"Let Auntie Ingrid open it for the first time. It is hers, after all."

Lucy stuck out her lower lip but handed over the key.

Ingrid kissed the top of her head. "Thank you. Next time, you may unlock it."

"Promise?"

"I promise." Ingrid slid the key into the lock and turned it. With a bit of a push, the door gave way, a little bell tinkling, announcing their arrival.

Glass display cases lined two walls. Both were filthy and in need of a thorough scrubbing.

Belle sidled up beside Ingrid. "This is what I imagine. In the case to your right, you can place your chocolate confections. All kinds of them—raspberry and nut and chocolate. In the one straight ahead, you can have Norwegian treats such as mandelstang." The stick of fondant covered in chocolate and crushed almonds was one of Belle's favorite treats.

She squeezed Ingrid's shoulders in a side hug. "There's a basement too, if you want to work on your photography. I can't have you using mine like you have been."

Now a genuine smile lifted Ingrid's lips. "Really? A place of my own to have my darkroom?" This arrangement might work after all.

Belle flipped on a switch, and light flooded the room.

Ingrid clapped her hands. "It has electricity."

"For when you work late at night. Your customers will be pleased."

Customers. Speaking to a stranger in Norwegian already sent her stomach into spasms. How much more when she had to speak to people here in English?

"This is so generous of you. With you busy on the farm, for you to take the time to help me get open is amazing. But are you sure? You'll lose my help watching the children, cleaning the house, and doing the chores. I don't want you to be shorthanded without me."

"Jennie is old enough to do some work, and so are the other girls. Not to mention this will help you overcome your shyness. It's one of your worst attributes." Belle frowned and shook her head, a few wisps of brown hair escaping their pins. "Besides, I'll soon have plenty of assistance. I got an answer to one of my advertisements."

Ingrid sighed. "Not another gentleman coming to try to make a match with you. I've lost count of how many there have been. Why don't you wait until God sends you the right person at the right time?"

"Because this man sounds delightful. Very responsible. He's arriving from Detroit where he was employed by his brother in an automobile dealership. I'm sure it's going to work out this time. I'm positive he's the right fit for our family and that he won't decide to return home or move west." A slight glimmer lit Belle's green eyes.

"For your sake, I hope you're right. I'll pray that this will be the time you find love and happiness." Though she said the words to encourage

Belle, the chances of her making a match were slim. Maybe as many as a dozen men or more had arrived at the farm to marry Belle. With her height and generous build, she could be intimidating. Perhaps that was why all of the prospective husbands so far had decided within a day or two to hightail it home or move on to other ventures.

If only Ingrid could convince Belle to stop placing these lovelorn ads. Some men were quite unsavory characters. Once Ingrid moved to town, Belle would be alone on the farm with the children. Given that situation, there was no telling what some men might do.

Detroit, Michigan
Tuesday, October 22, 1907

"Have you gone loony?" Nils Lindherud stared at his younger brother.

"What?" Sven shrugged his narrow shoulders, his light hair not quite tamed. "You're watching me as if I've grown horns from my head."

"You might as well have. I can't believe you're entertaining this ridiculous proposition for more than a second."

The door to Nils's Ford motorcar dealership swung open with a creak, and a man entered, crushing his dark hat between his hands.

"Looks like you have a customer," Sven all but crowed, his deep blue eyes sparkling.

Nils leaned closer and hissed at his brother, "Don't think this is over. Not for a minute. As soon as I'm finished with him, we will pick up where we left off." Pasting a smile on his face, he strode toward the gentleman, the sweet odor of leather and rubber filling the showroom. "Good afternoon, sir. How can I help you?"

Half an hour later, after he had sold a Model A, he returned to the back room, where Sven reclined in the chair with his large feet on the desk, a pile of money beside them. "I take it you made a sale?"

Nils raised and lowered his eyebrows.

"You always do. The good boy who works hard and takes care of everyone. You can do no wrong."

"Where is this coming from? With Papa's troubles, someone had to step in and keep the family from becoming destitute. I do what I have to do." Maybe a little more than he had to, but that wasn't anything Sven needed to know. He didn't need to know about the debt Nils had gotten himself into when he'd purchased the dealership. And he didn't need to know how Mr. Gillespie was pressuring him to repay it. Sooner rather than later.

"Well, I can't live in your shadow any longer." Sven swung his legs around and came to his feet. "This dealership was born out of your obsession with autos and your belief that they are the way of the future. This is not my dream."

"It may not be, but this dealership is providing for us and for Mama. Do you think taking a thousand dollars to a woman you don't know and marrying her is smart?"

Sven leaned over the desk. "Maybe it's smarter than you think. Maybe I want a home and a family, a simple life on a farm, a passel of children. Not this compulsion you have to make money, to provide, to be everyone's savior. You aren't, you know. You never will be. For crying out loud, I know the dealership is up to its neck in debt."

Nils gasped. "How did you find out?" He had covered his tracks so well. Perhaps, though, not well enough.

"Give me some credit. I can do figures."

"Then where did you get that?" Nils eyed the cash standing like a mountain between them on the table.

"Never you mind. You have your sources. I have mine."

"You didn't go to—"

"I'm taking it with me to help pay off the mortgage on the soon-to-be Mrs. Lindherud's farm. As part owner of a prosperous business, I'll be able to help out. I'm a grown man. I can make my own decisions. Don't you think it's time I lived my own life? Face it, we need the money. I can help you provide for Mama. If nothing else, I'll be one less mouth you have to feed."

"I've never thought of you as a burden."

"You haven't?"

Nils blew out a breath. Maybe sometimes he had, just a little bit. Sven had never been the most motivated to work. Without Papa here, though, someone had to think about keeping food on the table.

In the end, Sven was entitled to follow his dreams. Nils had never forced him to come into employ with him. It just made sense for them to work together, to keep the business in the family.

But this. This was nothing more than insanity. There were other, better ways to strike out in the world. Better ways to make money. Like staying put. And if Sven had put himself into debt the way Nils had, it might lead to disaster. "Does Mama know what you're about to do?"

"She knows I'm going to Indiana to get married. When I told her, she was very happy, said it was time one of her sons settled down and gave her grandchildren. I told her she would have four." Sven's eyes softened. "She was thrilled. You know how important family is to her. Now it's going to grow. Besides, LaPorte isn't so far away that she can't come visit or that we can't come here."

"But you didn't tell her about the money."

"No."

"Because you knew what she would say."

"Because I knew her reaction would be the same as yours. Neither of you see me as a man. I'm going to prove both of you wrong."

"Fine." Nils couldn't convince Sven otherwise. Trying any more would be as useless as shouting into the wind. "You're on your own. If things go wrong, don't come crawling back thinking I'm going to bail you out. That isn't going to happen. I came to your rescue when Miss White caught you putting a snake in Landon Higelman's desk. I stood up for you when Sammy Banks pushed you into the river for bad-mouthing his sister. Not this time. If this is a scam, then it's up to you to dig yourself out of the mess you've created. Do you understand?"

"Perfectly." Sven scooped up the cash, spun on his heel, and marched out the door, slamming it so hard the papers on Nils's desk floated on the resulting breeze.

Nils thumped into his chair, resting his elbows on the desktop. Sven had always been the stubborn one. Papa had said that all the time, and it was as true as the sky was blue. Trouble was, Nils didn't know what to do about it. He wasn't Sven's father. When Sven got an idea in his head, there was little to no talking him out of it. He was too much like Papa for his own good.

With a sigh, Nils picked up his pen, dipped it in the inkwell, and finished the paperwork for the day. Though it was a mite early, he flipped the sign on the door to CLOSED, turned the lock, and headed for home. Perhaps Sven had had some time to cool down, and now they would be able to have a calmer, more rational discussion.

Nils traversed Woodward Avenue and made his way home, strolling by the Greek Revival city hall and the Soldiers and Sailors Monument, the octagonal marble monolith topped by a bronze statue of an Indian queen. At least when life changed, these landmarks remained the same.

Though he prayed for a good talk with Sven, in his heart he was aware there would be no discussion, no rationalizing with him. No matter what Nils said or did, no matter what Mama said or did, he was determined to leave and chase this crazy dream of getting married and running his own hog farm.

He probably didn't know one end of a pig from the other. He probably didn't realize how hard farmwork was. He probably didn't realize hog farmers never got rich.

Before Nils even reached the front door of his home just off Woodward Avenue, it flew open, and Mama scurried onto the porch. "Your brother is gone."

Nils stared at the heavens. No help was forthcoming. "I had a feeling he would do this. Part of me hoped he would wait until I got home so I could have one more attempt at talking him out of this wild idea."

"No wonder he wanted to leave as soon as possible. What did you say to him?"

Nils approached his mother and pecked her on her still-smooth cheek. "Everything I could think of to make him stay. You know how headstrong he is. He wasn't about to listen."

Mama twisted her neat white apron in her hands. "Of course you're right. He was bound and determined to go marry that woman. We can only hope and pray she is a fine Christian lady and that their marriage will be successful, that Sven will be a good father to those four children. And that he will have the good sense not to drive all that distance tonight."

So, his brother hadn't told Mama about the money. No point in it now. It would only upset her more.

Heaven help Sven. No one else could.

Chapter Two

Wednesday,
October 23, 1907

Ingrid removed the almost-empty tray of chocolate truffles from the glass display case and rearranged the half dozen or so remaining sweets to make it appear almost full. These would have to last the rest of the day as she wasn't prepared to make another batch with the shop closing in only an hour or so. Once she replaced the tray, she picked up her towel and wiped the prints of a dozen or more little children from the glass. They all had gone home with a treat, regardless of their ability to pay.

The children, she could talk to. What a joy when they spilled through the door. The problem came when an adult wanted to make a purchase. With this being her first day in business, a good number of townspeople had stopped in to check out the new confectionary.

She was exhausted. A little something to eat and a hot bath, and she would be ready for bed. No time to get into her basement darkroom and work on photographs. No time to escape this madness.

Since business was winding down for the day, she turned to the kitchen to finish washing the dishes and start preparing for tomorrow. No sooner had she turned her back than the little bell above the door jingled. She swung around and tipped her head to the newcomer. A man. Her hands shook, and her heart raced. "G–g–good afternoon."

"Good afternoon." Even those couple of words he spoke gave away his Norwegian heritage.

"You speak Norwegian?" She could speak English enough to get by, but her native tongue was so much easier. She didn't stutter when she spoke it.

"I do." He answered in Norwegian. As the corners of his mouth turned up, the ends of his dark blond mustache rose too. "I'm Sven Lindherud."

"Ingrid Storset. I own this place. Well, I mean, my sister does, but

16

I. . ." Oh, goodness, this was why she should never open her mouth.

"It's nice to meet you. I'm new in town."

"Oh?" She sounded dumber than a stick.

"Yes. I've come in answer to, well, you might think it strange, but to an ad in the lovelorn section of the newspaper."

Ingrid chuckled, and the man's face reddened.

"I knew you would find it odd. Maybe even a little crazy. Everyone else I've told, even my own family, thinks it bizarre."

She sobered right away. "Oh no, I wasn't laughing at you." Now heat rose in her own cheeks. "You've come to meet my sister, Belle Gunness. Right?"

"Well, yes."

"I only hope you have good luck with her."

"Why?"

"There were others. They all left." Why was she telling him this? All she wanted was to close the shop for the day.

"Left? Why? Is your sister not—"

"She is rather tall and big-boned. But she is dear and sweet and has a good heart. I don't know why no one has stayed."

"I'm not easily put off, ma'am."

"Miss."

"Miss, then. I'm a hard worker, and I like children. And I believe that if God looks not to man's outward appearance but to the heart, then so should I."

Ingrid nodded. "That's a good attitude." She had just read this morning about God being a father to the fatherless. While that may be true, Belle's children needed an earthly father. Silence stretched between them, long and uncomfortable. She wiped an imaginary fingerprint from the case.

"Before I complete my journey, I would like to bring a small gift with me. It seems I've come to the right place, as you'll know just what confections your sister likes."

Of course. What kind of business owner was she if she couldn't speak well enough to make a sale? "I do. How much would you like to spend?"

He quoted her an amount, and she filled a white paper bag with all of Belle's favorites. Truffles and chocolates and a few mandelstang. Once he had paid, she handed the bag to him. "Good luck."

"Thank you. I hope to see you soon." With that, he exited.

Ingrid slumped over the counter. No matter what people said behind Belle's back about her size and her sometimes off-putting demeanor, she deserved happiness. She had worked hard to come as far as she had since arriving on these golden shores. Since the death of her second husband a few years ago, she needed love and stability in her life. Some help raising the children. Another pair of hands to work the land.

"Just what are you grinning about?"

At Ray Lamphere's deep, rough voice, Ingrid startled. "I—I—I'm sorry. I—I—I didn't hear you come in."

"Dreaming about that man who just left?" He spit a stream of tobacco onto her floor.

"P—p—please don't do that. I have to clean the mess."

"Is he your beau, or another intended for your sister?" Belle's former farmhand stared at her, his brown eyes narrow and hard, until she squirmed.

"What business is it of yours?"

"An awful lot of men coming and going from that place. Doesn't it make you curious?"

"Only I wonder why no one wants to marry my sister."

"Why might that be?"

"They are stupid." She wasn't going to stand here and have this conversation with Ray, even if she did know him from the months he had worked on Belle's farm. She spun on her heel and scurried to the kitchen, praying he wouldn't slip behind the counter and follow her.

As she stood at the sink, she held her breath. No footsteps sounded behind her. Good.

"You tell your sister I said hi." Ray's shout would scare away any potential customers she had.

"G—g—good day." She had no intention of informing Belle that Ray had put in an appearance. Belle had fired him some weeks ago, but he continued to hang around, and that was a constant source of distress to Belle. With all she had to worry about, Ray didn't need to be another problem.

Especially when it appeared that Belle had a good chance at finding love again. Sven just might be the answer to all of Belle's problems.

"You let me know if Belle has any troubles with that new suitor."

Ray hadn't left? No, the bell above the door hadn't jingled. "She won't."

"She knows I'll take care of her, no matter what. You be sure to remind her of that. If that guy pesters her, I'll be sure he leaves her alone. Got that?"

Now the bell above the door did ring.

A shiver coursed through Ingrid's body.

Thursday, October 24, 1907

"Auntie Ingrid, you're here, you're here!" Lucy hopped first on her left foot and then on her right as Ingrid ambled up the path that led from McClung Road to the front of Belle's farmhouse. A small porch greeted visitors to the narrow but long brick structure, its many windows glistening in the late-fall afternoon sunlight.

"Of course I am. It's Thursday night. Remember that I said now that I live in town, I will come for dinner on Thursday nights."

"I know." The big white bow in Lucy's hair bounced along with her. "That's what makes Thursday the bestest day of the week."

"You are a goose."

Lucy hugged Ingrid's waist, then danced and twirled away, her skirt billowing around her. "I know. Mama calls me that all the time."

"Where are the others?"

"Myrtle is in the kitchen finishing dinner. Jennie is in the dining room setting the table. They like to do that. I don't."

"Someday, when you're all grown up, you'll have to."

"Yuck." Lucy wrinkled her button nose. "I'll never grow up."

With laughter bubbling in her chest, Ingrid swept into the house, Lucy trailing her. Ingrid had to agree. Thursday was the bestest day of the week, because she got to enjoy the time with her family. After spending all day with strangers or people she didn't know well, having to speak English to most of them, coming here was like slipping on a pair of cozy socks. Comfortable and familiar.

"Ingrid, you've finally arrived. I thought we would have to have dinner without you. From what I hear, you've already met our guest." From her position over a pot at the stove, Belle nodded in the direction of the man sitting at the small kitchen table.

"Hello." Ingrid flashed him a small smile. "Has it been a good visit?"

"I'm enjoying it here very much. Your sister introduced me to much of the town, and this dinner smells divine. If it tastes half as good, I shall be very happy. Thank you, by the way, for the suggestions on the sweets."

"Yes, Ingrid." Belle stirred whatever bubbled in the pot. "They were just what I was craving. You do know me well."

Belle was considerably older than Ingrid and had left home when she was quite young. Once Ingrid had come to America, she cherished getting to know her big sister, and they had formed a tight familial bond. "I thought you would enjoy them. I'm glad they helped Sven make a favorable impression on you."

Jennie entered from the dining room. "We liked them too." She flashed a mischievous grin.

"I'm sure you did."

But then Emil Greening, the farmhand, strode through the door, and Jennie's smile was all for him.

"Mr. Lindherud has an automobile." Myrtle's green eyes sparkled. "Did you see it outside, Auntie Ingrid?"

"I did." How could she not spy the beautiful midnight-blue motor-car? That automobile was certainly big enough for a family. Perhaps they all could go for a ride. Though the request tingled the edge of her tongue, she couldn't bring herself to ask it of him. Instead, she studied the tips of her black boots sticking out from underneath her deep maroon skirt.

"And he can juggle." Phillip danced in a circle around her. "Did you know that, Auntie Ingrid?"

"I did not."

"Show her how you do it." Phillip leaned closer to Ingrid. "He's going to teach me."

"Not now." Belle cut off the performance before it had a chance to begin. "Dinner is ready. Lucy, Phillip, stop prancing about and go to the table. Ingrid, help me set the food out."

After prayers, everyone tucked into the fried beefsteak and mashed potatoes. Mr. Lindherud complimented Belle over and over again on her cooking. The chatter was pleasant, and they shared more than a few laughs over the meal. Even Ingrid said a few words. If Belle hadn't spoken for the newcomer, he might have turned Ingrid's head.

Jennie, however, could only stare at Emil. Despite the farmhand's presence, Jennie was quieter than normal.

Once finished, they all pushed away from the table. Mr. Lindherud came to his feet. "Now, who is going to beat me at checkers?"

Both of the younger girls squealed that they would have the pleasure and ran to the parlor to set up the game. Emil joined them. Ingrid and Jennie carried the plates to the sink to help Belle clean up. "So, what do you think of him so far?" Ingrid grabbed a dish towel. "He seems nice enough, doesn't he, and he was thoughtful in bringing you those sweets."

"I suppose." Belle plunged her chapped, cracked hands into the water. "I don't think he's going to last, though."

"What do you mean?"

"I can tell he doesn't like it here. In the next few days, he'll move on. Mark my words."

Jennie rubbed the plate she was drying with extra vigor, her gaze never leaving her mother.

Ingrid rubbed her sister's shoulder. "I know you've been disappointed so many times before that you want to protect your heart. But don't lose hope. I disagree. He appears to be enjoying his stay immensely." Giggling erupted from the parlor. "See how good he is with the girls? They adore him already. To me, he doesn't seem to be the type of man who is going to go back on his word. I believe he's here for good."

"You always see the sunny side of life." Belle scrubbed at a plate, ran it through the rinse water, and handed it to Ingrid to dry. "I refuse to get my hopes up, only to have them crushed again. You'd better learn to do that yourself, before you suffer a world of hurt. Life isn't kind. It's a cruel taskmaster. We work and work, only to lose everything we have."

"I like him." Jennie's voice was soft.

Ingrid nodded. "I can't believe you would be so negative on a night like tonight. I hope you can see Mr. Lindherud in the same light as I do. He would be good for all of you."

Perhaps Ingrid had at last uncovered the reason why every man who came to the farm with the intention of marrying Belle was gone within a day or two. If she was this negative with them, they wouldn't want to stay. "If you were a little nicer, if you paid him some attention and smiled at him, he might be more motivated to stay."

"You want me to flirt? At my age?" Belle held the knife in her hand just above the water.

Ingrid placed the plate on the open shelf above her. "You aren't that old. And I don't know if I would call it flirting. Just showing him your kind, cheerful disposition might do wonders. Don't be afraid to open yourself to him."

"Fine advice coming from a woman who has never been married. One who can barely talk to men."

Ingrid sucked in her breath. What had Belle in such a mood tonight?

"I've endured the loss of two husbands and two children. My home and my business in Chicago burned to the ground. I'm sorry if I'm realistic. Mark my words. Come morning, Mr. Lindherud will no longer be here."

Chapter Three

The late-night dampness seeped through Ray Lamphere's brown woolen coat, sending shivers up and down his spine. He huddled in the sweet-smelling pine trees that bordered Belle Gunness's farm. Though he couldn't make out the time on his battered silver watch, it was late. After midnight, at least.

Belle, his Belle. Strong as an ox, and built like one too. My, what a woman. No simpering, swooning females for him. Siree, he liked his women well-built and hardworking. She was the best he'd ever met. And he'd met plenty in his life.

He swigged from his brown paper–wrapped bottle, the fire of the liquor trickling through his veins.

Yet as he watched her, his chest burned. When she had sacked him a few weeks back, she had broken his heart. Hadn't she seen how much he admired her? How hard he worked for her? How he kept that farm afloat for her and her kids?

Instead, she had to place those ridiculous ads in the Norwegian newspapers. He'd read some of them. In them, she made herself sound like a weak woman who needed a man. If she was that desperate, why couldn't she see him standing in front of her? There was no need for her to advertise in the lonely-hearts column. Not when he was here and already loved her.

Then there was the parade of men she brought to the house. Each one in that stream of dandies added more weight to Ray's chest. He clenched the bottle. Every time another one of them showed up, hung his hat on the peg, and put his feet under the table, Ray's temperature rose. Couldn't they see, couldn't she see, that he was the only man for her? He was the one who truly loved her, who would stand by her side through thick and thin.

Belle would drive them up the lane, their trunks thrown in the back of her wagon. She'd bat her eyes at them a couple of times, and they'd fawn all over her. Why, it was enough to send a man's stomach to churning. Their laughter grated on his nerves. He hated each and every one of them.

When one of them showed up, Ray would warn him to watch his step. You never knew what could happen around the farm. Hay bales had a way of falling. Hog butchering knives were large and sharp. One wrong move with one of them could be disastrous. Fires could start and spread in an instant.

Within days, the men would be gone, much to Ray's satisfaction. He made sure they didn't stick around and interfere with his relationship with Belle. No man would come between the two of them.

Not while he had breath in his lungs.

The one who had come the other day arrived in an automobile. Even now, the machine sat glistening in the moonlight. Siree, and it was big too, with not just one row of seats but two. How Ray would love to get his hands on one of those. Perhaps that was why Belle had picked this one. She liked the finer things in life, things like this motorcar, things Ray could never give her.

He leaned against a tree. His favorite one. The one he leaned against many nights, just watching. She would be his. He'd stop the men from coming, and she would realize what she had in him. Just a little more time, and he would make her his forever.

The deep, deep darkness of the dead of night descended over Belle Gunness's farm, the time of night she enjoyed the most. All the earth lay still and quiet. Each of the farmhouse's thirteen windows was dark, including the one in the addition at the back of the place. Stairs led to a separate entrance to the room where Ingrid had stayed. Now she was gone, living above the shop Belle had bought for her. No one stirred. Emil, the hired hand, slumbered in the barn's loft. Even the hogs in the pen slept, snorting as they dreamed.

Though a low, chilly fog hung over the barn and the outbuildings, Belle hadn't grabbed a sweater. Instead, she drew in a deep breath of the cool fall air, relishing the odors of decaying leaves and burning wood. She couldn't hold back the sigh that escaped her lips. Not only her favorite time of night, but her favorite season of the year. A time when the old disappeared to make way for the new in spring. A promise of better things to come.

All her life, it had been about better things to come. Growing up in Norway, poor as the dirt her family attempted to scratch a living from, Mama and Papa had talked about better things to come. When she had arrived in this promised land, it was for the better things to come. Each time she married, each time she advertised in the lovelorn columns, it was for the better things to come.

Had she achieved them? True, she owned this farm, one her second husband, Peter, had wanted. Through stinky, backbreaking work, she'd scratched out a living for herself and her children. She had done the best she could. Here she had a big house. She and the children always wore nice clothes. Though they owned no motorcar—yet. That was just a matter of time. Still, it was a hard life, taking more than it gave.

This was not what she had dreamed of those long, dark winter childhood nights, staring at the stars through her bedroom window. She was meant to be a fine lady with silk dresses, a house with marble floors and paintings on the ceilings, a bevy of servants waiting on her. In her imagination, she was a princess at a ball, the room glittering in the lamplight, her fingers dripping with diamonds, every handsome man in the place with his attention trained on her.

That was what she had been born for.

One of the fattest hogs oinked, struggled to his feet, and lumbered to the trough for a drink.

Not this. This was not what life was supposed to hand her.

Another sigh, for all the good it did. Perhaps life would turn around soon. Perhaps she would achieve the future she was destined for. Then again, she wasn't getting any younger. Now in her forties, she was considered well past her prime. Time had etched away any of the little bit of beauty she had once possessed. Not that it had been much to begin with.

Well, there was no point in standing in ankle-deep mud pining for what might never happen, at least not without some action on her part. She set off to finish her chores. Slopping the hogs. Filling their water troughs. Cleaning up their waste. With arms strengthened by years of farmwork, she was able to make good progress in a short amount of time.

Farmwork was filthy and laborious but necessary. Pulling her shovel behind her, she headed for the pump to wash up. Though she spent a few short hours each night in bed, she liked to be clean before she slipped between the sheets. She worked the handle until clear, cold water ran over her fingers, washing the mud from underneath her short nails. Then she scrubbed her arms where her rolled-up sleeves exposed her white flesh. Finally, she splashed water on her face and rubbed until she was squeaky clean.

There. So much better.

The filth was gone, and she was spotless.

As she turned for the barn, a glint of something caught her eye. There, between the trees that edged the property. What was it? The hair on her arms rose straight up. She rubbed them. Shook her head. Likely nothing more than a coyote or fox, watching her, following her, wondering what she was up to, if she had anything good for them to eat.

She hung her shovel on a hook beside the other implements and leaned against the frame of the open barn door. Another good night's work completed. She had done a fine job. She always did. In the end, though the work was not what she enjoyed, she could rest her head in peace, knowing she had done what she needed to do for her family. To provide for herself and her children.

Once more, she glanced at the dark house. Lucy and Myrtle slept there in the bed they shared, Jennie with them in her own bed. Phillip had his own room. Her children. Everything she had in the world. She and her first husband, Mads, had tried so long and hard for them. What a shame he couldn't be here to watch them grow up.

Well, there was no use in dwelling on what couldn't be changed. He had passed away, and so had Peter, leaving her alone to scrape out a living, to keep them from sinking into the abyss of poverty. She pushed herself to a standing position, and with her boots slurping with each step through the muck, she clomped to the house.

Belle turned and stared in Ray's direction. Almost right into his eyes. As if she knew he was there. Had she spotted him? Making as little noise as possible, he backed farther into the fragrant pine trees, out of her sight. Blast the full moon. Tonight hadn't been the night to come. But he had to, especially once he heard around town about the new arrival at the Gunness farm. Yet another one who needed to be taken care of. Siree, another one who wouldn't be a bother.

She completed washing up, put away her shovel, stood straight and still for a moment, then slipped into the house. No lights lit the windows. An amazing woman, she had this way of moving about in the dark.

Even once she had gone inside, he waited, biding his time, until he could be reasonably sure that Belle was sound asleep in her bed. When he couldn't wait any longer, he carried a burlap bag to the outhouse. The pit was just large enough that, with a good bit of shoving, he managed to get it down. Way down, where no one would ever discover it.

He wiped his hands on his dungarees and blew out a breath. With that nasty job done, he turned and headed for the farm where he now worked, just down the road a piece. With Belle in the house, he didn't bother to keep his footsteps light and quiet. No need anymore. He spat a stream of tobacco and smoothed down his mustache. Once he got to the farm so much like the Gunnesses', he climbed to the barn's hayloft. While nothing fancy, he'd made it as comfortable as possible with a mattress, a trunk, and a parlor chair where he could sit and think. That was all he needed.

He slipped off his boots and plopped onto the mattress.

From outside of the barn, not too far away, came two deep male voices. One of them he recognized as John Wheatbrook, the man who owned the farm. By the way he slurred his words, he was three sheets to the wind. Nothing unusual there. Nothing Ray himself hadn't done a time or plenty.

What caught Ray's attention was what the men were saying.

"Heard Belle Gunness got herself a new beau. Saw them together in church yesterday." That was John.

"Wonder what she does with them. Probably shows them a good time then kicks them in the rear and tells them to hit the road. A strange one she is, at that."

"Never did understand what Peter saw in her. She brought him nothing but trouble. Now he's cold in his grave. Poor sot."

"Better off, I say." The friend barked a laugh. "Who'd want a cow for a wife? Face nothing to talk about, but that body. I shudder just thinking about it."

"Then don't."

Ray rose from his bed and peered through the barn's slats. The shaft of bright moonlight illuminated both men as if an electric bulb hung over their heads. John slapped his friend on the back, and both of them bent over in uproarious laughter.

How dare they say such things about Belle? That woman had never done anything to either one of them. She couldn't help how God had made her. In Ray's eyes, He'd made her just right. John and his friend were nothing more than a couple of drunken fools. If he didn't need this job so much, didn't need to stay near Belle, he'd hotfoot it out of here so fast, there'd be nothing to see but the dust he left behind.

"How's your new hand working out? Didn't he come from the Gunness place?"

"Sure did. Guess he works hard enough. Dunno. We'll see how long I keep him around. Wife says he's slovenly. She likes to use them big words." John stumbled around the yard. He tripped his way to his wife's prized rosebushes and upchucked in them.

Though he'd held himself back so far, Ray couldn't contain himself any longer. He flew down the ladder and raced from the barn, pulling on his boots as he went. "Wheatbrook, what's wrong with you?" he hollered as loud as he could.

John stood and wiped his mouth with the back of his hand. "Keep your voice down. Don't want the wife to hear."

"You drunk or something?" Ray didn't speak any softer.

John's friend clapped him on the back. "I gotta get going. See you later." He beat a path for the road.

John approached Ray. "You watch what you say and how you say it. What I do isn't none of your business. I suggest you go back to sleep. Morning's coming real soon, and those pigs are going to need to be slopped."

Ray didn't cower. "If I was you, I'd watch real careful what I said about Belle Gunness. Might cause you problems if you can't keep your mouth shut."

Chapter Four

Tuesday,
December 10, 1907

Darkness descended over the booming city of Detroit, traffic still heavy on Woodward Avenue, only a small electric bulb illuminating the desk where Nils Lindherud sat in the chilly dealership office attempting to formulate a letter to a woman he had never met.

Dear Mrs. Gunness,

He crossed it out. Goodness, he couldn't even get the beginning correct. She wasn't dear to him.

To Mrs. Gunness,

He crossed this out also, leaving a splotch on the paper and ink on his fingers. With a huff, he crumpled the page and tossed it in the trash can. How had Sven ever done this? Well, he'd have to go with *dear* even though he wasn't fond of the greeting. It was how you began a letter.

Dear Mrs. Gunness,
On October 22, my brother, Sven Lindherud, traveled to LaPorte to
meet you with the intention of uniting with you in marriage.

Nils bit the inside of his cheek. The wording of that sentence, especially the uniting in marriage part, wasn't quite right. He studied it for a minute or two. Sven had been a fool to run off and marry a woman he'd never met. But that was his brother.

Nils dipped his pen in the inkwell, blotted it, and continued.

He told us he would write and inform my mother and me of his safe arrival. We never received such a missive. Since that time, now six weeks ago, we have written to him multiple times a week without an answer. Did he arrive at your farm? Is he well? Any information you can give us about Sven would be much appreciated. I've enclosed a self-addressed stamped envelope for your convenience. Please write at your earliest opportunity and put our minds at rest.

Sincerely,
Nils Lindherud

Only the ticking of the schoolhouse clock on the wall behind Nils broke the silence as he read and reread the letter. Well, it said what he needed it to say. Perhaps Mrs. Gunness would be able to talk Sven into replying, at least with a line to let Mama and him know he was well.

All this worrying over her younger son wasn't good for Mama's heart. These days, she was wan and listless, saying little and eating less. She couldn't go on much longer without word of her son's whereabouts.

Then again, Sven might be sore enough from their last encounter to refuse to answer. That would be his way of punishing Nils for acting like the big brother and telling him what to do. True, he never should have told Sven not to come crawling back home if he got into trouble. Nils pounded his fist on the desk.

A soft knock sounded on his office door, and Mama peeked in. "Supper was ready over an hour ago. I kept it warm for a while then decided to bring it to you." She entered and set a napkin-covered basket on top of a pile of papers. Her breathing was labored. "You work too hard, you know. I wish you would slow down."

"You shouldn't have gone to all the trouble. It's too much for you." He rose and pulled out a chair for her, motioning for her to sit. "If we want to have food on the table and a roof over our heads, I have to make this automobile dealership a success. I promised to take care of you, and I will."

"You are doing a fine job, but not at the expense of your health or of having a family of your own someday."

"I have Princess." He rubbed the top of his King Charles spaniel's head.

"That's not the same." Mama tugged the napkin off the basket and pulled out roast chicken, the odor of garlic wafting from it.

"I've written a letter to the woman Sven was supposed to meet. Perhaps she'll be able to tell us something about him that he's unwilling or unable to share with us."

"Don't be too hard on him. He wanted to go and make his own way in the world. Working with automobiles was your dream, not his."

"Funny. He said almost the exact same words."

"Then you are forced to agree with us."

"But to marry a woman he didn't know? That's ludicrous. Insane. Marriage is a sacred institution, not a business proposition you run into headlong."

"What could we do?" A sheen of tears covered Mama's sea-blue eyes. "He's an adult. We couldn't keep him prisoner. God will watch over him. Most likely, he's enjoying being married, getting to know his wife and stepchildren, and working hard on the farm. You must imagine that with only a woman running it all these years, it must be terribly neglected. Don't fret so. Now, even though I brought you supper, I insist you come home and eat it."

She returned the chicken to the basket and covered it again. "I'll brew a strong cup of coffee for you. If you didn't drink it so late at night, perhaps you wouldn't have such insomnia. But I know you enjoy a good cup."

Nils folded the letter and slipped it into the envelope. For Mama, to ease her anxiety, he would go home. "Fine. I suppose whatever I have to finish here today will wait for tomorrow. I would, however, like to find a mailbox and get this letter on the way as soon as possible. I hear you pacing the floors at night."

"Don't you worry about me. You have enough to deal with." She patted his hand and, with a great deal of effort, came to her feet. "By the time you arrive, I'll have supper set out and waiting." She grabbed the basket and exited.

In no uncertain terms, she had told him he shouldn't dillydally.

Once he had straightened his papers, he shrugged into his camel-colored wool coat, called for Princess, and stepped into the brisk December wind, clutching the letter in his hand. Head down, they plowed forward until they reached the gray, cast-iron mailbox. As he opened the chute, it creaked. Nils deposited the letter and allowed the box to slam shut.

A gust of wind tore at his coat, and a damp page of a newspaper wrapped itself around his leg. "What's this, Princess?"

The dog stared at him with her big brown eyes.

He bent to untangle himself and discovered the paper was written in Norwegian. The language they spoke at home, one he was very familiar with. This was the classified section. One bold headline caught his attention.

Missing Son
Last seen on April 5, 1907, headed to LaPorte, Indiana,
and the farm of one Mrs. Belle Gunness. Ole Budsburg is 50,
light brown hair, green eyes, scar above his lip, walks with
a slight limp. If you have information on his whereabouts,
please reply to general delivery in Iola, Wisconsin.

As he got to the end, Nils sucked in his breath. Another man who went to meet Belle Gunness. Another man who hadn't been heard from. This one since April, poor family. Nils wrapped his coat tighter around himself, folded the newspaper page, and stuffed it into his pocket.

What was going on here? More importantly, what had happened to his brother?

Nils lugged his battered suitcase up the steep basement stairs and through the kitchen. He had to leave as soon as possible. Sven was in trouble. Though he didn't have any proof, his gut told him his brother needed him. And even though he had warned Sven not to come crawling home for help, Nils had only spewed that out of anger and frustration. He loved Sven more than anything. He would go to the ends of the earth to make sure he wasn't in any trouble or danger.

As Nils dragged the luggage through the kitchen, Mama stood with her arms akimbo. "What on earth are you doing now? Come, sit. I have your dinner ready. It won't be any good if I have to heat it up a second time."

"I'm sorry, Mama, but I can't. I have to leave. Now. Drive to LaPorte and get there as soon as possible."

She furrowed her already-wrinkled brow. "LaPorte? Did something happen between the time I left you and now?"

He couldn't—wouldn't—tell her about the newspaper advertisement he'd found. That would only cause her more worry and put more strain on her heart. At this point, he didn't know anything and couldn't explain to her why he had this strong urge to travel there and find out what his brother was up to. "I just got to thinking about Sven. I don't want to wait for an answer from that woman. She may never respond. It will be a short trip, I promise. You'll hardly miss me before I'm back with news of him."

A little of the stiffness in her shoulders eased. "What about your dealership?"

He stopped short, the suitcase thumping to the floor as he dropped it. His livelihood. His means of supporting his mother. What had gotten him into this huge hole of debt. Which mattered more—his brother or his business? It was a scale that wouldn't quite balance. On the one hand, a family member might be in need. On the other, they had to pay the mortgage on the house and the debt on the dealership. If he wasn't there to run things, Mama might end up hungry and homeless.

William, the young man he'd hired after Sven left, was fine. He just didn't have the knack for sales that Nils or even Sven had. He could handle the finances without a problem, but how many automobiles would he sell? Nils's stomach twisted into a knot.

Right now, Sven had to be his priority. "It will just be for a few days. We'll be fine." He couldn't afford much more than that. This was nothing more than a misunderstanding anyway. He would get there, catch a few hours of sleep, and then go to Mrs. Gunness's farm and give Sven a good calling out for worrying him and Mama so.

"This is why you should have hired more help. Then you could leave when you needed to without closing the doors."

"I won't close the doors. I have William." She didn't know that he couldn't afford to hire anyone other than this inexperienced young man. Now he had no time to bring on and train anyone else. He had to leave tonight, before Sven became another name in the classifieds. "I promise, I will always take care of you. I'll be back in a couple of days. I'm sure Sven is fine."

Mama twisted the corner of her blue-checked apron around her finger. She was as worried as he was. Neither of them could voice it.

He kissed her on the cheek, inhaling the sweet odor of cinnamon, onions, and roses that surrounded her. The scents of home. Whenever he thought of her, that's what came to mind. No one else smelled like her. "It's just like him to go off on an adventure and not think of us. He gets so wrapped up in what he's doing that everything else fades into the background. You know he's always been this way. I'm sure he's been meaning to write to us, but something else crops up and the letter never gets written. I'll go and give him a good scolding."

"Don't be too harsh on him."

Nils squeezed Mama before releasing her. "You know I won't. Now I really have to hurry. As it is, it will be a long ride in the dark."

"I do wish you would wait until morning. I hate the thought of you out there driving in that contraption on those lonely country roads."

"I love you, Mama, but I'm a grown man. If I work with these automobiles all day long, I think I can drive to LaPorte without trouble."

"I don't want both of my boys gone." She whispered the words.

She had lost so much in her life. *God, don't let Sven become another one of those losses. I'm not sure she could stand it. Then again, if You had stopped Sven from leaving, we wouldn't be in this boat.*

If God hadn't stopped him, Nils should have.

"You have nothing to fret about. Just a little trip. Now I really must pack. As you pointed out, it's getting later and later."

She pulled out the kitchen chair and pointed for him to sit at the table. "You aren't leaving this house without a proper dinner. That's my condition."

"Oh, Mama. You always know how to keep your sons in line."

"I have no other choice."

"Don't ever change."

"Why would I?" She set the dinner in front of him, the aroma of pungent garlic and rosemary wafting to him, sending his stomach rumbling and his mouth watering. No longer could he resist the temptation. He dove into the meal with a great deal of relish, cleaning his plate in record time.

Once he had his mother satisfied, he dragged the suitcase upstairs, filled it with enough clothes for several days, and latched it shut. Before exiting, he gazed at his brother's bed one last time. They had shared this room for many years. Laughed long into the night. Pulled silly pranks on each other. Wrestled on the floor. Everything brothers did.

What if he was truly missing, like the man from the ad? Nils pulled the newspaper page from his pocket and unfolded it. Ole Budsburg. That was the man's name. Ole Budsburg. Nils ingrained it in his brain. Perhaps when he went and spoke to his brother, he could find out what happened to Ole. From the looks of it, he had family waiting on word from him too.

Once packed and outside, Nils hefted the suitcase onto the back of his Ford Model R Runabout and strapped it down. Mama stood beside him, the wind whipping at her skirts. "Drive safely, you hear?"

"Yes, ma'am." He saluted her.

"No need to get sassy with me. You be careful. And find your brother. Please."

The pleading in her voice tore at his heart. For her sake, for her peace of mind, he had to discover where Sven was and what he was up to.

After several cranks, the engine rumbled to life. Nils lit the oil lamps, kissed Mama, whistled for Princess, who jumped inside, and the two of them tore off. For Sven, for Mama, for Ole and his family, he would uncover this mystery in LaPorte.

Chapter Five

Wednesday,
December 11, 1907

Bright morning sunshine streamed through the streaked display window of Ingrid's shop. Goodness, she had to do something about that. She'd given the job to Jennie the other day. No doubt she'd done the best she could, but they couldn't have streaks in the window. No one would buy the confections if they couldn't see inside.

Then again, if no one came in, she wouldn't have to speak to them. Perhaps she would even be able to spend time in her darkroom. When she was at the farm last Thursday, she had taken some photographs of the children. Yesterday, she had captured images of Mrs. Miller's eightieth birthday party she hoped to sell to the *LaPorte Weekly Herald*.

Belle would be upset with her, though, if she didn't make a go of the shop. With a sigh, Ingrid grabbed a bucket, soapy water, and a rag and went outside to complete the chore. At least the day was warm for early December.

No sooner had she put two feet outside than a strange sight caught her attention. A motorcar was parked on the dirt road right in front of her shop. The automobile was dark green with shiny brass accents and a black leather seat. Who did it belong to?

One of the few people in town who owned one of those contraptions was Mr. McGee, the attorney. And his didn't resemble this one in any way. His was more like a buggy, a LaPorte Carriage made right here in town. No one possessed such a fancy machine, except for Sheriff Smutzer, and his was red. So who had driven this auto and stopped it where they did?

She hadn't seen one of these oddities until she came to America a few years ago. She crept a few steps closer. It would be fun to ride in one, to experience the speed of it, to allow the wind to tease her hair. One of these days, she would get to know someone who had one. Too bad Belle's latest beau had taken off to parts unknown in his blue motorcar. Perhaps she might be able to save enough money to purchase one of her own someday.

At movement from inside the automobile, Ingrid jumped backward, clutching her heart. There was a person in there. He sat straight and finger-combed his mussed light brown hair. Her breath hitched. He was handsome, with eyes the color of cornflowers and a beard trimmed to a V. When he exited the vehicle, she stepped back a little more.

"Good morning." His voice was as smooth as pulled saltwater taffy but did nothing to calm her trembling.

"G–g–good morning." She said it almost more like a question.

"I'm sorry if I startled you."

Did she detect just a bit of a Norwegian accent in his words? "You didn't."

"Truly?"

She switched to her native tongue. "Maybe a little."

He swept the black fedora from his head. "Please, accept my apologies." He spoke the language reasonably well.

They stared at each other for a while, his eyes as blue as a rain-washed sky. "May I help you?" Perhaps he was lost. Or a vagabond. But a tramp wouldn't possess such a fine automobile.

"Can we go inside and speak?"

"Um, I don't know."

He shrugged his broad shoulders. "That's okay. We don't have to. I'm not here to buy anything."

"Oh." Then what was he doing here?

"I mean, I would at any other time, but that's not why I came to LaPorte."

"If you could tell me the reason." She didn't want to allow him into her shop if he was up to no good.

"I'm searching for someone." He approached her, drawing something from his pocket. "My brother came to the area about six weeks ago. We haven't heard from him since."

A funny fluttering churned Ingrid's stomach.

He held out the paper in his hand, a photograph of a young man.

There was something familiar about him, the way his eyes crinkled as he smiled, how he had smoothed his hair back.

Wait a minute. She did know him. "What is his name?"

"Sven Lindherud."

Had that been his last name? It certainly was his first one. If only she didn't forget names and faces so fast. "Why did he come here?"

"He was going to a farm owned by Belle Gunness. Do you know her?"

Ingrid puffed out a breath she hadn't realized she'd been holding. "Yes, I've seen him, but he isn't here anymore."

"Where did he go?"

Now it was Ingrid's turn to shrug. "I don't know. My sister didn't say. All she told me was that he had moved on."

"Your sister?"

"Yes." If this man was half as nice as his brother, he was safe. "Why don't you come in? I'll put the pot on for tea."

"Thank you. I'd be grateful for that. I drove all night to get here. Nils Lindherud, by the way." He gestured to shake hands.

She dried her fingers on her apron and reciprocated. "Ingrid Storset."

She opened the door, the little bell jingling. He held it for her, and they both entered. Once she had the kettle of already-warm water pulled forward, she settled at one of the small round tables in the shop.

He leaned forward in his scrolled iron chair. "Please, if you have any information about my brother, I'd be most grateful. Mama and I are very worried. We've written several times without receiving a response. That's why I thought I'd come here myself and see if I could get to the bottom of it."

"He stopped here on his way to the farm and bought some sweets for Belle. I had dinner with them the following evening. Everything seemed to be going well between them. He was so good with the children, I thought maybe this time it would work out for her. That this one wouldn't leave. But he did."

"I read about Ole Budsburg."

"Who?" The kettle picked that moment to whistle, and Ingrid jumped to heed its call. She measured the tea leaves and brought the steaming cups to the table, setting one in front of Nils. "That name isn't familiar."

"The piece in the paper said he was headed for the Gunness farm in LaPorte in April and hasn't been heard from since."

April. Yes, there was a man who was supposed to arrive soon after Easter. "My sister said he never showed up." Though Jennie later told her that a man had come but was gone within a few days. She must have been confused.

Nils studied his cup. "Have there been more?"

A wisp of steam curled from the amber liquid in her own cup. "Yes. Over the years, a good number. I couldn't say exactly how many."

"None of them stayed?"

She shook her head. People in town talked behind Belle's back about all the men who went to the farm, none of them finding her to be to their liking.

Nils pushed his teacup away and scraped back his chair. "If you would be so kind as to give me directions to your sister's farm, I must go there at once. Mama is frantic. I have to track down my brother as soon as possible."

"Is it an emergency?"

"Just that I'm concerned for Mama's well-being."

After Ingrid had drawn a map and pointed Nils in the right direction, he hopped in his motorcar and tore down the street, a cloud of dust obscuring her view of the auto as she stood on the sidewalk.

Under her breath, she wished him luck. But Belle would likely not be able to give him any more information. She never knew much about the men who left.

Having lost her will to clean the window, Ingrid picked up her bucket and turned to go inside. Could there be some truth to what the townspeople whispered about Belle?

Once inside, she slammed the bucket on the counter. No. Of course not. There was nothing wrong with Belle. The men who came and went were the ones missing out.

Imagine that. Nils had picked the right place to park when he rolled into the small city just before dawn. Mrs. Gunness's shy sister was the first person in the town he had spoken to. What a stroke of luck. Mama would remind him it was God's providence. Perhaps He had finally decided to smile a blessing on them.

No matter, Nils was on his way to the Gunness farm, and he would soon have answers about Sven. Though her rather pretty and charming sister didn't have much information, Mrs. Gunness was sure to. Sven must have told her where he was heading, what his plans were. Even a general idea of where he went would be a great help.

Though the day was young, a farm woman would be up and hard at work already. Her children would have to get ready for school. Princess sat on the seat beside him, her tongue hanging out of her mouth. She was eager to go. While many people were afraid to ride in an automobile because of the speeds it reached, Princess loved it. All Nils had to do was start the engine, and his faithful King Charles spaniel would run and hop into the seat.

They bumped over the rutted, uneven dirt road, Nils pushing the auto to go a little faster. Faster and faster. Pushing the envelope, the thrill of adrenaline coursing through him.

He glanced at the neat map Ingrid had drawn for him. If it was to scale, he would arrive soon. Though he hoped to get the information he needed right away and get back on the road within the hour, it would be nice to see Miss Storset again. She was enchanting. Tall, thin, regal, with a heavy Norwegian accent, much like Mama's. A soothing, lulling melody. A woman he might well like to get to know.

Almost too bad he wouldn't be in town long enough for that.

There, ahead on the left, must be the place. On the top of a small hill sat a brick home surrounded by a fence and pine trees. Several sheds, a small barn, and a hogpen filled out the farmyard. Just like Miss Storset had described it. He pulled up the lane and, once near the house, cut the engine. Silence descended, save for the snorting of the hogs and the clucking of the chickens.

"You stay here." He flashed Princess his sternest gaze. She returned it with her best puppy-eyed look but failed to sway her master. "I don't know if she would take kindly to dogs. You can't come this time."

Princess turned around twice and settled onto the seat. Nils tucked her blanket around her again. "Good girl."

Time for some answers. He strode to the farmhouse door and knocked. A black-and-white barn cat slunk toward him, sniffing and rubbing against his leg. No answer. He knocked harder. "Hello. Is anyone home?"

No one came to the door.

His next stop was the barn with its slanted, asymmetrical roof. He stood in the entrance. "Hello?"

"Just a minute," a male voice answered. Ingrid hadn't mentioned it, but perhaps another man had come and stayed this time. An average-sized but muscular young man approached, wiping his hands on his dirty overalls. "Hi there. What can I do for you?"

"Nils Lindherud." He reached out to shake the boy's hand.

"Emil Greening."

"Nice to meet you. I'm looking for Belle Gunness."

Emil shook his head. "Here we go again."

"Pardon me?"

"Nothing. I believe Mrs. Gunness is in the henhouse. She said something about the girls not getting all the eggs this morning."

"Thank you. I'm obliged."

Indeed, as he neared the red wood structure, he spotted a large-boned woman bent over, a basket in her hand. "You lousy birds. Can't you produce more than that? I should stew each and every one of you."

Nils cleared his throat. "Excuse me."

She screeched and dropped the basket, a few eggs breaking as they hit the ground.

"Pardon me. I didn't mean to scare you." Though now he had frightened both of the sisters.

"Mean it or not, you sure did. Do you always sneak up behind people? I'm going to have to charge you for the broken eggs."

"Of course." This woman couldn't be more different from her sister. Heavyset, heavy lidded, perhaps once a beauty but now a wrinkled, middle-aged woman. Not what Nils had expected at all. Not the type of woman he would have guessed his brother to be interested in. Perhaps Sven hadn't even seen a picture of her. Perhaps she hadn't presented herself truthfully. That might be why Sven decided not to stay.

"Was there something you wanted?"

Nils shook his head to bring himself from his musings. He withdrew Sven's photograph from his pants pocket and handed it to her. "I'm searching for my brother, Sven Lindherud. He was supposed to arrive here in late October. Your sister said he was here, but he didn't stay."

"My sister? When did you see Ingrid?"

"In town, when I was trying to get directions to your place."

She thrust the photograph at him. "Sure, he was here. He stayed several days. One night I went to bed, and he was gone by dawn's first light."

"Where did he go?" Waiting for the answer, Nils held his breath.

"Didn't say. Just that this wasn't what he expected, and he was leaving. That's all I can tell you."

He released his pent-up breath. "He must have told you something, must have given you some clue of the direction he was headed, at the very least." Though it seemed rather strange that he wouldn't come home. Perhaps he hadn't wanted to face him and Mama. Nils shouldn't have been so hard on him. If only. . .

Mrs. Gunness wiped her hands on her dirty, yellowed apron. "If I said that's all I can tell you, that's all I can tell you. Quit badgering me, or I'll have my hand throw you off the property so fast, you'll catch up to tomorrow."

At that precise moment, a shorter man with wavy hair and a dark mustache sauntered into the yard and up the small rise to the chicken house. He spit a stream of yellow-brown tobacco onto the ground, just missing Nils's polished boot. "This here fellow giving you any trouble, Belle?"

"Ray, you're another ugly face I don't care to see again."

Nils slid backward. Looked like it was best not to be between these two.

"Good to see you too, sweetheart."

"I've told you, I am not your sweetheart. Quit hanging around here."

"Siree, you got another one with a fancy automobile here. One day

I'm going to get one of those. Then maybe you'll look my way."

This man was a regular on the farm? Nils slipped Sven's picture from his pocket. Perhaps he knew Sven's whereabouts. "Have you seen this man? He arrived here in a blue automobile."

For less than a second, Ray glanced at it, then turned his attention to Belle. "Another one of those who keeps showing up?"

"Both of them, apparently."

"No, no." Nils raised his hands to stop them before either one ended up with the wrong impression. "I'm not here seeking to marry Mrs. Gunness. My brother came about six weeks ago. He's the one who answered the ad, and now we haven't heard a word from him. That's why I'm here."

"Never saw him."

"He left." Mrs. Gunness answered at the same time as Ray. "Now get off my property. You aren't welcome here."

What else could he do? He dragged his way back to his auto, Princess simpering in the front seat. Once he had cranked the car, he jumped in, shifted into gear, and proceeded to leave.

Ray appeared just then, kicking at stones as he too left the farm.

Princess gave a deep-throated growl.

Chapter Six

Mr. Klein peered over his wire-rimmed glasses at Ingrid, sucking in his already-sunken cheeks. He rubbed his wrinkled face, the muttonchops a relic of the past.

Ingrid was about to faint right here in the office of the editor for the *LaPorte Weekly Herald.* This wasn't a good idea. Not at all.

The man, who should have been enjoying his final years in a rocking chair on his porch, glanced back at the photograph in his hand. "Miss Storset."

"Yes?" The word squeaked by her tight vocal cords.

"Why did you bring me this photograph?"

"Um." She reminded herself to breathe in and out. "I—I—I know you p–p–put photos in the p–p–paper of special birthdays. Mrs. M–M–Miller turned eighty. And she had all f–f–fifteen grandchildren there."

"Hmm." Mr. Klein adjusted his spectacles and studied the photograph a moment longer. "You've done a good job."

She slumped in relief so much, she grabbed the edge of the desk to avoid crumpling to the floor. "Thank you."

"I will purchase the photograph from you and include it in next week's paper."

"R–r–really?"

"The photograph is well composed and tells a wonderful story about Mrs. Miller and her family."

"Thank you." Her first sale. She had done it. Spoken to the editor and gotten her photograph published. Perhaps this was the first step toward her becoming a newspaper photographer.

She wouldn't tell Belle. Not now. Not until the paper hired her and she was sure she could make a living. No use in upsetting her sister until then. Belle never read the local paper, only the Norwegian ones, so she wouldn't see Ingrid's photograph.

Upon returning to her shop, instead of opening it for just an hour, she grabbed a broom to sweep the red and orange and yellow leaves that littered the walkway. A gust of chilly wind greeted her, eating through the thin knit shawl about her shoulders, scattering the leaves at her feet. Goodness, the temperature had plummeted in the last fifteen minutes. The sunny skies of earlier had given way to roiling clouds, promising an outburst of rain or maybe snow at any time.

And today was Thursday, her day to have dinner with Belle and the children at the farm. As another gale buffeted her, she abandoned the idea of sweeping away the leaves and hustled inside, already chilled to the bone. While a bowl of soup and fresh bread in Belle's warm kitchen would be delightful, walking all the way there in a deluge would not be so pleasant.

What was she going to do? Perhaps if she hurried, she could make it out before the clouds released the downpour. At least she'd be dry one way. She shoved her broom in the closet in the little room behind the counter and pulled her heavier coat from a set of hooks. Once she'd filled a bag of treats for the children, she turned out the lights.

The bell jingled, and the door opened, bringing another burst of cold air. If it was Tommy come for more sweets, she would have to explain to him that she was closed.

But it wasn't Tommy who entered. Instead, Mr. Lindherud doffed his fedora. "Good evening. I'm afraid I've caught you at a bad time."

"Yes. I was on my way to my sister's for dinner. I must hurry to beat the storm."

"Could I take a moment of your time? Allow me this, and I'll drive you to your sister's place in my motorcar. We can put the top up."

A chance to ride in one? How could she resist, even if it meant speaking to him? "Fine." She worked to keep from sounding like a giddy schoolgirl. Or a blubbering fool. "Shall we go?" While she retrieved her wide-brimmed hat and tied the purple tulle ribbon under her chin, he put up the motorcar's top.

Once she had locked the door, he led the way to his automobile and held the door open for her. She slid in, and his brown-and-white dog crawled onto her lap, staring at her with the most beautiful chocolate eyes she had ever seen.

He cranked the engine until it chugged to life then joined her inside. At least she would stay somewhat dry, as long as the wind didn't blow from the wrong direction. They puttered down the road, Ingrid sitting forward in her seat. While the automobile was not as swift as a galloping horse, they were certainly making good time.

"You have a sweet dog."

"She can make a pest of herself. Feel free to push her off your lap if you don't want her."

"No, she's fine company. What's her name?"

"Princess."

She stroked Princess's silky head. What a darling creature.

Mr. Lindherud steered around a rut in the road. "Your sister wasn't able to provide any information on my brother's whereabouts."

"Not a surprise. These men disappear, usually without telling her where they're going." She leaned back against the seat.

"I got the feeling that she was withholding information."

"Why?" Belle had no reason to do such a thing. What would lying gain her?

"Are you familiar with a man by the name of Ray?"

"Unfortunately. Ray Lamphere was a hand at the farm until a few weeks ago. He showed up at Belle's house?"

"Yes, he appeared while I was there. Something about him set my teeth on edge. If he was there at the same time as my brother, I'd like to talk to him. There has to be someone in town who knows where Sven went."

"We go to church with the stationmaster. I can introduce you tomorrow. Perhaps he remembers your brother."

"That would be a tremendous help. Thank you."

They arrived at the house just as the clouds burst. Had she walked, she would have been soaked to the skin within seconds. She turned to Mr.

Lindherud. "Thank you. You have saved me from a drenching. Even if I carried an umbrella, this wind would have blown the rain right under it."

"It was all my pleasure." His smile sent a warmth radiating through her.

She smiled back at him and relaxed. Talking to him, at least, wasn't too scary, especially when he spoke Norwegian. "Why don't you stay for dinner? Soup and bread, the girls told me. If you'd spend some time speaking with my sister, you might jog her memory."

"That is possible, but I don't want to intrude. I got the impression earlier that she doesn't care too much for me."

She waved off his concerns. "She can be prickly, but deep down, she's a wonderful woman. Life hasn't always been kind to her."

He raised his eyebrows. "A wonderful woman?"

"She has fostered an orphan girl for many years. She's doing an amazing job running the farm and raising her children on her own. Please say you'll stay." Something about him, about his lazy grin, his gentle ways, his adventurous spirit, drew her in.

"What about Princess? I can't leave her in the cold and rain."

"Belle won't abide dogs in the house, but you can tuck her into the barn."

"Are you sure she won't mind on either count?"

"Of course not."

"And you aren't doing this because you'd like a ride home in my auto? I noticed how bright your eyes were the entire way out here."

"It was my first time to ride in one. I enjoyed every second." And she'd give her left arm for another ride. "But that's not the reason." No, the reason was that Mr. Lindherud was someone who might be worth getting to know.

Ingrid didn't have a thought like that every day. Or ever.

"Then I accept." He splashed through muddy puddles to her side of the car and helped her out. She dashed for the protection of the front porch while he raced to the barn, Princess under one arm. Once he had her settled, he joined Ingrid on the porch.

She led the way inside. "Belle, children, I'm here, and I've brought a guest." She took Mr. Lindherud's coat and hung it on the hook by the door, then showed him to the kitchen.

Belle hunkered over the stove, stirring the soup. When she turned in their direction, a deep frown stretched her lips. "I didn't know we were going to have company."

"It's good to see you again, Mrs. Gunness. I'm sorry for the intrusion. If this isn't a good time, I'll understand and leave."

"No, no. Since you're here, you might as well stay."

"Thank you."

"Make yourself comfortable in the parlor, Mr. Lindherud. Dinner will be ready soon." Ingrid got out another place setting and helped Jennie adjust the layout of the dining room table.

The girl glanced at her mother, who bustled between rooms, and back at Ingrid several times before grabbing her by the arm and holding tight. She whispered in Ingrid's ear. "Can I talk to you later? In private?"

"Of course," Ingrid whispered back. "This sounds important."

"I need to tell you something very serious. And kind of scary."

"We'll find a time after dinner, okay?"

Jennie nodded, the blue bow in her blond hair bobbing, but she kept her gaze on the table. Whatever was going on had the girl deeply troubled.

A tense silence hung over the dinner table at the Gunness home, only the clink of spoons in steaming bowls of soup breaking the stillness. That and the howl of the wind buffeting the house, tree branches scraping the windowpanes, rain battering the roof.

Nils should have listened to his own instincts and left after dropping Ingrid here. This had been a bad idea. A very bad idea. Even Lucy and Myrtle, whom Miss Storset had said were rather chatty, sat without uttering a word, their attention on the dinner in front of them. Jennie focused on her supper. Emil, the farmhand, didn't join them, as Mrs. Gunness had sent him on an errand to Michigan City.

Nils cleared his throat. "This is very good chicken soup." Perhaps it was made from one of the hens she'd threatened to stew that morning. "Thank you for having me, Mrs. Gunness."

In reply, she harrumphed.

"I told you my sister is a wonderful cook." Miss Storset, the color high in her cheeks, swallowed another bite.

"And you were right."

Several long minutes stretched in front of them. Well, he was here with another chance to question the lady of the house in regard to his brother, so he might as well make the most of this opportunity. "Sven was very excited to meet you, Mrs. Gunness. That's what has me so puzzled about his leaving. He was sure this was where he was supposed to spend the rest of his days."

"Can't figure most men." Mrs. Gunness slurped another spoonful.

"He wanted to settle down and have a home and a family. Nothing pleased him more than discovering that you had four children."

Lucy peered up from her bowl. "Mama, I—"

The girl's mother threw her a pointed look. One Nils recognized from his days as a boy. One that said it was time to keep your mouth shut before you got into trouble. What had Lucy been about to say?

"My apologies, Mr. Lindherud. Sometimes Lucy forgets that children are to be seen and not heard."

"I don't have a problem—"

"But I do. And that is the rule."

Miss Storset buttered her slice of bread. "We regularly chat—"

"I've had enough of chatting. The girls can sit and eat without running their mouths like a river over rapids."

"Are you sure my brother didn't mention where he was going?"

Mrs. Gunness shrugged. "How am I supposed to remember something like that? He came here, and when he discovered that he would have to do some actual work and that hogs are a dirty business, he decided this wasn't the life for him after all. He hotfooted it out of here without so much as a how-do-you-do. That's all I can tell you. Don't bother me about it anymore."

Unfortunately, that did sound a good bit like his brother, one to do whatever he had to in order to get out of chores. Though there was the risk of alienating her, he had to ask one last question. "Did he mention in which direction he might be headed?"

Mrs. Gunness pushed her chair back and picked up her bowl and plate. "I said not to pester me again, and here you go. You're worse than the children at knowing when to hold your tongue."

"What about Ole Budsburg?"

"Who?"

"He supposedly arrived here in April. His family is searching for him. I saw a classified inquiring into his whereabouts."

"Ole Budsburg isn't your concern. Now, I will have to ask you to leave the property."

Miss Storset stood and gathered her own dishes. "He's my ride into town. I'll catch my death if I don't go with him, and I can't leave you with a sink full of dirty dishes."

Mrs. Gunness eyed the overflowing pile of plates and pots and nodded. "Fine. He can stay. But after tonight, he is not to come back. Is that understood?" She swept her gaze around the room and received nods of assent from both Miss Storset and Nils.

He had no desire to return anyway, unless she held some useful information into Sven's disappearance. For whatever reason, he couldn't shake the feeling that she did. He had to get back into her good graces. "Why don't you relax and spend some time with your children? Perhaps read the paper. Miss Storset and I will do the dishes."

"That's a splendid idea." A wide smile spread across Miss Storset's cherubic face. "You don't take enough time for yourself."

"Mama, can we play checkers with you?" The older girl's voice held a hint of pleading.

Mrs. Gunness grunted at Myrtle's question but lumbered away to the parlor with her ducklings in tow.

Miss Storset filled the sink with water, her hands trembling slightly. Did he make her nervous? "I apologize for ruining your supper and if I've made you uncomfortable."

"No." She studied the suds in the sink. "You make me less nervous than most people."

That boded well for him. "I'm glad of that. You can trust me."

She didn't glance at him but grabbed a dish to wash. "I'm sorry about this evening. I don't know why Belle is in such a mood."

"Maybe it's this weather. Awful, unless you're a duck."

A delicate smile graced her smooth face. "I hate rain. And mud."

"No mud pies for you growing up?"

She shook her head. "Chocolate is much nicer to work with than dirt."

Nils chuckled.

"Are you laughing at me?"

"With you. And I would have to agree. Except that I'd rather work with motor oil than dirt."

"Isn't that messier and harder to wash away?"

"Maybe, but it's necessary to make autos run. And the faster they go, the happier I am. That and selling them."

Now Miss Storset laughed. "To each his own. You sell cars?"

"I have a Ford dealership in Detroit. Automobiles are the way of the future, and I wanted to get into the business in the very beginning. I still can't understand why Sven would leave a lucrative business for a hog farm, but he said it would make him happy. That it was his dream. Motorcars were mine, not his."

"I hope the stationmaster can give you some answers tomorrow. You must miss your brother a great deal."

"I do. I'm worried."

"I'm sure there's a simple explanation. Perhaps he wanted to see another part of the country before he came home."

"He never mentioned wanting to do anything like that. Then again, we weren't on the best terms the past couple of years."

"That's too bad. I'm glad that most of the time, Belle and I get along."

"Do you have other siblings?"

"Family in Norway. Belle is all I have here. If we fought and couldn't reconcile, I don't know what I would do."

Perhaps Miss Storset saw the softer, gentler side to her sister. He, of all people, shouldn't judge. Familial bonds were strong, and so they should be. "How long have you been in the candy business?"

"Not even two months. But can I tell you something?" Though her words were hesitant, her face lit up like sunshine through a cloudy day.

"Of course."

She leaned toward him, her voice soft. "I found out today that the paper is going to publish the photograph I took of Mrs. Miller's eightieth birthday. Isn't that grand? I've never had one of my photographs in the newspaper before."

"I didn't realize you enjoyed photography."

"Oh yes."

This was the most animated he'd seen her. "What about your confectionary shop?"

She shook her head. "That I do for my sister. What I really want, what I've always wanted, is to be a photographer. It's taken me this long to work up the courage to submit a picture to the paper, and they bought it."

"That's wonderful news. I'm happy for you."

"Thank you." She colored, and he doubted it was from the heat of the kitchen. "I'm sorry, I'm talking too much."

"You have nothing to apologize for. You have a beautiful voice, and I love to hear you speak." That was the truth. The timbre of her words was almost like music.

"Psst."

Both Miss Storset and Nils turned at the sound. Jennie stood in the doorway, her blond hair flowing over her narrow shoulders.

Miss Storset dried her hands on the too-big apron she'd borrowed from her sister. "That's right. You wanted to talk to me about something. Would you excuse us, please?"

"Of course."

Before they could step from the kitchen, Mrs. Gunness bellowed from the parlor. "Jennie Olsen, you get back in here right away."

"But I wanted to talk to Auntie Ingrid."

"I said right now. They have to be going."

"Mama."

"No more arguing."

Miss Storset bent in front of Jennie. "Why don't you stop by the shop tomorrow on your way home from school? We can have our talk then."

Jennie gave a solemn nod and shuffled away.

In a short time, he and Miss Storset were headed to the car. He opened the door for her then turned to the barn for Princess. As soon as he released her, she bounded out. "Come back here, you."

The wind carried away his shout, and he took off after his mischievous pooch. Princess raced toward the hogpen, Nils hot on her heels. Just when he reached out to grab her, he slipped and fell face-first in the mud. He struggled to his feet, only to fall again. After several more tries, he found his footing. By then, Princess was busy digging a hole in the yard.

He approached her, and she growled. The second time today. So unlike her. "Stop that right now. Let's go."

She leaned over the hole and pulled something out. He went to grab it from her. A bone. A good-sized one. Perhaps from a cow. "Give me that." He took hold of one end. She grasped the other between her teeth. A tug-of-war ensued.

When Nils landed in the mud on his backside, Princess dropped the bone and trotted to the car.

Chapter Seven

Friday,
December 13, 1907

As his breath puffed in front of his face, Nils paced the walk that ran alongside Miss Storset's sweet shop. She said she would go with him to the train station to question people there but couldn't leave until lunch. Though he understood, he shouldn't have agreed to wait for her. Even though he and Princess spent the night at the hotel, he hadn't slept well. Every little creak of the building and each snore from next door kept him awake. He could be at the station already, conducting his own investigation. Every minute he wasted was another minute farther away from where Sven was.

A balding gentleman wearing no coat over his shirt and vest exited the building. Nils tipped his hat as the man went by then continued his pacing. As he strode back and forth, Nils racked his brain for possible places Sven might have traveled. Other than very early in their lives in Norway, Detroit was the only home they had ever known. Sven didn't even remember much about the old country. Nils was the one who filled him in on those details.

Not to mention that Sven didn't have enough money to travel far, not by any means of transportation. Unless he hadn't handed his money over to Mrs. Gunness the first minute he arrived. Why hadn't he asked that question last night? Since she had banned him from having further contact with her, that would be one for the bank manager. Perhaps he should find out how much longer Miss Storset would be. He could run over there while she finished.

At that moment, she stepped outside and wrapped her heavy blue wool shawl around her thin shoulders and over her head. "I'm sorry to have taken so long. Like I said, you could have waited inside."

"I can't sit still."

"I understand." Her eyes shone, even in the dim light of a cloudy winter day.

"You appear to be in a good mood."

"Goodness. I guess I'm still excited about my photograph in the paper. I can't believe I blurted the news to a stranger." She studied the ground as she toed the walk. "Shall we be on our way?"

He stepped in stride beside her. "You have nothing to apologize for. I was happy to share in your joy." They continued in silence for a few moments. "Is the bank on the way to the station? I'd like to stop there first, if possible."

"Oh, I didn't realize you had business to conduct."

"Just finding my brother."

She turned to him and scrunched her forehead. "Why the bank?"

"Did Sven or your sister mention that she asked him to bring a large sum of money, enough to help cover the mortgage on the farm?"

Miss Storset stopped short, drawing a sharp intake of breath. "That can't be right. My sister is a proud woman. She wouldn't ask such a thing."

"But she did. I saw the advertisement and the large wad of cash my brother left Detroit with."

"She wouldn't have taken it."

"I'm hoping he didn't give it to her."

"That must be it." She resumed her stroll beside him.

"Still, to be sure, I'd like to inquire at the bank."

She shook her head, a few golden curls escaping from their pins. "I don't think you'll discover anything useful, but if you want to, we can." Her voice held a soft hint of resignation.

He would make it brief. Not a block later, they arrived at a three-story brick building that housed the First National Bank of LaPorte. The marble lobby bustled with activity. How would anyone remember his brother? This branch was much larger than he had anticipated.

Miss Storset pointed at a mustached, bald-pated man behind the counter. "That's Mr. Larson. He knows everyone in this town and remembers everybody who comes through. If your brother was here, Mr. Larson would know."

They approached the man, who nodded and gave a small grin. "Good afternoon, Miss Storset. Nice to see you again. Who have you brought with you?"

"This is Nils Lindherud. H–h–he has some things to ask you. If you have some time free. Alone." Her voice trembled.

"Of course."

Nils's pulse pounded in his neck as Mr. Larson led the way to a desk in the back of the lobby where there was less traffic. Nils held out a chair for Ingrid then seated himself across from the banker.

"What brings you in?" Mr. Larson leaned back in his wooden chair.

Nils explained the situation. "Do you remember seeing my brother here?" He pulled out Sven's picture. Already, the edges were ragged and one corner was folded.

Mr. Larson slipped on his spectacles and studied the photograph.

"He's about six foot three, my height, and similar in build as well. Dark blond mustache. He would have been with Mrs. Gunness and would have had a large sum of cash with him. They would have been here in late October, most likely."

"Hmm." The man stroked his dark facial hair. "I don't recall your brother being in here. I never forget a face. What I do remember is Mrs. Gunness coming in around that same time to make a large payment on her mortgage. If memory serves, it was all in cash. Would you like to wait here while I pull her record?"

"Of course." Nils slid forward in his chair and faced Miss Storset. "I had a feeling that he would have handed over that money upon his arrival or that your sister would have demanded it of him."

Miss Storset straightened her spine and all traces of her timidity vanished. "I know you don't care for Belle. The two of you have gotten off on the wrong foot. However, don't jump to conclusions about her when you don't know her at all. She never would have stolen your brother's money or not returned it to him when he decided to go."

At her sharp words, he sat back in his seat. "Fine. You've put me in my place. Let's wait and see what Mr. Larson comes up with. Then we—I—can make my conclusions. Just to be fair about this, my brother brought one thousand dollars with him. Let's see what size your sister's transaction was."

"Certainly."

They remained seated in silence while the bank customers buzzed around them. Miss Storset folded her hands in her lap. Nils resorted to tapping his foot. While they waited, he couldn't help but glance in her direction a few times. She sat straight and tall in the chair, every inch the proper lady. So much the opposite of her sister. A curl brushed her cheek, whispering against her face. She blinked her green eyes a few times, her long lashes brushing her fair skin.

After too long of a wait, Mr. Larson returned, a folder in his hand. "My apologies for the delay. I do believe I've gotten to the bottom of this. I did remember that Mr. Lamphere came with her that day."

"Ray?" Miss Storset sagged a bit.

"I'm positive. Like I said, I never forget a face. Anyway, she put eight hundred dollars into her savings account. I hope that is helpful."

Before Miss Storset could say a word, Nils jumped in. "And what day did you say that was?"

"October twenty-fifth."

A couple days after his brother arrived.

Ingrid turned to him. "There. She only had eight hundred dollars with her, not one thousand."

"She could have held some back."

"Or perhaps Ray got the cash from somewhere."

Nils turned to the banker. "What about a man named Ole Budsburg? Did he ever come in here with Mrs. Gunness? It would have been April or thereabouts."

Mr. Larson scratched his head. "No, that name doesn't ring any bells. Can you tell me any more about him that might jog my memory?"

Nils recited the advertisement.

"I'm sorry. I don't recall the gentleman."

Nils stood and shook Mr. Larson's hand. "Thank you for your time. You have been a great help."

Though Miss Storset dismissed it, there was too much of a coincidence in the timing with the deposit in October. That money must have come from Sven.

Unfortunately, he would have to write to the Budsburgs and inform them that he hadn't been able to locate their family member.

Ingrid blinked in the December afternoon as she stomped out of the bank ahead of Mr. Lindherud. She told herself it was because of the cold that she hurried, but she had another reason.

He caught her by the elbow and tugged her to a stop. "What has your knickers in a bind?"

"That is not the way to speak to a lady, Mr. Lindherud."

"You're right. I shouldn't have said that." His words were contrite, but a muscle jumped in his jaw. "What's the matter? Have I offended you in some way?"

"Do you even have to ask?"

The noonday crowds of housewives and businessmen and farmers slowed their activities and stared at them. She resumed her jaunt but at a slower pace.

"I'm afraid I do." He was at her side once more.

This time, she worked to keep her words low. "You blew into town yesterday, not knowing a soul here, and today you proclaim my sister guilty of taking your brother's money."

"I never said she took it."

"But you did." She gazed sideways at him, and his cheeks reddened. Possibly not from the chill in the air.

"Sven might have given it to her. We don't know what happened."

"Maybe it wasn't his money at all. Belle is frugal." Although, was she? She and the children had the nicest clothes. Not that long ago, she had purchased a piano. Plus, she had put out the money for Ingrid's shop. Where did all those funds come from? Was the farm that prosperous?

No, she shouldn't be thinking such thoughts. Belle was the only family she had in the States. Without her sister, Ingrid would be all alone in a country that frightened her, with no way to return to her native land.

Family was everything. Without it, a person had nothing. Besides, Belle was a good and honest woman.

"She did deposit a large amount of cash all at once."

"A deposit she had likely been saving for quite some time to make." But that didn't make sense. Wouldn't Belle have been making small deposits? Then again, she didn't like going into town much.

"I'm not accusing her of anything."

Ingrid chortled. "I'm afraid it sounds like it to me."

"Please." His pleading tone slowed her frantic steps. "I'm only trying to determine what happened to my brother and where he might be. My mother suffers with heart issues and isn't in the best of health. My father is, well, not around. She's worried about Sven. All I want to do is locate him and be able to return home and let Mama know that her son is safe and well. Is that too much to ask?"

"No." The fight drained from her body. "Not at all."

"Thank you for understanding."

She didn't, really. Hoped she never would have to. Then again, she would be frantic if Belle disappeared without letting her know where she'd gone.

The wind gusted, and Ingrid bent her head against it. This afternoon had been so upsetting, she set her sights on returning to the shop. She was going to hide in her darkroom for a while and lose herself in developing some photographs. Perhaps the ones she'd taken at the farm a week or so ago.

Mr. Lindherud grabbed her by the elbow and pulled her backward. She gazed up, only to see Sheriff Smutzer barreling down the walk in their direction. Before she could sidestep him, he slammed into her, her breath whooshing from her lungs.

"Oh, my dear, I'm so sorry." The sheriff smiled at Ingrid, his cheeks round, his neat mustache rising with the action. "If you'll excuse me, I really must go. There's been an automobile crash near McClung Road." He touched the bill of his cap and scurried away.

Ingrid couldn't draw in a deep breath until he left. She turned to Mr. Lindherud, who continued to hold to her elbow. She wrenched from his grasp. "I have to get there. This might be another chance to get a picture in the newspaper. I just hope no one was hurt or worse."

"Would you like a ride? I would be happy to take you."

"I thought you wanted to get to the train station."

"Accept this as my apology."

How could she turn him down? This way, she would arrive at the scene faster and perhaps get a good shot before another photographer beat her.

"I accept your apology and your offer of a ride. Thank you."

They hustled toward the shop, where he had parked his motorcar. After she grabbed her camera, they drove to the crash site. Already a small crowd of farmers had gathered. Ingrid slid from the machine before Mr. Lindherud had a chance to come to her side.

She moved forward, gazing downward at the scene. A scratched blue motorcar had rolled down the embankment toward Fish Trap Lake. No one was near the automobile. Something about the vehicle was familiar, stirred some kind of memory, but she couldn't put her finger on it.

As Mr. Lindherud came around the car, a gasp escaped him.

Ingrid turned toward him. All of the color had drained from his face, even from his lips. "What is it?"

"That's Sven's automobile."

"No." A chill raced through Ingrid. "How do you know for sure?"

"See the storage box on the side?"

She nodded. And hugged herself. There, burned into the wood, were the initials SL. Sven Lindherud.

Mr. Lindherud pushed his hand through his hair. "This doesn't make any sense. It's been almost two months since anyone has seen him. Now his motorcar shows up. Where has he been? Where is he now?"

The sheriff pulled up in his red automobile and ambled toward them, his gun holstered at his hip. "You look like you've seen a ghost."

Mr. Lindherud opened his mouth, but no words came out. Ingrid needed to inform him of what had happened. She wiped her hands on her black skirt. "The c–c–car is Mr. Lindherud's brother's."

"You're sure of this, sir?"

Mr. Lindherud nodded and, using few words, informed the sheriff of Sven's situation.

"Then we must begin a search for him at once. We have no time to lose in finding him." Sheriff Smutzer turned to the gathered crowd. "Fan out, every one of you. Let's find this man."

The group dispersed. All except for Mr. Lindherud and Ingrid. She tugged him by the arm. "Let's go. You have to find him."

"I can't seem to move." Though that was what he said, he took a few steps toward the motorcar.

Ingrid followed him. A glint of something on the floor of the automobile caught her eye. She leaned over. A silver watch.

One she recognized.

Chapter Eight

N ow you're the one who looks like they've seen a ghost." Nils leaned over Miss Storset's shoulder in an attempt to see what she had pulled from Sven's automobile. A silver watch lay in her open, trembling hand.

She gazed at him and bit her lip, her green eyes wide.

"You know who this belongs to?"

"Ray Lamphere."

Just the sound of the man's name sent goose bumps skittering across Nils's arms. "Are you sure?"

"I was there when Belle gave it to him. She made a big deal out of it, made sure the children and I were all there. He grinned from ear to ear when he opened the package. He said he had never owned such a fine timepiece."

Nils swallowed hard, as if he could wash away the metallic taste of disappointment from his tongue. "Then it was Ray who was driving this machine and not my brother."

"That's what it looks like."

"We have to inform the sheriff." Nils raced off, hollering for Sheriff Smutzer, who soon appeared from the reeds lining the lakeshore. Nils told him what Ingrid had found.

Smutzer shook his head. "I'm sorry, Mr. Lindherud, but it appears you haven't found your brother after all. It does seem that I need to have a bit of a talk with Mr. Lamphere. Perhaps I will be able to get some information from him."

"What was Lamphere doing with Sven's automobile? Where has it been all this time?" Nils spun in a small circle. Far from answering questions, this entire scene only brought up more.

"Let's go take another look at the motorcar," the sheriff suggested.

Together, they climbed the bank to where Miss Storset leaned against Sven's automobile, staring at the watch in her hand. Smutzer approached her. "May I see that?"

She handed it to him, and when he asked, she recounted the story of how Ray came to own it. By the time she finished, she was breathless.

The sheriff and a couple of his deputies combed the vehicle for more clues. Nils couldn't stand by and do nothing. He traversed the area, squinting at the ground, searching for something, anything, that would provide the elusive answers.

After he had circled the automobile several times, Miss Storset came to him and touched his shoulder. "Don't make yourself crazy."

He flashed a wry smile. That was exactly where he was headed. To insanity. "Too late for that, I'm afraid. This just doesn't make sense. None of it does."

"I know."

"I don't believe Sven would leave without taking his automobile."

"What if he went to California?"

Nils heaved a long, slow sigh. "I suppose that would be kind of far to drive. Then it makes sense he would leave it behind. Why wouldn't your sister mention that, though? Why wouldn't she let me know that Sven had left his motorcar behind?"

"Perhaps Ray took it the same night your brother left."

He gazed at her, standing so straight, so sure of herself. Perhaps she was more than a wilting flower. "You're smart, you know that?"

She shook her head, a faint blush rising in her cheeks like the first brushes of dawn across the sky.

"My mind jumps to the thought that my brother has met with a sinister fate. Your explanations make sense, though, when nothing else does. If Sven went west, he would leave his automobile behind. The first time I met Ray, he mentioned wanting a motorcar. That would explain everything." He held himself back from the improper urge to hug her.

"What will you do now?"

"Now it's time to go to the train station and see what I can find out there."

"I'll come with you."

"Don't you have to get back to the shop?"

"No, the business won't fail if I'm not open for a couple of hours."

Once she had snapped a few photographs, he led her to the motorcar and held the door open for her while she climbed in. He cranked the engine and, once he slid in, he studied her. Even her face and her expression were soft and gentle, just like the woman.

He turned the automobile toward LaPorte. "Your sister should listen to you more. Like about the confectionary." Then again, wasn't that just what he had done with Sven? He hadn't paid attention to his brother's wishes. Perhaps if he had, Sven would have been content to stay in Detroit.

Nils had driven Sven away.

Ingrid returned to town in Mr. Lindherud's motorcar, the cold wind whipping about her face sending the ends of her hat's ribbon fluttering. She welcomed the bracing chill. Anything to cool her cheeks.

Mr. Lindherud's compliment had affected her more than she cared to admit. No one had ever called her smart before. She had never allowed herself to believe that she might be. There went her face warming again. She had to stop this nonsense. He was being nice, nothing more. Yes, he was a thoughtful gentleman. He probably told all the women he met that they were smart.

Then again, she had helped him, had gotten him to see that the puzzle pieces might fit together after all. That was an accomplishment she could be proud of.

Perhaps some of the photographs she had snapped at the scene would wind up in the newspaper. That would be another mark in her favor.

No matter what, though, Belle would never listen to her. She was much too headstrong and independent for that. Maybe another reason why men fled from her.

Mr. Lindherud steered his automobile around horses and buggies and wagons and soon arrived at the train station. The building's boards ran up and down, a small overhang protecting passengers from the elements. The arched windows on the second story marked the hotel. They entered the large waiting room. "The stationmaster's office is to the right." She hadn't forgotten a detail of the day she and Belle and the girls had arrived from Chicago, mourning the loss of Belle's first husband, Mads Sorenson, and the destruction of her home and store by fire. At least she hadn't been alone. Not like Mr. Lindherud was.

They left the hubbub of the crowded waiting room behind and entered the stationmaster's office. "G–g–good afternoon, Mr. Botchkiss."

The man was slouched over his desk, but at their arrival, he unfolded his lanky frame and came to his feet. "Ah, Miss Storset. Shouldn't you be at your shop? School will let out soon, and I know more than one child who will be beating a path to your door."

At least once a week, Mr. Botchkiss's brood of three appeared at her shop, their nickel allowances in their grimy, chubby fingers. She always had a little something special waiting for them. "I'll be back in time." Especially since she was anticipating Jennie stopping by for their talk. What could the girl want? She shook away the thought. "This is Mr. Lindherud from Detroit."

Nils nodded. "Pleasure to make your acquaintance." The two men shook hands.

Mr. Lindherud proceeded to explain the situation to Mr. Botchkiss. "I was wondering if you might have seen my brother leaving and if you could possibly remember where he was going."

Mr. Botchkiss tsked and shook his head. "As you can see, Mr. Lindherud, there are many, many people who pass through here on a daily basis. Most of them are strangers, here for the night or to grab a bite to eat. I don't have the kind of memory to tell you if your brother was among them."

"Please, look at the picture again."

He studied it for a minute more. "I'm sorry, sir, but I don't recognize the gentleman. I wish I could be more help to you, but I can't. You might want to ask the porters and the other staff. They have more interaction with the passengers than I do. They might recall something."

"Thank you very much." Mr. Lindherud shook Mr. Botchkiss's hand once more. "I appreciate your time. If you don't mind, I believe I will make a few more inquiries."

"Suit yourself."

They left the office, returning to the chaos that was the busy station. People flowed around them, some arriving, some departing to destinations all over the country. A young boy shined shoes near the platform while porters pushed carts loaded with trunks and carpetbags.

Between all the commotion and all the people, Ingrid's head buzzed. If only she could escape to the comfort of her darkroom in her shop's basement. There, she could drink in the solitude, the peace and quiet. Not to mention that she had photographs to develop.

Before Mr. Lindherud started his questioning, Ingrid stopped him. "I have to get back to the confectionary. Once school lets out, that is my busiest time of the day. Let me know what you find out. I'll pray for success."

His light blue eyes brightened. "Thank you for everything you've done. I will keep in contact. I'm sure I'll see you before I leave."

"Of course."

As she stepped backward, he tipped his hat. She hoped he would find out where his brother went. And that he went there with a pocketful of money.

The cold weather pushed Ingrid to make short work of returning to the shop. That and her anticipated talk with Jennie. Already, the school bell had rung. A gaggle of children hung about the store's exterior, their noses pressed against her window. Good thing she hadn't had a chance to clean it.

Though she searched the wide-eyed faces, Jennie wasn't among the children.

Chapter Nine

A steady stream of children flooding the shop kept Ingrid busy all afternoon. By the time darkness fell and the tide slowed, her feet screamed at her and her back ached. Worst of all, her stomach clenched, because Jennie hadn't shown up. Ingrid shouldn't be overreacting. Likely, the girl had gotten busy with friends or chores and had forgotten. Perhaps whatever issue it was had already been cleared up.

Not too much time had passed since Ingrid was almost a young woman. At such an age, girls could be mortal enemies one day and the best of friends the next. They could be fickle and petty. That must be what Jennie had wanted to speak to her about. Or perhaps it was something of a more personal nature girls of that age needed to know. Belle could take care of that.

With a huge sigh of relief, Ingrid turned the shop's sign to CLOSED.

Because the stairs to her two rooms above the shop were outside, Ingrid locked up the store and headed for the side of the building. With her head down against the wind, she ran into someone. Someone with wing-tip shoes and a solid chest. Goodness, she already knew who it was. She peered through her lashes to discover Mr. Lindherud staring at her.

"I was hoping to run into you, but not quite in this way."

She couldn't help but chuckle at his comment. He had an easy way about him that was appealing. "How did things go at the train station?"

His smile faded. "Not well. I spoke with a dozen people or more. Not a single one of them remembered Sven. Not one. With his height and blond hair, he stands out in a crowd. You can't forget him. If he had been there at any point, someone would have remembered him."

"Just because no one recalls seeing him at the station doesn't mean he didn't take the train elsewhere."

"I suppose you're right. If, as your sister claims, he left in the middle of the night, there would have been different staff on duty."

"You should ask tonight."

"That means that right now, I'm no closer to having any idea where he is. Where he went."

"What will you do now?"

"I don't know. I just don't know. Maybe I will get some rest. Tonight, in addition to the station, perhaps I should also check the taverns. Though Sven wasn't taken with drink, maybe someone there might have run into him on the street the night he left."

"That's a good idea. I really must hurry now."

"Evening plans?"

She shook her head. "I'm just a little worried about Jennie. She was so intent on speaking to me, but she didn't show up after school today. I'm going to Belle's to talk to her."

He tipped his hat. "Have a nice time. I hope you find out what's bothering your niece and that it isn't anything too serious."

She nodded and flashed him a smile. He was such a gentleman. "Thank you. I hope you get some rest."

Once he turned in the direction of the hotel, Ingrid headed to the farm. Fridays weren't her usual day to be there, but she wouldn't rest easy until she knew what was going on with Jennie. Last night, she was so serious. Insistent on not speaking with her mother about her troubles. In fact, it was like she wanted to keep them a secret from Belle.

The brisk walk invigorated Ingrid enough that she was quite warm by the time she reached her sister's farm. Lamplight streamed from the barn's loft where Emil spent his nights. A yellow glow shone through several of the house's windows. A blanket of serenity covered the entire scene.

"Ingrid."

At the sound of Ray's voice, she jumped a mile and clutched her chest. "Goodness, don't you know it is not nice to sneak up on people?"

"What are you doing here? It's not Thursday."

"I can visit my sister any time I want."

He spat his tobacco. What a disgusting habit. If only he wouldn't chew it in front of her. "Seems like you've been here a lot lately. Can't seem to stay away. Doesn't have anything to do with that fellow who's been poking around, does it?"

"That's not your business. Why are you here? You're not working for Belle anymore."

"This is a free country. I can come and go as I please."

"This is not your house. It is not the same. Good evening, Mr. Lamphere. Please go back to the Wheatbrook farm." Without waiting for any sort of reply, she swept up the steps and knocked.

Lucy answered, hopping first on one foot and then the other. "I'm so glad you're here."

Ingrid would hug her niece if she would stand still for one second. "That's quite the greeting."

"You'll make everything all better."

"What do I need to make better? You aren't fighting with your sisters, are you?"

Lucy gave a solemn shake of her head.

"You aren't disobeying your mama, are you?"

Another shake. "It's worse than that."

Ingrid's heart rate ramped up, much like the engine in Mr. Lindherud's automobile. "I'm sure it's not that terrible."

"Mama has sent Jennie to a finishing school way out in California. We're never going to see her again."

Nils sat alone at a table in the hotel lobby, conversation swirling around him. He tuned it out and sipped his hot, creamy coffee. Though his stomach complained of hunger, he didn't order a meal. His money was dwindling fast. He needed to solve this mystery and return to Detroit. He couldn't remain away from the dealership forever. Bills piled up, and collectors wouldn't be far behind.

One collector in particular.

He had plunged the family into enough of a financial hole already. There was no way he was going to dig them in any deeper. He couldn't stay but a day or two more.

Home beckoned to him. His responsibilities weighed down his shoulders. The family wouldn't survive long without a source of income. Sven had run away, or so it appeared, leaving Nils to provide for their mother. He sighed and stirred more sugar into his coffee. Hopefully tonight's canvassing of the train station and saloons would shed some light on Sven's whereabouts.

"Are you waiting for someone, or may I join you?"

Nils gazed into the ruddy face of Mr. Larson from the bank. Had the man been searching him out? Did he have more information for Nils? "No, I'm alone. Please, have a seat."

"You look rather forlorn."

"Just anxious to know where my brother is."

"That's understandable. I'm sorry I wasn't able to be more help to you today."

So he didn't have any further details. Perhaps, though, all wasn't lost. "Does Mrs. Gunness often make large deposits into her savings?"

"She does, as a matter of fact. Sometimes she brings one of her suitors with her. Sometimes Mr. Lamphere, her former hand, comes. Most often, though, she comes alone."

"Always cash?"

"Always."

"You don't find that bizarre?"

"I try not to stick my nose where it doesn't belong. My job isn't to question people or what they do with their money. Not even to ask them where their money comes from. My only responsibility is to keep their money safe and earning interest."

"People often do such things, then?" Nils had never been able to bring a large amount of cash to his bank.

"Not really."

"But you've never questioned her."

"Like I said, it's not my place."

Just then, the telegraph operator burst through the door, bringing a bite of cold air with him. Nils recognized the short, dark-haired young man. Earlier today, he'd questioned him about Sven.

The man doffed his cap, swept his gaze across the room, and hurried to Nils. "Thank goodness I found you and I know who you are. I've had a telegram come for you. The message sounded urgent, so I thought I'd track you down." He held out a yellow envelope.

With shaking hands, Nils ripped it open.

MOTHER ILL *Stop* COME HOME

No one had signed it. Was it possible Sven had returned in the time Nils had been here and sent this message? Whoever it was, there was no doubt. Mama needed him. He had to get home.

Tonight.

He scraped back his chair and threw a few coins on the table. "Please excuse me. There's a family emergency. I must return to Detroit as soon as possible."

"The next train's not until the morning." The telegraph operator nodded as Nils pressed a coin into his hand.

"I have my motorcar."

"Ah, so you're the chap with that fancy contraption. Good luck getting anywhere tonight. This storm's looking to be a doozy."

Nils stared out the large window at the front of the dining room. Big, wet flakes swirled in a howling wind. On a night like this, you wanted a sleigh and a dependable horse. But he had no other choice. He had to get home to Mama. "I'll be fine." It might take him all night and possibly into the next day, but he would make it home.

He raced upstairs to his room, gathered his belongings, grabbed his hat from the table and his coat from the back of the chair, and whistled for Princess to follow.

He all but shot from the hotel into the icy night. Slipping and sliding on the slick walk, he hustled to his auto as quickly as possible. If he had a difficult time walking, imagine what driving was going to be like. *Lord, protect me.*

Nils cleared the snow from the front seat, and Princess climbed into the automobile, tail wagging, and burrowed underneath the pile of blankets Nils placed for her. After cranking the auto to life, he puttered down the street. At this rate, it might be July before he got home. This was crazy.

Mama needed him though. Ever since Papa had been put away, she had relied on Nils. Even before that. He'd always risen to the occasion. Despite the conditions, he wouldn't let her down.

Princess climbed into his lap. He didn't need the distraction, but the warmth she provided was welcome. Little by little, they inched their way toward Michigan.

He leaned forward, peering through the swirling, blinding storm. Where had the road gone? So much snow covered the ground, he couldn't find it. How would he see trees? Curves? Other vehicles?

With a great deal of caution, he proceeded forward. The slick tires slid on the snow-covered street. He turned the wheel.

The auto didn't obey his command.

He cranked it the other way. His slow slide continued.

Another turn of the wheel, and he spun in a complete circle. The auto tipped as it left the roadway.

Chapter Ten

The wind howled around the corners of the farmhouse, sleet pinging on the windowpanes. Even though the stove and the fire kept the inside cozy and warm, Belle shivered. The memory of too many cold nights in Norway chilled her to the bone.

At least she had gotten the hogs fed and bedded before the worst of the storm struck. Lucy and Myrtle giggled in the kitchen as they washed the supper dishes. Phillip was already in bed. Belle relaxed in the chair and sipped her hot chocolate. All was right with the world. At least for now.

Ingrid sat across from her, sipping her own hot chocolate. She was curvy and svelte, had their mother's build. The beautiful child, her parents called her. Belle had been unfortunate enough to inherit their father's makeup, including his less-than-average looks. Life just wasn't fair.

"You are crazy to come out on a night like this. Didn't you see the dark clouds in the west?"

"As I told you before, I was worried about Jennie."

Belle worked to keep her demeanor calm, even though what she had decided for Jennie was none of Ingrid's business. "There is nothing to worry about. Jennie is fine. Couldn't be better, in fact."

From the kitchen, Lucy and Myrtle appeared, the fronts of their dresses damp. "Now that you're finished, girls, it's time for you to get to bed."

Lucy stuck out her lower lip. "But we want to play with Auntie Ingrid."

"Not tonight. You do as I say."

Myrtle heaved a sigh. "Yes, Mama."

The two of them bid good night to Ingrid then clomped upstairs, mumbling the entire way.

"No dessert for either one of you tomorrow. I don't abide grumbling, and you know it." Belle repositioned herself in her roomy armchair, the springs groaning under her weight. "Now we can speak a little more freely."

Ingrid sipped her chocolate then set it on the polished mahogany table between them. "Then something did happen to precipitate Jennie's sudden departure."

"Nothing more than her age and demeanor. And the way she carried on with Emil. She wasn't serious about her studies or her chores at all. Every time she opened her mouth, it was to speak about Emil. They sat across the dinner table from one another and made eyes at each other. I was afraid she was going to do something foolish. It was high time for her to learn to be a lady."

"I don't understand how fast it happened. You never mentioned this to me. Neither did Jennie."

Good. Belle had been able to keep the girl from opening her mouth. "I didn't tell her until last night after you left. You know how upset she would be, making a fuss about leaving home, crying and carrying on. I didn't want you to have to deal with so much emotion. This was for the best."

"But why send her away at all?" Ingrid's otherwise-unlined forehead creased.

"The girl is seventeen years old and wild as they come. If she's to make a good match, she needs to be tamed. Emil is nothing more than a farmhand. You know how I want a better life for her. I have the money to make that possible, so why not give my daughter the best?"

Ingrid tipped her head. "Why didn't you tell anyone? You never discussed it with me."

Belle smoothed her skirt over her ample waist as she worked to smooth the words flowing from her tongue. "I do appreciate the advice you give me, but Jennie is my daughter. In the end, the decision is mine. That is one benefit to not being married. I answer to no one but God." Belle scraped some dirt from underneath her cracked fingernails. "When I told her, she was quite happy to go. Excited, in fact."

"I never got a chance to say goodbye and wish her well." A shimmer of a tear sparkled in Ingrid's green eyes.

"Now, now, there's no need for such theatrics. You know I can't stand them. She's not gone forever. One of these days, she'll be back, all grown up and settled, a proper young lady."

"Do you have her address? At least I can write to her. I'm sure it would cheer her to have a letter from home soon after her arrival."

"Give the girl a chance to get there and get settled. She'll be home-sick, and a letter will only make it worse. I'll give you her address when I feel she's ready to hear from us." Belle rose. "That's enough of that. It's only right that our children grow up and make their own way in the world. Are you finished with your cocoa?"

Ingrid tipped the mug to drain it and handed it to Belle. "That was wonderful. I'm good and warm for my trip home. I'll just make sure the children are all tucked in and head toward town."

"Are you sure you don't want to spend the night? I'd hate for you to get lost in the storm."

"No, I'll be fine. I'll heat a water bottle when I get to my place and slip it into bed under the quilts. In fact, it sounds quite inviting."

"If you're sure." Frankly, Belle thought Ingrid was crazy, but young people tended to be that way. By the time you were Belle's age, you were more practical. She lumbered to the kitchen to wash the cups and wipe the counters. As she did so, she hummed a little tune to herself. Yes, life was good. The time had come to place a new advertisement. Time to seek out another man.

Just as she reached to put the cups in the cabinet, Ingrid called for her from upstairs, her voice so urgent it stopped Belle's heart for half a second.

She raced up the stairs as fast as her bulk allowed. There Ingrid stood, the wardrobe door open, her face as pale as a whitewashed wall.

Ingrid's hands, her entire body, trembled as she stood in front of the girls' wardrobe. Jennie's clothes were still here. Her sweet smocked dresses that Belle had sewn for her. Her winter coat, a fake fur one that Jennie wore all the time. The wide-brimmed hat she insisted on putting on anytime the sun shone. If she would be gone for an extended period of time, what were the clothes doing in here?

"What's the matter, Auntie Ingrid?" Myrtle rubbed her sleepy green eyes.

"Do you know why Jennie didn't take her clothes with her?"

Myrtle shrugged. "I never thought about it. We went to bed last night and Jennie was here. When we woke up this morning, she was gone. Mama told us not to say anything about it. If someone asked, we were to let them know she was in California. That's so far away."

Belle stood in the doorway, panting. "What is all this commotion about?"

"Jennie's clothes." Ingrid pointed to the cherry wardrobe. "They're here, even her favorites. What's going on?"

"First of all, I don't know what you're doing snooping about my business." Belle lunged forward, slammed the doors shut, and leaned against the wardrobe. "Second of all, it's warm in California. She won't need her winter clothes."

"She wouldn't go anywhere without that hat, especially to a place where the sun is always shining."

"Do you think I would send my daughter to a sophisticated city like Los Angeles in such provincial clothing? Here they may have been the best and the latest fashion, but not there. She had to have all new things. I've been buying and sewing like crazy the past few weeks."

"She didn't suspect anything?"

"She was excited to have new clothes. Almost like a trousseau."

A dull ache pounded behind Ingrid's right eye. Jennie would have told her if Belle was measuring her for new things. She would have shared those plans with Ingrid. But she didn't. Never breathed a word of it. That couldn't be what she wanted to discuss last night, could it? She wouldn't have been so secretive. Instead, she would have been making quite the fuss.

If Jennie had left last evening, wouldn't the stationmaster have mentioned it today? He knew Jennie and knew her well. Everyone recognized her by the blue bow in her hair. Surely he would have remarked on her departure. Then again, if she took the overnight train, the stationmaster wouldn't have been there. Oh, Ingrid couldn't make sense of what was happening. "I don't understand this."

Belle, arms akimbo, pierced Ingrid with a fierce gaze. "It's not for you to understand. Jennie is my child, and I made the best choice I could for her. We will miss her, that's for sure, but we couldn't hang on to her forever."

Yet when Jennie had returned to her biological father soon after the death of her mother a few years ago, Belle had mourned over the child and pined for her so much that Jennie's father agreed to return the girl to Belle's care. What a joyful reunion.

Now Belle wasn't playing the part of a mother longing for her child who was traveling across the country alone. "Is that why you wouldn't let anyone into the room off the parlor? Were you storing Jennie's new clothes there?"

"Yes, that's where I keep my surprises. You know how fun that is. So that room will remain off limits. Now, don't you think you should be off? By the time you get home, it will be quite late. I'm afraid the storm is worsening."

With no other explanation forthcoming, Ingrid had to accept her sister's word. On some level, it did make sense. Belle always dressed her children in the best and wanted them to be more than she ever was. The secrecy was what was puzzling Ingrid. "Yes, I'll bid you good night and be on my way."

After Belle insisted Ingrid borrow her buggy, a short five minutes later, Belle sent Ingrid on her way with a hot brick for her feet. Sissy—the girls had named the mare—plodded along, bobbing her head as she plowed through the snow. A thick, wet blanket now covered and hid what road there had been. A few inches must have fallen in the short time she'd been at Belle's. Perhaps going home tonight had not been the best of ideas.

She urged Sissy forward, though she shook her head and turned to the side. "Come on. Now is not the time for you to get stubborn on me."

Though she slapped the mare's rump with the reins, she refused to move. What was going on? Maybe she had run off the road or had missed the turn toward town. Ingrid set the brake on the buggy and hopped down to inspect.

Through the driving snow, a pinprick of light shone just on the side of the road. What on earth was that? She stepped closer. The light came from a lamp. A lamp that illuminated green paint on a motorcar.

No, not Mr. Lindherud. He was the only one in town with such a conveyance. Though cold snow soaked her shoes and stockings, she tramped through a drift to the driver's side of the vehicle.

Mr. Lindherud sat inside, slumped forward. In his lap, Princess lifted her nose through a pile of blankets. She gave a happy yip when she spied Ingrid.

Her heart thumped inside her chest. She had to get him out of there. See if he was still alive. Though there weren't signs of blood, the light wasn't good. "Mr. Lindherud, can you hear me?" She shook him as hard as she dared. No response. "Mr. Lindherud!" The screeching wind carried her words away.

Though she tugged on the door handle, it refused to budge. Like an animal scrambling to dig a hole, she shoveled the snow away with her hands, her mittens wet, her fingers numb. At last, the door gave way.

"Nils." *Please, God, let him be alive.*

He groaned and sat up. "You came." A light smile graced his undamaged face.

"Do you remember what happened?"

"The auto skidded. There was nothing I could do. My poor car. Is it damaged badly?"

"Let's not worry about that now. You can take care of it in the morning. Belle loaned me her horse and buggy. Let me drive you to town. Can you get out on your own?"

He slid across the seat, moaning as he did so. "My ribs."

"I wouldn't be surprised if you cracked a few. When we get to LaPorte, I'll call for the doctor."

"I need to get to Detroit. My mother is ill."

"You aren't going in this storm. She would want you to be safe."

"No. I have to leave. Right now. I've wasted too much time. I have rope. It's a long shot, but maybe your horse can pull me out."

Chapter Eleven

Thick, heavy snow swirled about Nils, sticking to his eyelashes so it was almost like he was attempting to read a book through a snow globe. But Mama needed him. Even with everything going on with Sven, Mama came first. Nils had to get home.

"Hand me that rope from the back of the auto." He shouted so Miss Storset would hear him above the howl of the storm.

"Here you go." Her gloved hand brushed his open palm and all of a sudden, the night wasn't quite so cold.

He attached the rope to the front of the motorcar and then to the horse's harness. He slapped the reins and urged the mare forward. Though she pulled with all her might, the auto didn't budge. Not an inch.

"Let me see if she'll do better with a treat." Miss Storset left his side and disappeared into the white darkness.

Did she carry a carrot or apple in her pocket?

"Ready!"

Again, though he yeehawed and giddyupped, the poor animal wasn't strong enough to move his heavy auto.

As if stepping out of a fog, Ingrid was by his side once more. "You aren't going anywhere tonight. Why don't I drive you into town?"

He gazed at the sky, the swirling flakes sending his head spinning. Mama, Sven, the dealership. They competed for dominance in his life. How could he neglect one for the other? Tonight, God was making that decision for him. One Nils didn't like. "I don't have much of a choice, do I?"

"No. Can you help me hitch Sissy so we can get going?"

Hitching the horse was more time consuming than it should have been. By the time they climbed into her buggy, his toes had gone numb, as had his fingers and the tips of his ears and nose. When he warmed up, it was going to hurt. Princess shivered, and he wrapped her inside his coat.

With visibility so low, the going was slow. After a silent, tense trip, they arrived in the near-quiet city. Everyone else had the good sense to stay inside tonight.

"Do you need any help with the horse when you get home?" The two- and three-story buildings lining the road blocked some of the wind. Speaking was easier here.

"No, thank you. I'll bring the buggy to the livery, and they can help me."

"I owe you a favor."

"You don't. How are your ribs?"

"Not bad. No need for a doctor. With a little rest, they'll be fine."

"If you're sure. Otherwise, alert the hotel staff. They'll send for Dr. Clark."

He tipped his snow-laden fedora to her, and she rolled away toward the livery.

Oh, to be home with Mama and Sven. Safe and warm where he belonged. Tonight, it would have to be the Teegarden Hotel in LaPorte. He had no other options. If only he had a way of knowing what was going on with Mama, how she was. He could try to telephone the drugstore near their home, but the shop would be closed for the night. No one would answer.

Upon entering the red-carpeted lobby, he set Princess on the floor and removed his hat and coat and shook them out. Before he climbed the stairs to his room, he strolled to the empty dining room. Not a soul was out and about tonight.

The waiter scurried over, no doubt glad for a customer. "Good evening, sir. A table for one?"

Nils suppressed his laughter. No one else was around. "Yes, please."

The man, dressed in a dark suit and a white tie, seated him at a table close to the fire. "What can I get you?"

Nils placed his order, and the waiter left. Princess turned around three times and settled herself on the floor at Nils's feet. Soon the waiter was back with a steaming cup of coffee. "What brings you out on a nasty night like this? Hey, I've seen you around. Aren't you the chap with the motorcar?"

"*Was* the chap with the motorcar. Right now, it's resting against a tree on a road just outside of town."

"Tough luck. That's when I say those modern contraptions aren't worth it. Give me a horse any day of the week."

"You may be right in this case. I was trying to get home to my mother, who is ill. Now I'll have to wait until at least the morning."

"What brings you to town in the first place?"

Did Nils care to share his personal problems with a total stranger?

The waiter pulled out the chair across from Nils and sat down. "I'm Henry, by the way." A smile spread across the man's round face, so much like Sven's.

Like melting snow, Nils's resolve disappeared, and he poured out his story to Henry. "So that's why I'm here, though it appears that my brother isn't."

"I wish I could have spoken to him before he went to the Gunness place."

Nils raised his eyebrows. "Why is that?"

"I could have warned him."

The warm coffee turned to ice in Nils's veins. "About what?"

"The nasty business that has gone on at that place for a few years now."

Nils pushed his cup away, the bitter brew souring his stomach. "Tell me."

"About eight months or so after Peter Gunness moved to town and married Belle, he died under some rather mysterious circumstances. She claimed he was putting his shoes by the stove to warm before they went to bed one night. Somehow, he managed to knock part of the sausage grinder from the shelf above the stove. The grinder hit him in the back of the head, leaving a nasty gash. She also claimed the hot water on the back of the stove spilled and scalded him."

"That's terrible." The nausea worsened.

"The suspicious part is that there were no burns anywhere on Peter's body. His nose was broken, and though she claimed he lived for four hours after the hit on the head, she never noticed his nose. By the time she called for the doctor, Gunness was dead on the parlor floor. Though she told authorities he had just died, he was already stiff. The whole town was buzzing about it. Still is."

Nils leaned forward. "Did she receive any type of punishment?"

"Nope." Henry rubbed the top of his bald head. "The coroner ruled it an accident, and she got off scot-free. Although anyone with a lick of sense knows what happened in that house that night."

Was that the fate that had befallen Sven?

No, Nils couldn't allow himself to entertain the notion for a single second. He had to give Mrs. Gunness the benefit of the doubt. She may have had nothing to do with her husband's death. In the end, it may have been nothing more than a bizarre, tragic accident.

Besides, Sven was too smart. He would have gotten away before it came to that.

Wouldn't he?

"Well, well, well, what do we have here?" Ray crunched through the sparkling snow around the mangled green automobile, the morning air carrying a bite. Mr. Lindherud wasn't such a good driver after all, was he? From the looks of it, he was headed out of town. That would be a good thing. Belle didn't need anyone like him sniffing around her place. She'd had enough trouble when Peter died a few years back.

Ray spit a stream of tobacco onto the white snow, dirtying it. No time like the present to help the man get on his way. In the early-morning light, Ray picked out footprints dancing around the car, along with hoof marks. Looked like someone in a wagon or buggy picked him up. Likely brought him to town for the night. That was the first place Ray would search.

He headed in the direction of LaPorte. The bitter cold that swept in after the storm bit at his cheeks and streamed through his thin wool coat. Maybe if he helped Belle get rid of that good-for-nothing, there would be a reward in it for him. He'd be able to buy himself a new coat. Wheatbrook hardly paid him enough to survive. Then again, the saloons around the city profited greatly from Ray's business.

He trekked into town, the deep snow making the walk more arduous.

He wasn't there long before he spied the man striding down the road, his black fedora and long camel coat standing out in a crowd of farmers and ordinary folk. Good that he should go back where he came from. No need for the likes of him around here.

But Ray's breath hitched when Lindherud turned into the sheriff's office. He shuddered. What did Lindherud want there? Was he filing a report with the officials about his brother? This couldn't be good. Ray moved closer in an attempt to glean some information.

"Oh, excuse me, I didn't see you there." Before the feminine voice had a chance to register, the scent of lilies filled his nostrils. Ingrid.

He gave her his best, most charming smile. "Miss Storset." He had no bowler to tip, only a knit cap to keep his ears warm.

"Mr. Lamphere." Her words were as icy as the weather.

Before he could inquire after her health, she too disappeared into the sheriff's office. For sure, something was going on. Something Ray had to find out about.

He inched along the sidewalk, closer to the office. No good. He couldn't see anything or hear anything. Much as it made his skin crawl, he'd have to make up an excuse to go inside. Perhaps a concerned citizen reporting a motorcar accident. Yes, that was the ticket.

He straightened his shoulders and entered the building. Several officers sat scribbling on paper or typing, the clacking noise giving Ray a headache. There they were, both of them, in the back of the room, speaking with Sheriff Smutzer, a man with whom Ray was all too familiar.

"Mr. Lamphere." The paunchy deputy who approached Ray spoke with more than a hint of disdain in his voice. "What can I help you with?"

"I'd like to talk to Sheriff Smutzer."

"As you can see, he's busy at the moment. I can assist you with whatever you need."

"I'll wait." Ray plopped himself into a chair and crossed his arms to keep the deputy from bothering him. He was still too far away from Lindherud and Ingrid to hear what they were saying. But from the way they gestured, neither one was too happy. Good. They shouldn't be.

"And now my brother is missing." Ah, Lindherud had finally raised his voice for Ray to hear what was going on. "And so is Jennie."

Jennie? Belle's oldest girl?

"M—m—my sister told me she went to Los Angeles, but to me that isn't right. All her clothes are here."

"Miss Storset, if your sister wishes to send her daughter to school in California, there is nothing I can do about that. It's not a crime." The sheriff stroked his neat, wiry mustache. "And Mr. Lindherud, I understand your frustration, but unless we have concrete proof to the contrary, we are going to have to assume that your brother left LaPorte of his own volition and may not want to be found."

"Do you have any more information about my brother's motorcar? Have you questioned the farmhand?"

"He claims to have found it hidden in the woods and said he was driving it to town to turn it in. Seeing as he had never driven before, he didn't do too well or get too far."

"And you believe him?" Mr. Lindherud's voice now carried clearly to Ray. "The automobile was pointing away from town."

"There was evidence that it spun when it slid down the embankment. There was nothing else in or around the vehicle to indicate that Mr. Lamphere was lying."

The sheriff believed him. Good. Why was it that whenever there were any out-of-the-ordinary happenings in LaPorte, he was the first person to be questioned?

"What about the inquest into Mr. Gunness's death?" Lindherud leaned forward, now nose to nose with the sheriff, who was dressed like a dandy in a turtleneck sweater and a tailored jacket.

"That is neither here nor there. His death was found to be an accident, and the case was closed. Listen, I wish I could help both of you, but there is no evidence of a crime in either instance."

"S—s—so you can do nothing to find Jennie?" Tears laced Ingrid's words.

The sheriff shook his head.

"And nothing to help me locate my brother?"

Another shake of the sheriff's head. "I'll keep my eyes and ears open.

That's the best I can do. If there's nothing further, I'll see you out."

They allowed the sheriff to lead them to the front of the room. Ray stepped in their way. "Mr. Lindherud. Funny to run into you here."

The big-city man knit his eyebrows together. "Mr. Lamphere. I would say that it is quite a coincidence."

"I believe I came across your automobile up against a tree in a snowdrift." Ray tapped his chin.

"You may well have."

"I'd like to lend you a hand in getting it out." Ray struggled to keep his words syrupy sweet.

Lindherud glanced at Ingrid, like he needed her permission. What a sissy. No man should be led around by a woman like that.

Ingrid shrugged.

Just then, the Western Union boy scurried into the office. "Ah, Mr. Lindherud. There you are. I've been searching all over. Telegram for you."

Chapter Twelve

Nils's heart almost beat out of his chest as he stood in the middle of the police station and held the yellow slip of paper in his hand. Everyone knew that only bad news came in telegrams. This one had to be another one about Mama. He hadn't made it in time. She had passed away alone. His only prayer was that Sven had somehow returned and hadn't thought to contact him.

With shaking fingers, he slit the paper open, holding his breath the entire time.

HAVE YOU FOUND SVEN *Stop* WHEN WILL YOU BE HOME *Stop*
PEOPLE ASKING TO BUY CARS *Stop* LOVE MAMA

This had to be some kind of a joke. Yesterday, barely twelve hours ago, Mama had been on her deathbed. Today she was fine? Asking about him?

At least he had the answer to one question. Sven wasn't home.

Before he jumped to any conclusions or made any decisions, he had to glean more information.

Miss Storset touched his arm, her fingers as light as butterflies. "Is it bad news?"

"Confusing news. This telegram is supposedly from Mama asking what I've found out about my brother."

"I thought she was so ill you had to hurry home."

"That's what last night's telegram led me to believe."

"How very odd."

"That's what I think. Does the station have a telephone? I need to speak to someone in Detroit directly."

The Western Union boy, still standing beside Nils, pointed to Smutzer's desk.

"Thank you." Nils tipped the young man and headed to Smutzer. "I need to make a call."

"Of course." The sheriff handed the telephone to Nils.

After speaking to the operator, he was put through to the drugstore down the street from the house. "Paul, this is Nils Lindherud." He spoke slowly and clearly so Paul would be sure to understand him.

"Nils. Good to hear from you. How are things in LaPorte?"

"I'm confused about something. Have you seen my mother recently?"

"Sure. She was in here this morning for some liniment. Said this cold weather and the storm were making her hands ache."

"That's all she mentioned?"

"Yes. Why?"

"How did she seem to you? Sick at all?"

"Not at all. In fact, we had a nice long talk. She's worried about you and about your brother. Said she was going to try to get in touch with you. Did she?"

"She did." He went on to inform Paul about the telegrams.

"Well, that is very strange. To me, she looked fit as a fiddle. Said she'd even shoveled the front walk this morning after the snow then tromped all the way here. I didn't notice a thing wrong with her, and she didn't mention anything other than her hands bothering her."

"Thank you, Paul. Tell her I'm well. No news on Sven. Give her my love."

"Will do."

Nils ended the call and thanked the sheriff for allowing him to use the telephone.

In a flash of blue from her dress, Miss Storset was at his side. "What? What did he say?"

"Mama's fine. He saw her this morning. Her only complaint is her rheumatism."

"How odd." A small frown marred her face.

"I know. Why would she send that first telegram?" He bit the inside of his cheek. "Don't you have to get back to the confectionary?"

"I should." She shook her head, a blond curl escaping her pins. "I suppose I do need to go." Her voice was flat. She didn't enjoy that job. Why didn't she just tell her sister the way she felt? Surely Mrs. Gunness would understand.

Then again, had Nils understood when Sven had wanted to follow his own dream?

"Let me walk you back, and we can talk along the way." Nils gave Ray a glance. Had the man been standing there the entire time?

Ray had the good grace to slink away.

Nils and Ingrid both buttoned their coats and stepped into the day as shimmering white as angels in heaven. Yet Nils shuddered as he wrapped his muffler around his neck. That whiteness hid a great deal of ugliness. He offered Miss Storset his elbow so she wouldn't slip and fall on the walk.

"I'm sensing you have a theory about that first telegram."

"I do. I don't think my mother sent it."

"Who would have?"

"I'm not exactly sure. Someone who doesn't want me here investigating my brother's disappearance. Maybe Ray. Or your sister."

Ingrid gave a sharp inhale of breath. "Not Belle. She wouldn't do such a thing. It must have been Ray. Do you think your brother met with some. . . ?"

"Misfortune?"

"Yes."

"I'm beginning to strongly suspect it." This town was filled with shadows and secrets. Things they would rather have remain buried. Figuratively and possibly literally. Among them might be the answers Nils was seeking. "Why didn't you tell me about your brother-in-law?"

"Which one?" The gaze she gave him was pure innocence.

"Belle was married more than once?"

"To Mads Sorenson in the '90s, before I arrived from Norway. He died of heart failure soon after their home and business in Chicago burned. She married Peter Gunness not long after moving here."

"I'm talking about Peter."

She came to an abrupt halt in the middle of the street and faced him. "You've heard the rumors around town about him."

"You think they're rumors?"

"My sister is a loving and kind woman. She's taken in a number of children who have no place else to go and has saved them from a life on the streets. She would never hurt another living soul." Yet, as she spoke the words, she averted her gaze to stare at the icy walk.

He tilted her chin and forced her to look him in the eyes. "Do you believe that?"

Without hesitation, she nodded. "I have no evidence to the contrary."

"What about the evidence collected at the time of Peter's death?"

"The coroner ruled it an accident. If that was his finding, it must be so. The others are newspapermen and busybodies searching for a juicy tale. Not everything is as sinister as you make it out to be, Mr. Lindherud. Bad things happen to people sometimes." She quivered. "Perhaps your brother wasn't the man you believed him to be. Perhaps he has gone off without telling you. Disappeared on purpose. Why don't you consider that possibility?"

As she stepped away, she huffed then marched down the street toward her shop. After a minute, he hustled to catch up to her, but by the time he was close enough to holler to her, she had entered the confectionary.

She'd been a true friend to him. Most likely, she had saved his life last night. He didn't want to lose that friendship. Well, he wouldn't intrude on her business hours. He'd have to talk to her later.

As he turned to go, the flash of a blue jacket against the white snow caught his eye.

Ray Lamphere. What was he doing hanging around here?

Thursday, December 19, 1907

Belle allowed the lace curtain at the window to fall back into place. A thrill passed through her at the sight of the man striding up the lane, suitcase in hand, a long, gray fur coat that reached to his knees embracing his body.

Unlike the effort it took to get Sven Lindherud to accept her invitation, John Moe had been more than eager to move to LaPorte. As she waited for him to make his way to the door, she inspected the parlor. A luxurious red settee dominated the middle of the room, and a hand-knitted lace runner covered the mahogany coffee table. Not a speck of dust to be found. All the throw pillows were in place. Too bad she didn't have a bouquet of flowers to set on top of the spinet piano in the corner.

She lumbered into the kitchen to check on dinner. The carrots bubbled away in the pot and the potatoes were baking in the oven. Soon the aroma of beefsteak frying would fill the air. She cracked open the icebox to check on the cream cake. She lifted the corners of her mouth. Perfect.

In the dining room, her good china gleamed in the glow of the electric lights. Nothing was too good for her. She might live on a hog farm, but she had the finest house around.

Mr. Moe gave a firm knock at the door, and Belle scurried to admit him as fast as her oversized body would allow.

"Sir, what a pleasure to make your acquaintance, though I feel I already know you from your letters."

He doffed his hat. "Woo-wee. You weren't kidding about the house and the farm. All looks mighty fine. I've never seen such a pretty place out in the country before. And you run this place by yourself?"

She slipped the smile from her face and replaced it with a frown. "You wouldn't believe what a difficult time I've had. Two husbands dead, every hand I've hired run off." She grinned again and pointed at him. "But you, Mr. Moe, are cut from a different cloth, I can tell. You aren't going to be like the others. You will stay around, won't you? Together, we can make this one of the finest places in all of Indiana. No, in all of the Midwest. You did bring the money, didn't you?"

He slipped off that expensive coat of his and handed it to her. "Of course I did. And may I say that you, lovely lady, are charming enough to convince any man this is the place for him. I don't understand why you have had such a difficult time keeping help."

"You know how men like to take advantage of a woman on her own. Some I've had to fire. Some don't tolerate the thought of having to listen to a woman. Who knows about the others? But you're here now, so life is looking up. Why don't you take your trunk to the first bedroom on the right at the top of the stairs? I'll get the beefsteaks going. You can meet the children at dinner."

He licked his lips. "Yes, ma'am."

"You and I are going to get along just fine." Belle chuckled as she sauntered to the kitchen. "Myrtle, get the butter out for the potatoes. Lucy, don't be dawdling now. There are still no napkins on the table. Everything needs to be just right for Mr. Moe."

Myrtle sighed a rather long, dramatic sigh as she opened the icebox. "I don't know why you think this one is going to work out when none of the others have."

"Phillip, you keep away from that stove, you hear? And no sassing me, miss. I've prayed hard about this, and this time, I think God has sent us the perfect man."

Lucy pulled Belle's best white napkins from the cupboard. "Is he going to be our new daddy?"

"We'll just have to wait and see on that. Now get to your jobs. If we want him to stay, we must be proper little ladies and gentleman. Phillip, I'm talking to you. Stay out of the icebox."

In no time, Mr. Moe clomped down the stairs and seated himself at the dining table, napkin tucked under his chin. He was pleasant enough to look at. Middle aged. Graying hair. Still lean and muscular but not too brawny. Yes, he would do just fine.

The children prattled on and on to him over dinner, but she didn't scold them.

"Do you have a motorcar like Mr. Lindherud?" Phillip stuffed his mouth full of potatoes.

Mr. Moe widened his dark eyes. "A motorcar? No, I'm afraid not."

"I want to go fast in one. When I grow up, I'm going to drive a motorcar."

"That's a fine ambition."

"Please, Phillip, don't talk with your mouth full. And quit pestering Mr. Moe. Let him enjoy his dinner."

"Our sister has gone to finishing school in California." This from Lucy, who picked at the carrots she hated. "You wouldn't send us to California, would you?"

"That would be something for your mother to decide. I've never been, but I understand that California is quite beautiful with palm trees and sunny weather all the time."

"But I like snow." Lucy stuck out her lower lip.

What was wrong with her children this evening? "Lucy, do not pout. No one has talked about you going away. You're much too little. Jennie was a young lady."

And so the dinner went along. At last, everyone cleaned their plates. Myrtle washed the dishes while Lucy put Phillip to bed. "School tomorrow, children. The last day before Christmas. Off with all of you. Sweet dreams. I love you." The girls pecked her on the cheek and climbed the stairs.

The peace and quiet of the evening, the part of the day Belle enjoyed most, settled over the house. She brought Mr. Moe a cup of coffee and settled on the couch beside him. They drank in relative silence, conversing only about his trip from Wisconsin.

As soon as he drained his cup, Belle hefted herself to her feet and took it from him. "I expect that you are tired after your journey and are eager to get to bed. I'll bid you a good night. We'll get down to business later."

Chapter Thirteen

Monday,
December 23, 1907

The bleak darkness of December descended on the confectionary shop while Ingrid worked. Thank goodness for electric lights, their glow casting eerie shadows on the walls.

Christmas was almost upon them, the busiest she'd been since she'd opened the shop. Every one of LaPorte's eleven thousand residents, or so it seemed, wanted to purchase candy for a gift for a sweetheart or a child or a dear friend. Perhaps soon, if this season went well, she would be able to hire an assistant, someone who could mind the front of the store while she spent more time in her darkroom. She had photographs waiting to be developed.

She whisked the ganache for her truffles in a large bowl. Not long into the process, her arms ached. How was she ever going to complete this order for the mayor? While it was a great honor to have him buy from her as opposed to the grocery or elsewhere, fashioning the sweet delights for all of his employees and major donors was a daunting task.

She almost had the ganache to the right consistency when a creak sounded from upstairs. "What was that?" She spoke into the air, praying no one would answer.

For a long moment, she held her breath. When all remained silent, she released it in a gigantic whoosh. She was exhausted, and her mind was playing tricks on her.

There. She stared into the bowl. Perfect ganache. Now it needed to cool so she could shape it into balls. Once she put it in the icebox, she chopped some pecans to add to it.

Though the silence around her was heavy, almost oppressive, the atmosphere inside her mind was just the opposite. Her thoughts chased each other round and round like a pair of frisky dogs.

Mr. Lindherud had found out about that debacle with Peter's death. He, and most of the city of LaPorte, believed that her brother-in-law's demise was no accident. She would grant them that the circumstances were unusual. How many people passed away because part of a sausage grinder fell on their heads? None that she knew of. But accidents, even strange and bizarre ones, happened all the time.

Take Thomas Swanson's untimely passing. He died when he tripped and fell on a pitchfork, the tines piercing his heart. No one questioned his widow about what happened. No one accused her of running him through.

Why were they so hard on her sister? Yes, she could be abrasive at times. She didn't possess many social graces, but look where she had come from. Growing up, they'd struggled for every scrap of food for the large family. There was little time for school, little time for niceties. From a young age on, Papa and Mama expected them to work and to work hard. Nothing refined about that.

Why shun Belle because of her background?

Perhaps that's why she had sent Jennie to the school in California. It made sense that Belle would want to give her daughter a better life. Jennie wouldn't have to grow up with the stigma of being big and working like a horse.

But then there was that closet full of Jennie's clothes. Even a couple of her signature blue hair bows.

Belle's explanation made some sense. A little. Still, Ingrid couldn't wrap her mind all the way around it. Jennie wouldn't have left everything behind. There were precious possessions she had that she would never go anywhere without, especially the necklace her papa had given her and the small porcelain shepherdess Emil had gifted her.

Without Jennie there, Emil had quit as Belle's farmhand.

Ingrid set her knife down, added the pecans to the ganache she had pulled from the icebox, and rubbed her aching temples. Though her mind wasn't on the task in front of her and fatigue weighted her eyelids, she had to finish these sweets.

There it came again. The squeak from upstairs. Groaning floorboards or a door opening or shutting. Hadn't she locked the door to her rooms like she always did? Once more, she picked up the sharp-bladed chef's knife. She lit the lamp she used to walk upstairs. This time, she crept from the kitchen and stepped outside, the bitter cold stealing her breath. On tiptoes, she climbed the steps to her simple two-room apartment.

The front door was closed and unlocked. She must not have latched it after a quick bite of lunch a few hours ago. How careless of her. No light shone through the windows.

Panther-like, she stole inside, careful to avoid the one section of the floor right inside that always squeaked. She turned on the electric bulbs and light swept across the room, over her small settee, the lounge chair, and the coffee table where the book she'd been reading sat.

All normal.

She glanced to her right, toward the bedroom. The door was closed. She never left it that way. Only when she slept. Was that a sliver of light peeking from under it?

Someone was here. In her private space. Her most personal area. What were they doing?

Well, she wasn't going to keep standing in this one spot, and she wasn't going to investigate. The best thing to do was to inform Sheriff Smutzer. Let the professionals handle it.

Before she even had a chance to turn and leave, the perpetrator flung open her bedroom door, a candle illuminating his long nose and hooded eyes, deepening the crevices of his face.

He approached.

She screamed. Turned to run.

He caught her one-armed. Yanked her to himself. Covered her mouth.

"Don't make a sound. You understand?" He reeked of alcohol.

She nodded.

"Drop the knife."

She'd forgotten she held it. With a clatter, it fell to the floor.

He kicked it away.

"If you promise to be quiet, I'll let you go. No more screaming. Got it?"

Again she nodded.

He released his grasp.

But she had no intention of allowing him to harm her without putting up a fight.

For most of the first day after the accident, Nils had made a few inquiries and telephone calls to try to get his automobile repaired. Though Lamphere had offered to help, something about the man didn't sit right with Nils. At last, he had managed to employ Mr. Wheatbrook and his Clydesdales to pull the machine out of the snow and tow it to the livery. Though the livery owner had had a good laugh at Nils's expense, his auto was now safely under a roof.

Over a week had gone by while he worked on his motorcar, getting it into driving condition once again. Even though the local manufacturer in LaPorte didn't build Fords, it did make parts for automobiles. Nils had managed to finagle what he could get, make it fit, and return his motorcar to service. He'd finished late today. Too late to head home now.

The frustration was that all those days in this town working on his vehicle were days he didn't spend tracking down his brother. Time wasted while Sven moved farther away.

If he had left at all.

Now the holidays had arrived. First thing in the morning, he would head to Detroit to spend Christmas with his mother. Was it even worth it to return after the first of the year?

So much time gone.

So few answers.

Before he quit LaPorte tomorrow, he needed to sit down and have a long talk with the sheriff, who dismissed the sudden appearance of Sven's automobile a little too easily. The vehicle had to yield some clues. Sven had come to LaPorte. Nils had yet to be convinced he left.

Nils gave a deep-throated growl as he threw his suitcase on the hotel bed. Princess gazed at him, her eyebrows raised.

"Sorry. Guess I'm not much in the holiday spirit."

Princess relaxed again, and her eyes fluttered closed.

What he needed was a stroll to Miss Storset's confectionary. Through-out the past eight or nine days, they had enjoyed each other's company. A couple of times, they had dined together at the hotel. One pleasant evening, they had ambled along Main Street, admiring the electric light displays and the Christmas decorations in the store windows. Now the time had come for him to bid her farewell.

He had known her for such a short time. Why, then, did his heart ache at the thought of leaving? Of possibly never seeing her again?

He finished stuffing his clothing into the suitcase and left his room, Princess content to stay curled up close to the fireplace.

He waved to the young man at the hotel's front desk as he shrugged into his coat and made his way to the door. The clerk, James, who spoke into the telephone, motioned him over. He covered the speaker. "I'm glad I caught you. This call is for you, actually."

Nils stepped to the desk and took the receiver as James slid the speaker toward him. "This is Nils Lindherud."

William's tinny voice came over the line. "Nils? Isn't this crazy? I can be in Detroit and talk to you way down there in Indiana."

"What's going on, William?"

"Well, sir, I was wondering when you were going to return to the city."

"Tomorrow. How are things at the dealership?"

"That's why I'm phoning. Since you've been gone, I haven't been able to sell a single auto. Not one. The bills are coming in, and when I looked at the books, there isn't much money to pay them. Then there is a Mr. Gillespie who continues to come around, claiming you owe him money."

Nils squeezed his eyes shut. Not Gillespie. He was supposed to give Nils more time to come up with the cash, time for the dealership to take off and turn a profit. Now was not the moment for him to show up. Nils didn't have the funds. Didn't know when he would get them.

If only he hadn't made that investment that crashed. And then borrowed money from Gillespie for the business. Now he knew how a drowning man felt. To say the least, it wasn't nice. "Put him off. I'll deal with him after Christmas. And while I'm home, we'll need to sell some cars. A bunch of them."

"Whatever you say, Boss."

They ended the call a minute later.

As Nils shuffled out the door toward Miss Storset's place, night taking hold, he kicked at a clump of snow, his temples pounding. Being badgered by Gillespie was the last thing he needed. Didn't he have enough to deal with? Sven missing, the dealership struggling, Mama's health poor.

After dashing through dirty puddles of melting slush and skirting numerous wagons, buggies, and the streetcar, he arrived at the block where the confectionary stood. Most of the businesses sat dark, lights streaming from the top floors where families ate their suppers and chatted together.

A sudden wave of homesickness washed over him. If only he could turn back the clock a few months. He hadn't cherished the times around the table with Mama and Sven. He should have. How suddenly life changed.

Would it ever be the same?

He came to Miss Storset's shop. Light tumbled from the upstairs panes. Two shadows passed in front of the window. One form was curvy and decidedly feminine. The other just the opposite. A flash of blue.

Ray.

From the way they danced back and forth in front of the glass, Miss Storset wasn't happy he was there.

Pulse pounding in his neck, Nils sprinted to the back and took the stairs two at a time. He flung the door open, and it slammed against the wall, sending a shower of plaster to the ground.

Ray held Miss Storset in a choke hold. "Get it." She squeaked out the words. Her eyes were large in her peaked face, her lips void of color.

He followed her gaze to something shiny on the floor. A butcher knife. He bent to grab it.

"If you want her to stay alive, I wouldn't do that."

Nils straightened. Stepped between the weapon and Ray and Ingrid. "You're drunk, Lamphere. Let her go."

"Not till I get what I want."

"Which is? What is your problem with her?"

"Not her." Ray spit a stream onto the floor. "Her sister."

"Why not take it up with Mrs. Gunness?"

Miss Storset wobbled on her feet.

"Don't think I haven't."

Miss Storset slumped. What had Ray done to Mrs. Gunness? "Let Miss Storset sit down, and we'll talk about this like sane adults."

"You saying there's something wrong with me?" Ray also wobbled.

Nils bit his tongue. "Just let her go."

"No funny business. Keep those hands where I can see them."

Nils raised his arms above his head as Ray half dragged Miss Storset to the settee and plopped her down. "You sit down too." He motioned to Nils, who complied.

"Now explain yourself, Lamphere."

"Another man showed up at Belle's farm a few days back. I'm getting tired of it. Belle is always making me look like the fool. I aim to make her pay."

"How did you get in here?"

"You just make sure Belle gets the message. I poured my blood, sweat, and tears into the farm. She promised me it would be ours together, then she reneged. I ain't gonna put up with it any longer. No more."

Chapter Fourteen

Ingrid sat straight and rigid on the settee as Ray stomped from the house, slamming the door behind him, shaking the entire building. Or maybe she wasn't so rigid. Maybe she was trembling.

Mr. Lindherud touched her arm. She had almost forgotten he was sitting there beside her. "How are you holding up?" The warmth of his hand seeped through her lacy shirtwaist clear into her bones and drove away the chill.

She swallowed the lump in her throat. "What would I have done without you? He might have killed me."

He scooted closer to her. "I don't think that was his intention. He's not upset with you but with your sister. He thought that by getting to you, he could get to her."

"I need to warn her. Tell her to keep away from him." She jumped to her feet, the world tilting at an odd angle. Then it spun.

He grabbed her by the elbow and steadied her. "Be careful there. You've had a fright and need time to recover. Please, sit a while longer. I'll go downstairs and telephone the sheriff."

"I suppose that's what I should have done when I heard the noise up here instead of coming to investigate. Ray was waiting for me." She gave a small laugh that sounded weak even to her own ears.

"That would have been a good idea. You take it easy, and I'll make the call."

"Please do. And hurry." Both because she was concerned for her sister and because she didn't relish being alone right now.

He was gone in a flash but returned in a few minutes. "All done. Sheriff Smutzer is going to check on her now. Let me get you some coffee."

"No, thank you," she said, standing. "I have to finish an order. The mayor is expecting it first thing in the morning. After all, it will be Christmas Eve. I mustn't let him down. If I do, I could lose him as a client, and he's a good one. Belle would be so upset with me if the confectionary went bankrupt."

If Ingrid didn't make a go of it, Belle would holler and shout. Might even cut her out of the family. The last thing Ingrid could afford to lose was her sister and those children. She depended on them. *Please, Lord, help me keep the store and my loved ones. I need them. We need each other.* When you didn't have family, you didn't have anything.

"In a bit. First of all, I'll fix you something to eat."

Though she had to get downstairs, with the way her knees were as soft as melted chocolate, she couldn't argue with him. She stumbled back to the lumpy davenport.

As if he had been in her kitchen before, he got to work stoking the fire, putting the percolator on, and heating some soup he found in the icebox.

"Let's get our minds off tonight's incident. Tell me something good that's happened."

She sat forward. "Mr. Klein bought two of the photographs I took of your brother's car."

"That's wonderful news."

"The best part is that your brother's story will be in the local paper. Maybe a lead will come from it. I'm sure you'll find him very soon."

He stilled and stared into space for a long moment.

"Mr. Lindherud?"

"Call me Nils. I'm not going to get my hopes up about the coverage in the press. I go home in the morning for the holidays. That will give me time to sort through what I know and what I don't. Then I can make a better decision about the direction I will take."

"Will you return, Nils?" His name tingled on her tongue.

"I'm not sure. Perhaps not."

A little chill returned to the room.

He stirred the soup in the pot. "But I feel like, if I leave, I'm letting Sven down. And Mama. I owe it to her to find out what happened to him.

To find him and bring him home." He sighed and stared once more. "I only wish I could have done it before Christmas."

She came to her feet a little slower this time and stood behind him. She went to embrace him but stopped herself. She didn't know him that well, yet something about his quiet, gentle manner drew her. "You speak like you don't think you're going to find him alive."

"I know my brother better than anyone in the world. When we were young, we were best friends. I used to know everything about him. If he isn't here, he should be at home. But he's not. No one saw him after he went to the farm. Then his car shows up. Without him. That's all I have to go on. I won't rest, Mama won't rest, until we have the answers we crave. The answers we need and deserve. But I do have to provide for myself and my mother. I have, well, I have obligations I have to meet."

What did he mean by that? "You will. I think tonight proved to you that my sister had nothing to do with your brother's disappearance. Ray has been obsessed with Belle for years. He hates that she doesn't return his affections. He'll do whatever is necessary to keep Belle for himself."

He turned to her, so close his breath was hot on her cheek. "And what about your brother-in-law?"

"Ray could have done something to him."

"Then why didn't your brother-in-law point the finger at Ray before he died? He had every chance to tell your sister who hit him on the head, and he didn't. Don't you find that strange?"

"That blow might have knocked him into confusion."

"Hopefully time will bring the truth to the surface. I am not giving up until I find my brother."

She set two bowls on the table and took two coffee cups from the cupboard. Soon they were sitting down to a meal of *Bergens fiskesuppe*, a Norwegian soup loaded with carrots, parsnips, and fish. Nils slurped it. "Delicious. You are a very good cook, Ingrid."

She sipped the tasty soup. "Thank you, Nils." She enjoyed another bite. "You never mention your father. Has he passed away?"

Once again, Nils stared into the distance.

Giving him time to answer, she savored several bites.

Without warning, he scraped his chair back and came to his feet. He cleared his half-full bowl and set it in the sink. "I don't talk about him." He drew in a breath and blew it out. "When you're ready, I'll walk you down and keep you company while you finish your work. I don't want you to be alone there tonight. You never know who might come along."

What had she said to elicit this response? "I'm sorry. You don't have to tell me anything if you don't want to."

"Well, I don't. Are you ready?"

Her appetite had fled, so she too set her bowl in the sink and followed him to the shop. While she worked, Nils stared out the window and didn't speak much. He'd been so good to her, so kind and gentle with her after Ray's attack. Her question about his father turned him completely around.

He was wrong about Belle. Ingrid would never believe anything ill of her sister. Belle was one of the most caring, God-fearing women Ingrid knew. Why, she'd even gifted this business to Ingrid.

No, Nils was very much mistaken. *Lord, let him be mistaken.*

He should be looking harder at Ray. Ray was dangerous. He'd been crossed in love, and that made him more ferocious than a lion.

The silent stillness of the winter evening wrapped itself around Belle like a cloak as she stepped outside and breathed in a deep lungful of the chilly, bracing air. Cool and cleansing.

She turned to where bright moonbeams bathed the dark house in light. Inside, her children slept soundly, safe and secure in their beds. She scanned the yard with its hogpen, small barn, shed, apple orchard, all of it. Yes, through shrewd dealings and hard work, she had built a better life for herself and the little ones. After many years of labor, she was what people would consider a successful woman.

Then again, there was always more that needed to be done around the place. More items for herself, her children, the house that needed to be paid for. It never ended.

Mr. Moe was gone. Yet another one. While it was hard at first to see them leave, she was used to it by now. There would be others. Already, she was corresponding with a set of brothers from Wisconsin. Perhaps one or the other of them would work out.

She wiped off the bloody butcher knife on her apron. What a mess the slaughtering had been. At least it was over. This had been a tough one, leaving her exhausted. She would go to bed now and finish the cleanup in the morning.

Before she reached the porch steps, the puttering of a car broke the quietness of the night. At the sound, she spun on her heel. The moon illuminated the red Ford Roundabout that Sheriff Smutzer drove.

As he pulled into the yard, climbed from the car, and approached, she couldn't move. Even if a tornado had been bearing down on her, she wouldn't have been able to take a step.

"Mrs. Gunness?" The sheriff stroked his large, well-trimmed mustache.

"Good evening, Sheriff Smutzer." She smiled at him.

He glanced at the knife in her hand. She gripped it tighter.

"Looks like you've been busy tonight."

"Butchering. Trying to get some bacon for Christmas morning and a ham for Christmas dinner for my family. If I didn't do it tonight, they wouldn't be cured in time."

"Yes, that does sound good."

"What brings you out here this time of night?" Or at all?

"Your sister, Miss Storset, was concerned for your welfare. I came to see that you are safe."

"Why wouldn't I be? What led my sister to believe I had come to some harm?"

"Ray Lamphere paid her a visit tonight and gave her a pretty bad fright. Apparently, it was his way of threatening her to get you to resume a relationship with him."

Belle creased her forehead. "I'm not sure I understand."

"He wanted her to tell you to pick up your relationship with him or he would hurt her in some way or another."

"That would be mighty hard to do, since there was never anything amorous between us. Really, I wonder where Mr. Lamphere comes up with these things. If the world knew who he was carrying on with, they would shun him and run him out of town on a rail." She chuckled. "Honestly, it's the funniest idea I've heard in quite some time."

"I'm glad you find some humor in the situation."

Right away, she contained her mirth. "How is my sister? Did he hurt her?"

"Thankfully not. She's shaken but not a scratch."

"Praise the Lord. That's the best news I've heard in a long while. And what about Mr. Lamphere?"

"He absconded, and we're working right now to locate him."

"That man is crazy. You know that, don't you? When you find him, you need to lock him up and never let him out, ever again. He's been hanging around here for months, spying on us, causing disturbances at all times of the day and night, even some property damage when he broke a window throwing pebbles at it."

"Why is this the first I'm hearing of this?"

"Why?" Belle slapped her knees for dramatic effect. "Why? Ray is a scary man. I was afraid if I said something, if I told the police, he would follow through on his violent threats and would hurt either me or my children or all of us. That's one reason I had to send Jennie away. She's young and pretty, and I didn't want him to do anything to her. He had made advances toward her."

The sheriff removed his hat and slicked back his hair. "These are serious allegations, Mrs. Gunness. Perhaps I should come inside and take a statement from you."

Inside? She couldn't allow him to see the state of her home. What a mess it was. That wouldn't do. Not at all. She rubbed her hands together. "No, no." She commanded her voice to keep from betraying her. "Can't I do it at the station in the morning?" She yawned big and wide. "Sir, it's very late, and you must understand how tiring butchering can be. After a good night's sleep, which I won't get while Mr. Lamphere is running loose, I'll be able to better help you. I think your time tonight would be better served in working to bring this menace to justice."

"I have deputies—"

"That's all for tonight, sir. I hope that when I see you in the morning, you'll have apprehended Mr. Lamphere and this nightmare will have come to an end. Until then." She marched up the steps and into the foyer, slamming the door behind her.

She leaned against the door, her breath coming in rapid spurts, until the roar of the engine faded and silence once again took hold.

Only then did she slump to the floor, shaking from head to toe.

Chapter Fifteen

A steady *drip, drip, drip* of melting snow woke Ingrid the following morning after a restless night. Every little sound, every creaking of the building, had sent her bolting upright. Her heart couldn't take much more of this. Ray had gotten under her skin and discomfited her.

No use in trying to go back to sleep. The mayor's truffles were ready for her to deliver. As soon as she did that, she would go to Belle's and speak to her. Make sure she was all right. Ray's words about wanting to get even with Belle rang in her ears.

Not bothering to light the stove, she slipped into a heavy wool skirt and a high-necked shirtwaist with a warm sweater. Ray was likely to be sleeping off the effects of his intoxication, so she scurried down the stairs, packed the truffles into little boxes tied with string, set them in a bag, and bustled down the street to city hall. This way, she would get this chore checked off her list for today. The last thing she looked forward to was speaking with the mayor.

As she had hoped, the early-rising mayor was already in his office, even though it was Christmas Eve. "Come in, Miss Storset. I hope you've brought me those candies I ordered."

She held her canvas bag loaded with numerous small red boxes of truffles even as her heart thrummed in her chest. "I—I—I have."

He maneuvered around his desk, took the proffered bag from her, and peeked inside. "Oh, how nice these look. I knew I could count on you. Thank you. Our town is blessed to have you as a resident."

"Y—y—you're welcome." Her quiet darkroom beckoned to her.

"Let me get you a cup of coffee. You're up very early."

She waved him off. "N—n—no, thank you. I do have to get going." Before he could attempt to detain her any further, she raced from the office and was on her way to Belle's.

The thaw that had set in during the night left the road from LaPorte to Belle's farm a muddy mess. The trip took a bit longer than usual, so morning was wearing on as she wandered into Belle's farmyard. From the corner of her eye, she discovered Belle hard at work in the hogpen. No wonder she advertised for men to come and assist her with this back-breaking job. No woman should have to do what she did. Though she was built for this type of labor, it wasn't feminine.

Lifting her skirts against the wet dirt that made up the yard, Ingrid picked her way to the hogpen with ginger steps. "Good morning." She waved to her sister. "Thank goodness you're all right." Ingrid tromped through the slush and mud and gave her sister a light hug, careful not to soil her own clothes.

"And why wouldn't I be?"

"I was so afraid." Ingrid drew in a breath to combat the wavering in her voice. "Ray surprised me at my place last night and threatened you. Didn't the sheriff stop by and check on you?"

"Yes, he did. Came at a most inconvenient time, just when I had butchered a pig. What a mess I was."

She butchered a pig last night? Then why wasn't she busy this morning with the smoking and sausage making and everything that went into that process? Why do it so close to Christmas? Ingrid shook off her thoughts. "Did Ray show up here?"

"No, I haven't seen him. Good thing too. He's been hanging about. I told him next time he comes, I'm going to file trespassing charges. That's what you need to do. March yourself right back into town and file a report against him. If we allow him to get away with such behavior, it's only going to embolden him. You must take swift and severe action—otherwise he will continue to pester you."

"He did more than pester me. He frightened me terribly, trying to get back at you. If not for Nils Lindherud, I don't know what would have become of me." A shudder coursed through her.

"All the more reason to hightail it into LaPorte and get that report filed as soon as possible."

"The sheriff already knows. Won't he handle it from there?"

"In my experience, not unless you demand that charges be brought against Ray. In fact, if you give me a chance to clean up, I'll go with you and make sure the sheriff takes you seriously."

Ingrid relaxed her shoulders. "Would you do that for me? You must be so busy with the pig from last night."

"Nothing that won't wait. You, my dear sister, are more important to me than anything."

Together, they ambled toward the house so Belle could clean up and they could collect Phillip to bring with them. The girls could stay alone.

Belle slowed her pace as they approached the brick dwelling. "You said that Mr. Lindherud is still in town?"

"Yes. He came to my rescue last night. I owe my life to him."

"I would have thought he'd be home for Christmas by now."

"Getting his automobile repaired took quite a while."

"Did he ever find out who sent him that fake telegram?"

Ingrid had told Belle about it last Thursday at dinner. "No. He has no idea who sent it or why."

"Could be Ray. If he thinks Mr. Lindherud is a rival for my affections, he wouldn't hesitate to do whatever it took to remove him from the picture."

"Why would he believe that?"

"You never know. I suspect Ray is insane. Any more antics, and I may be forced to try to have him declared and committed."

"Goodness, is that necessary?"

"You never know. Anyway, what's most important is to get you to LaPorte and follow up with Sheriff Smutzer. We have to stop Ray before he harms anyone else."

"I need my money sooner rather than later, Mr. Lindherud." Even through the tinny telephone, Nils didn't miss the menacing tone of Gillespie's voice. William must have cracked and told Gillespie where to locate him.

Nils tapped a pencil on the hotel's marble-topped front desk. What could he do to buy more time? His money was running low. He had a business to run that needed his attention, but he was no closer to an answer about Sven than when he arrived almost two weeks ago. Not knowing what happened to her son might be all it took to stop Mama's heart for good. He had to take care of her. And of his brother.

What was the right thing? Did Mama need him more, or Sven? How would any of them survive without the dealership's income?

When he'd made that bad investment, bought those stocks in a company that went bankrupt a few short weeks later, he'd let them down. He wouldn't do it again. He'd prove to them he was different than Papa. "Just a little bit longer. I'm begging you to be patient with me. I'm, uh, away due to a family emergency."

"William told me all about that."

So it *was* William who had given away Nils's whereabouts.

"I don't like to hear that you aren't giving your dealership the attention it needs. If you aren't bringing in an income, how are you going to bring in cash to repay me? What will happen to your family if I take away your business?"

That was the question for which Nils had no answer. He had to earn a living, had to keep his family from going destitute. Though the temptation was strong to follow in his father's footsteps and get the money through any means necessary, he wouldn't do it. He wasn't like Papa. "I will. I promise you, you'll get your money. You have to understand."

"All I understand is that I loaned you a considerable sum last year to purchase that Ford dealership. You told me that under your care, it would be a profitable venture. Perhaps my mistake was putting my faith in you."

"No, sir, I assure you, your faith was not misplaced. I'm returning to Detroit today. When I arrive, I'll be able to make a payment."

"I expect to see you in my office the day after Christmas, cash in hand. Otherwise, I'll be forced to go to your mother and inform her of your predicament. I hear she has heart problems. You wouldn't want her death to be on your hands, now would you?"

Nils swallowed hard. He would do anything to protect Mama. Well, almost anything. "I will see you then and have your money." He returned the receiver to the hook on the telephone.

Now what was he going to do? He didn't have the money. There was no way he'd be able to get it in two days. But he couldn't allow Gillespie to go to Mama and tell her how he'd sunk the family into debt to buy the dealership. All his life long, she'd pounded into him to neither a borrower nor a lender be. Hadn't that been his father's downfall, what had landed him in prison? When the collector had come to call in Papa's debts, Papa went after the man, seriously injuring him, landing Papa in prison, leaving Nils to take care of them.

Now Nils found himself on the other side of the coin.

Between Sven being missing and the debt, the strain would be bad for Mama's heart. Gillespie was right. While the telegram may have been a hoax, her condition was all too real. The doctor had warned her to avoid stress as much as possible. This revelation could well be too much for her.

"Is everything okay, sir?" The front desk clerk raised one dark eyebrow above his round, wire-rimmed glasses.

"Fine." Nils clipped the word.

His time in LaPorte was running out.

Without bothering to grab his coat, Nils stormed toward the sheriff's station to confront Sheriff Smutzer. Princess trotted alongside him. He flung open the station's door and marched to the sheriff's desk almost as if he had blinders on, concentrating only on the lawman. "The time for playing around is over. You and I both know who is responsible for my brother's disappearance. I demand that you arrest Ray Lamphere at once."

"Mr. Lindherud—"

"No more excuses."

"Mr. Lindherud." This time the voice was quiet and feminine.

He turned. "Ingrid. Mrs. Gunness." He really must have been focused on Smutzer not to have noticed them.

Ingrid peered at him through her lashes. "Belle convinced me that we needed to file charges against Mr. Lamphere. The sheriff picked him up at the Wheatbrooks' farm late last night."

Belle nodded her large head. "Right now he's cooling his heels in the jail downstairs. The sheriff is about to sweat him. Get him to admit to the crimes he has committed. Perhaps while he's at it, Ray will give us some kind of clue as to what happened to your brother."

"Really?" Nils focused his attention on the sheriff. "Is this true?"

"Most certainly. Under our pressure, Mr. Lamphere is sure to give us the information we've been seeking on your brother."

"Such a horrible, horrible man," Belle wailed. "Thank God in heaven that he is about to face his judgment."

Nils plopped into the chair, and Princess came to his side. "How long until we have information?"

"There's no telling how long it will take for him to crack." The sheriff rubbed the back of his neck. "I'll let you know as soon as I know something."

"Perhaps today?"

"It's possible. Then again, it might not be until after the new year. No telling."

He would have to pray that Ray would cough up the truth before the holidays. Perhaps the good cheer of the season would force him to cleanse his conscience.

Then again, there just might be something Nils could do to speed up the process. "I want to see him. Alone."

Chapter Sixteen

The dank odor of the jail filled Nils's nostrils. Here and there, a vagrant or drunkard occupied one of the barred rooms. Maybe a thief or two. The sheriff led Nils farther down the corridor before stopping at the last cell in the hall.

He eyed Nils. "Ten minutes. That's all you have, understand?" With a jangle of keys against his hip, the sheriff retreated.

"So now they got you doing their dirty work," Ray sneered.

"I asked to see you."

Ray crossed his arms. "Is that so?"

"It is." Nils grasped the cell's bars and pulled himself toward Ray, now nose to nose with him. "I like you safely tucked away. Much better than our meeting last night."

"I wasn't ever going to hurt her, you know. Just scare her a bit, so she'd beg her sister to take me back."

"What you did to Miss Storset is despicable. Right now, though, I'm not here about that. The police have all the information they need for that case."

"Then why did you come?"

Nils's tongue went dry. "You're going to tell me what you did to my brother and where he is. Now. I know you know, because you had his motorcar."

Ray spit in Nils's face, sending Nils stumbling backward. "Who do you think you are, coming in here and demanding information from me? If I haven't told the cops, what makes you think I'm going to tell you?"

Nils wiped his wet cheek with his sleeve. "So you do know something?"

"Never said that."

"You implied it. Just as good for me."

"Listen." Ray lowered his voice, forcing Nils to step closer. "You're barking up the wrong tree. It's not me you want to sweat—it's the old lady."

"Which old lady?"

"You know. Belle Gunness. Siree, she may be trying to get me committed, but she's the crazy one, I tell you. Ruthless and mean. She has no heart. Or if she does, it's as black as night."

"Don't you have a motive for getting rid of the suitors who come to the farm? Aren't you insanely jealous of them? You've admitted you want to be her paramour. It must drive you crazy, having all those men come seeking Belle's hand when you're the one most suited for her. Being jilted doesn't feel good, does it?"

"What about those stories she told you about your brother? Do they stay consistent? Do you buy any of them? Because you shouldn't."

"Listen, Lamphere, I've had about enough of your antics, throwing dirt on a respectable woman." Did Nils believe what he just told Ray? Not 100 percent, but perhaps Ray wouldn't call his bluff.

"Ha! Belle is far from respectable. Take it from me. No one knows her better than I do. The things I could tell you."

Nils rattled the bars on the cell, his pulse pounding in his neck. "Tell me." His shouts echoed down the hall. "Tell me now. Where is my brother? Is he alive? I have to know."

"Hmm." Ray stroked his spit-crusted mustache. "What would you be willing to give up in order to get this information?"

"Are you blackmailing me?"

"Well, let's see what you have to offer."

Nils released his death grip on the cold steel and marched down the hall, away from Ray, fuming, clenching and unclenching his fists. He had to keep the man from seeing how he affected him. How he got under his skin.

Ray could be bluffing, just as Nils had been. A game of cat and mouse. Who would blink first? The possibility did exist that Ray might not have a drop of information, just as he claimed. Someone that arrogant, who flaunted his indiscretions, would never be able to keep his mouth shut if he had information on Sven.

Then again, he could be the one responsible for Sven's disappearance. He might be in possession of every ounce of knowledge about Sven's whereabouts. Had he kidnapped him? Was he holding him prisoner somewhere? Or had he committed an even more dastardly deed against Sven?

Nils shivered and rubbed away the goose bumps on his arms.

He might have to play Ray's game, at least long enough to discover if he knew anything about Sven. If Ray wanted money, that would be difficult, if not impossible, to come by. That's what everyone wanted from Nils right now.

Cash he didn't have.

Too bad Mama had forbidden Papa to teach Nils how to play poker. Some of those skills would come in handy.

Mama. For her, he had to do whatever it took to bring her information about her younger son.

After steeling his spine, Nils returned to the cell where Ray lounged on the cot. "So." Ray came to his feet. "You've come to a decision."

"Maybe. You see, we both have to act in good faith. If you share just a tidbit with me, a hint of what you know, I'll see what I can do about getting you sprung from here just in time for Christmas. It would be a shame to spend the holidays behind bars. You'd rather be with your mother and the rest of your family, wouldn't you?"

"Not good enough. Before I talk, I walk."

"And if you walk and don't have details or refuse to share them with me? Sorry, but that's not a risk I'm willing to take." He wasn't about to put his reputation on the line only to spring a murderer from jail. Time to put what little card-playing skills he did possess to the test. "Let me know when you're ready to spill." Nils turned and took three steps away from Ray, all the while holding his breath.

"Wait." Ray's call reverberated off the walls.

Nils halted. Still didn't breathe.

"I know something. Just come back."

For a moment, just to draw out Ray's agony, Nils hesitated. Then he headed back once more. "This had better be good."

"It'll be worth your while. You just have to promise to get me out of this stinking place. And get the sheriff off my back. You can't share with him what I'm about to tell you, do you understand me? Otherwise, there will be dire consequences," Ray snarled.

More goose bumps rose on Nils's arms. Was it wise to allow a criminal like Ray to go free just so Nils could find his brother? Was he selling his soul to the devil? But for Mama's sake, he had to make this move. "I promise to do what I can to get you released."

"Did your brother have a long gray and tan fur coat?"

An expensive Christmas gift from Nils. One he could ill afford, but he'd bought it anyway as a show of goodwill between Sven and himself. A way to mend the divide between them. "Yes."

"It's hanging in Mrs. Gunness's wardrobe."

While Nils was downstairs with Mr. Lamphere, Ingrid paced the tiny room where the sheriff had told her and Belle to wait. "What could he have wanted to say to that man? Does he believe he can get him to confess to some nefarious activity involving his brother?"

Belle twisted her plain white handkerchief in her hands. "I don't know. I just don't know. Why did he want to go down there? What might Ray say to him?"

Ingrid paused in her pacing to stare at Belle. "Like what?"

"Since I rebuffed Ray, you never know what he'll spout. He might try to implicate me in the entire matter, just to get even with me. It wouldn't surprise me one bit. That man is insane." A couple of tears flowed down Belle's weathered face. "Then what will I do? I'll lose my farm, my children, my entire life."

Ingrid enveloped her sister in an embrace. "Please, you're getting worked up over nothing. You've done nothing wrong, so you have nothing to worry about." Then again, since Nils had uncovered the sordid affair with Peter, Ingrid hadn't been able to shake the thought from her mind.

No. She couldn't allow herself to believe such things, not of her own flesh and blood. All she had in the world. If Belle lost everything, so would Ingrid.

"You're such a comfort and a joy to me. What would I do without you? I praise God for you every day."

Nils was wrong. Whatever suspicions anyone had about her sister, there was no basis for them. The coroner had acquitted her. That was the end of that matter. Ingrid couldn't allow Nils to sway her thinking. Family was family and always came first.

Two pairs of footsteps clomped up the basement stairs. As soon as Sheriff Smutzer and Nils opened the door to the windowless room, Ingrid swept toward Nils. "What did you find out? What did he tell you?"

He gazed over her shoulder toward her sister then leaned over to whisper in her ear. "Not here. Not now. Meet me at the hotel dining room in thirty minutes. I'll explain then. Right now, I need to speak to the sheriff in private. Please."

"Of course."

The sheriff nodded to Belle and Ingrid. "I have your statements. I'll keep you informed of the progress of the case. Thank you for coming in today. Let me show you out."

Belle waved him off. "That's it? Just like that, we're dismissed?"

"Yes, Mrs. Gunness, that's it." The sheriff's words were firm. "Like I said, I have all I need from you. Right now, I must speak to Mr. Lindherud."

"And what about Mr. Lamphere?"

Ingrid trembled. What if the sheriff allowed him back on the streets? Wouldn't he make good on his threats against Belle? Ingrid would faint dead away if he showed up at the shop again.

"He's my problem, not yours."

"I beg to differ." Belle raised her voice.

Ingrid grabbed her by the arm, murmuring, "The sheriff is doing his job. Let's leave him to it. He won't do anything to put you at risk. He'll make sure you're safe."

Phillip pulled on Belle's skirts. "Mama, I don't like this place. Can we go home now?"

Like a mama bear, she slicked back his hair. "Of course, my darling.

You're right. We've been here long enough. Now it is time to let the sheriff do his job. The one I pay my good tax dollars for."

"Can we have hot cocoa when we get home?" Phillip's blue eyes were wide in his round face.

"Yes, since it's Christmas Eve, we can all have some after church. How does that sound?"

Phillip grinned, his hair flopping in his eyes.

Once outside the station, Ingrid hugged her sister and her nephew and made her way to her shop. She had little time to get much work done before she had to meet Nils at the hotel, but she straightened up a bit and put a few things in order. She made several sales, as customers were anxious to purchase their last-minute gifts. All the hustle and bustle and commotion wore on her nerves. She hadn't been in her darkroom in a while.

Time flew, and she was frazzled as she hustled down the sidewalk, threading her way through the late-morning shoppers and business-people to get to the hotel. She entered the lobby just behind Nils, who turned into the dining room.

She followed but didn't sit down. All the noise and hubbub grated on her. "C–c–can we go somewhere quieter?"

He gazed at her for a moment then nodded. "I know a peaceful spot in a far corner of the lobby."

She followed him past the front desk to a corner hidden by a potted palm. She sank into a plush red-velvet chair. "This is perfect. I'm so glad I didn't have to make you wait."

"My meeting with Sheriff Smutzer took a little longer than I had anticipated. Thank you for agreeing to meet with me."

"I'm anxious to hear what you had to say to Ray."

"Well, I'm not sure I was altogether successful in what I set out to do." Nils took his coat off and draped it on the back of his chair. "I thought if I was stern enough with him, he would tell me where my brother is."

"So you're convinced my sister is innocent."

He scrubbed his face. Little lines had appeared around his eyes and his mouth in the two weeks since he'd come to town. "I don't know.

I was. Now I'm not. I don't know what to think."

Ingrid scooted forward in her chair. "Whatever he told you, please let me know. I can handle whatever you have to say."

"He wanted a trade for his information."

"What kind of trade?"

"If I talked the sheriff into releasing him, he would tell me what he knew."

"I hope you didn't agree to his terms." She quivered like a poplar in the breeze, and her heart threatened to vacate her body.

"I did." A shadow passed over Nils's face. The news Ray had shared must have shaken him something awful.

She drew in a tremulous breath. "Was it worth it? Worth putting my life at risk again?"

He nodded and grasped the arm of the chair so hard his knuckles turned white.

"What aren't you telling me?" Ingrid worked to force the words past her tight vocal cords.

"He shared with me some damaging information against your sister."

"It can't be true."

"But we can verify it."

"What is it?"

"She still has my brother's coat."

"Perhaps he ran off without it."

"In October? Not likely."

"Even if she does, it doesn't mean anything."

"I'm returning to Detroit for the holidays and to take care of some business. Please, don't say anything to your sister about this. We can talk more when I return."

At least he said he would be back. "I—"

"I'm begging you not to say a word to her. Can you promise me that? Please?"

The pleading in his voice was her undoing. "Fine."

He rose. "I must head home if I want to make it before dinner. Even then, I'll be pushing the top speed of my automobile." He stared at her so intensely that she turned away. He lifted her chin and forced her to return his gaze. "Goodbye for now, Ingrid."

"Goodbye. Have a safe trip." Her world wouldn't be quite as bright with him gone.

"You are the one thing I will miss about this awful town. May you have a very merry Christmas."

"Merry Christmas, Nils. I will miss you too."

He strode away, taking a tiny piece of her heart with him. His footsteps faded on the stairs. When he was gone, she exhaled.

Yes, she had promised she wouldn't tell Belle about the information Ray shared with Nils.

But that didn't mean she wouldn't investigate.

Chapter Seventeen

With a sigh—whether from relief or from sheer exhaustion, he couldn't tell—Nils parked his now-repaired automobile, walked through the front door of his home, and dropped his bags in the entrance. In an instant, Mama was there, wrapping him in a hug, squeezing him like she had when he was little. "My boy, my boy, how good to have you home."

He kissed her on the forehead. "It's good to be here."

"What news is there of your brother? In all this time, you must have found out something." She patted his cheek then led him to the kitchen. The aromas of a roast and pumpkin and cinnamon enveloped him, much like Mama's embrace.

Her coloring was good, and she spoke without gasping for breath. Nils had walked in not knowing in what condition he would find her. For now, she was fine. But what about when he answered her question? He drew in a deep breath, his mouth going dry. "Nothing to report."

"Oh." She leaned against the counter, some of the color draining from her face. "I was so hoping. All that time, and no leads on where he is?"

"A few, but nothing definitive. We located his automobile, but there was no trace of him."

Mama gasped and clutched her chest. "My baby." She whispered the words.

"Mama, are you okay?"

She nodded but wobbled. He raced to pull out a kitchen chair and motioned for her to sit. This news was too much for her to bear. "I hate to disappoint you. LaPorte is quite the interesting place with colorful characters, but I don't have much more information than when I first left home to investigate." Since he hadn't been able to verify it, there was no point in informing her about Sven's coat. Ray could have been bluffing.

"The Lord will give you the answers at just the right time."

The Lord. Yes. He'd been such a great help to Nils so far. Why didn't He answer his prayers for Sven? Why had He allowed Sven to go missing? Where was he? Too many questions without any resolutions. His neck and shoulders ached. He rolled them to try to relieve some of the tension.

Mama put the kettle on the stove for tea and piled a plate high with cookies. "If nothing else, it's good that you're back. The house was so empty without either of my boys."

He bit into one of the sweet treats. No one baked like Mama. No one. "I do want to stop at the dealership before dinner and check on the situation there. I know it's late and it's Christmas Eve, but I can't wait."

Mama frowned and furrowed her forehead. "Don't make the same mistake your father did."

Now it was his turn to scrunch his eyebrows together. "What do you mean?"

"He was so concerned about taking care of us. No, more than that. So concerned about providing more than the necessities that he allowed the acquiring of wealth to consume him."

"I'm not."

"I see it starting in you, wanting to go to the dealership on a holiday. Keeping poor William there late when he should be with his family."

"You make me sound like Scrooge."

"That's not how I meant it. I don't want to see you following in your father's footsteps."

"I never will." He'd raised his voice without meaning to.

At his bellow, Mama startled.

"I'm sorry. I shouldn't have yelled. But I'm not going to be like him. Just the opposite. I'm going to show him you can earn a living, a good living, in an ethical manner."

"Just don't go about it in a way that costs you what is most precious in life."

"I won't. I promise." As soon as they located Sven, their lives could get back to normal. Nils could focus on running his business and selling cars. With that money coming in, he could pay Gillespie and get him to stop threatening him. Things would be good again. Like they'd been before he left, when he had labored to provide for his family, to keep food on their table. Then, they had been together, had all they needed, and had been happy.

As happy as they could be under the circumstances.

All too soon, he left the warmth and comfort of home for the automobile dealership, with no idea in what state he would discover it.

He needn't have worried. Everything was in its place, just as he had left it when he set off for Indiana. All the same autos were in the showroom, the papers on the desks neat and organized, the floors swept clean. Any second, Sven would appear from the back room.

If only.

When they had spoken on the telephone, Nils had told William to wait for his arrival so they could chat. At Nils's entrance, William peered up from the paperwork on his desk. A grin broke like the dawn across his thin face. "Welcome back, Boss. You sure are a sight for sore eyes."

"Good to see you too. How are things going?"

William shrugged. "Could be better. Could be worse, all things considered."

"Well, I'm home, at least for a while. Let's sell some cars. Why don't you get me the financial books? I'd like to take a gander at those."

William scurried off to do Nils's bidding. Behind him, the bell on the door chimed. Who in the world would be coming at this time of the evening on a holiday?

"Mr. Lindherud." The deep voice came from right behind Nils. "So good to see you home at last."

Nils spun around, his pulse hammering in his wrist as he stood face-to-face with the round, cherry-cheeked man. "Gillespie. How did you even know I was back?"

"I have my ways. Been keeping my eyes open for you."

All Nils could do was blink several times in rapid succession.

"Let's get down to business, shall we?"

"My assistant is here."

"He knows about your problems. Where is my cash?"

"I told you I'll have it day after tomorrow, so I don't know why you're here. You will get your money."

"That's what your brother kept saying to me."

"What?" Nils scrubbed his face. "My brother?"

"Yes. He borrowed money from me in September. Said he needed it to invest in a farm in Indiana. Soon he would have all of it back and more, once he married the wealthy widow. I never saw a dime of it."

That cleared up the mystery of where Sven had gotten the funds to meet Mrs. Gunness, just as Nils had suspected. Could Gillespie have something to do with Sven's disappearance? Could he have traveled to LaPorte and kidnapped Sven? "Have you heard from him since he set off for Indiana?"

The beefy man shook his head. "I sent several letters to that Gunness woman at the address Sven gave me. She said he hadn't wanted to stick around. Said he was going to California to see if he could strike it rich in gold." Gillespie snorted. "I thought the gold rush was sixty years ago."

That was a completely different story than the one Mrs. Gunness had spun for him. According to her, she had no idea where Sven was headed, just that he had up and left without warning. "Did she give you a specific town or area?" If Sven was out west, Nils would find him. An energy that had been waning in recent days once again surged through his veins.

"Nah, that woman just told me he wasn't satisfied with the comfortable living the farm was earning. He wanted more and more. Your brother, according to Mrs. Gunness, had gold fever."

That was the first time Nils had heard anything about that.

He had to get back to LaPorte. Had to start the search for Sven from square one. The first step was to confront Mrs. Gunness. True, she had lied to him and kicked him off the property, but he had no other place to begin. With enough persuasion, if you wanted to call it that, he might be able to get her to talk. Perhaps if he could verify that Sven's coat was there, he would be able to hold that over her head. Get her to talk.

In the meantime, he had Gillespie to deal with. "How about a motorcar? What if I give you one? Would that satisfy part of our debt?" How Nils would pay for the vehicle was a bridge he'd have to cross when the time came. He rubbed his hands as he waited for Gillespie's answer.

Gillespie stared at the ceiling and chewed on his lower lip. "That might do me for a bit. A few months, anyway. But I want my money by the first of March. No more excuses. Only cash. Cold, hard currency. Otherwise, there will be a very steep price to pay."

Nils swallowed hard, understanding all too well.

The first of March bought him some time. Perhaps long enough to find Sven and get back here. Time to return to business and sell a few more autos and get out from under this load. "Pick one out. Whatever you want, it's yours."

As soon as Christmas was over, Nils would be back on his way to LaPorte. He would have his answers. This time, Mrs. Gunness was going to tell him the truth.

Wednesday, December 25, 1907

"Merry Christmas, Auntie Ingrid, Merry Christmas!" Lucy and Phillip swarmed Ingrid as she swept into Belle's house, ushering in a blast of cold air and snow flurries with her, her arms loaded with presents wrapped in red paper. Myrtle hung back. Getting a little too old for the hullabaloo.

"Look at what Santa brought to my house. He must have gotten mixed up, so I had to deliver them myself."

"Yeah!" Phillip jumped up and down.

"But you won't get to see any of them until I take off my coat."

With squeals, both Phillip and Lucy backed away, enough for her to set down the gifts, unwrap her muffler, and hang up her coat. Belle entered from the kitchen, her face flushed. "What took you so long to get here? I almost have dinner ready. Your help would have been nice."

Ingrid lowered her gaze to the spotless wood floors. "With the weather so cold and nothing else to do, I'll admit to staying in bed a bit longer today than usual. That was thoughtless of me. Why don't you sit and relax while the girls and I finish the meal preparations?"

Belle nodded, tossed Ingrid her apron, and marched toward the parlor.

Myrtle followed Ingrid into the kitchen. "Mama's been in an awfully terrible mood all day. I don't know what's been eating at her, but she's been storming around and grumbling under her breath."

"There's much to do to get ready for a holiday, plus she has all her other farm chores. We'll treat her extra nice today, and she'll feel better. You'll see." Ingrid hoped that would be the case.

With help from the girls and even a little from Phillip, they got dinner on the table in a short amount of time. The children chattered about all the presents Santa had stuffed into their stockings and even a few that were under the tree. A new dress for Myrtle. A baby doll for Lucy. A train engine for Phillip.

All the time they prattled, Ingrid studied Belle, who ate her baked ham and sweet potatoes without saying a word. Just a steady *clink, clink, clink* of her fork against the bone china plate. For dessert, she served cream cake, a favorite with all around the table. While Ingrid reveled in the luscious goodness of the vanilla cream, Belle sat stone faced, hardly eating a bite.

That wasn't like her sister at all. Something was wrong, no doubt about it.

After the last plate had been licked clean, Belle and Ingrid set to washing them while the children played in the parlor. Ingrid allowed the silence to stretch between them for a few minutes before she summoned enough courage to confront her sister. "Is something the matter?"

"No." Belle clipped the word.

"There is. You love Christmas and are never this solemn."

"I just. . ." She stared out the window across the snowy farmyard.

Was that a tear that shimmered in her eye?

"I just miss Jennie so."

"If that's the case, you can bring her home, can't you?"

Belle shook her head, her jowls jiggling. "She's in a far better place. Sometimes a mother has to put her children's welfare above her own, no matter what the cost. That's what I've done for Jennie."

"We could write her a letter. All of us could contribute a section. It would be wonderful for her to hear from her entire family, and for us, it will be like talking to her. Like she's here with us."

Belle swiped away the single errant tear. "You're right. She is with us, in spirit, closer than we think."

Ingrid wrapped her sister in a hug. "That's a beautiful way to put it. Imagine how she's missing us and wishing she could be here too."

"Do you think that's the case?"

"Of course it is. Remember how much we missed Mama and Papa when we came to this country? That's how Jennie is feeling."

"I don't know."

"Where is this coming from? There is no doubt in my mind that she loves you and wants to be near you."

"I do feel her near me."

"Good. Now let's enjoy the rest of the day."

The holiday sped by with much laughter and silliness on the part of the kids. Belle remained quieter and more reserved than usual but did partake in the activities, even in writing the group letter to Jennie. For sure, Jennie would reply. It would be good to hear from her. When she got home, Ingrid would also write a private letter to the girl.

The evening deepened and stars sprinkled the dark winter sky. Phillip crawled into Ingrid's lap as Belle lit the candles on the tree. The soft light washed over them, and the meaning of this day stole the breath from Ingrid's lungs. God descended in humble human form to save the world from their sins. What a thought. What a concept.

Phillip yawned, the contented sigh of a little boy who'd had the most perfect and exciting day of his life. Ingrid squeezed him. "Are you ready for bed? Do you want me to tuck you in?"

The child nodded. "Yes, Auntie. And tell me a story?"

"Don't I always?"

"That's what I love about you best."

With her own happy sigh, Ingrid carried the boy upstairs to his room. "This is the last year I'll be able to do this. Next year you will be six and much too heavy for me to carry."

"Then I never want to have another birthday."

Ingrid lifted the bedcovers, and Phillip slid between the sheets. She mussed his hair and kissed his brow. "Sweet dreams, my darling boy." Part of her never wanted him to have another birthday either. If only he could remain five forever.

But time marched on.

She slipped the door shut, but before it latched, Phillip called to her. "Auntie Ingrid, I left my blankie in Mama's room this morning. I need it."

"I'll get it for you." Her heart rate ticked up a notch. This was the opportunity she had been waiting for. The chance to prove or disprove Ray's claims about Sven's coat.

In no time, she located Phillip's blanket on Belle's huge walnut bed. The matching wardrobe beckoned to her, singing its siren song. Downstairs, Belle and the girls laughed. Good, they were preoccupied. And noisy. Perfect. Because if Belle discovered her in here, poking around, it might cause a permanent rift between them.

Drawing in a deep breath, she pulled open the two doors and exposed Belle's personal belongings. Nothing out of the ordinary. Nothing Ingrid wouldn't find in her own wardrobe.

She was about to shut the door when a garment tucked in the back caught her eye. So different from the mundane clothing of a twentieth-century farm woman. A gray fur coat. Ingrid glanced over both her shoulders. Then she yanked out the coat's sleeve. The fur beneath her fingers was softer than anything she'd ever touched.

A whiff of cologne filled the air. Men's cologne. Nothing feminine about its muskiness.

"Ingrid?"

She jumped, dropped the coat's sleeve, her heart pounding in her ears, the whoosh drowning out everything else. When she whirled around, Belle stood behind her, arms akimbo. Her green eyes had darkened, a storm brewing in them that she would soon unleash.

"I—I—I was just getting, um, Phillip's blanket. He asked me to."

"Get out of my room. Get out of my house."

"Where did it come from?"

"That's not your business, you little snoop. Leave. Now. And don't come back."

Chapter Eighteen

Friday,
February 21, 1908

Nils drove into LaPorte, his ever-faithful Princess curled under a pile of blankets at his side. As he motored by Ingrid's confectionary, his heart warmed. An OPEN sign hung on the door. He would visit her right away.

While he was home, he had sold a few autos. Enough to pay some bills and put a little cash in his pocket. Besides, he wasn't going to be here long. He had put enough money aside to take a train to California if necessary, but he still had funds for a few nights at the Teegarden Hotel.

He'd even managed to make a payment to Gillespie, buying him time until the end of March to come up with the balance. Still, he would never have enough. All he kept doing was putting the man off and putting him off again. At some point, Gillespie would stop being so cooperative.

Once he was properly greeted by the staff and settled into his room along with Princess, his single bag set on the luggage rack in the corner and the heavy curtains pulled back to let in the daylight, he set off for Ingrid's.

When he entered the shop, Ingrid was nowhere to be found. He rang the little bell on the counter and called for her several times before she emerged from the basement, a heavy apron over her dark blue skirt and her white shirt. She must have been in her darkroom. When she saw him, her countenance brightened, and her green eyes widened. "I'm so glad you've returned."

"It's good to see you." And it was. Until this moment, he hadn't realized how much he'd missed her. Her lilting laughter. The way she tilted her head when she concentrated. The lightness of her touch on his arm. He placed a soft kiss on her cheek, his lips on fire as he stepped back.

Ingrid's eyes sparkled, and she didn't throw him out on his ear. His advance hadn't been unwelcome.

"Are you taking a day off from the candy business?"

She shook her head. "Since the holidays are over, business has been slow. I needed the solitude."

"I'm sure. You told me in your letters that you sold a few more pictures."

"I have. Two of them. Including the ones Klein bought of your brother's car, that makes five altogether. He will have to hire me soon."

"That's wonderful."

"I didn't think you'd ever be back. You kept saying you were coming, and you never did."

"Like I wrote, I had to deal with my business. Problems kept cropping up that I had to take care of. Always just before I planned to leave. This time, I'm only here for a few days, because I have a lead about my brother I want to check out. Add that to the information you gave me about my brother's coat, and this was the logical place to start."

"I haven't seen or spoken to my sister since Christmas Day. She'll have nothing to do with me. She's even forbidden the children to visit here after school."

He reached out to embrace her but thought better of it. "I'm so sorry. How difficult that must be for you."

She nodded, staring at the floor. "It is. They're the only family I have in America. Everyone else is thousands of miles away. When she banned me, she might as well have ripped my soul from my body." Her voice caught.

The poor woman. What she must be suffering.

Then she turned her attention toward him. "What did you discover?"

"Your sister told an acquaintance of mine that Sven caught gold fever and made his way to California in hopes of striking it rich."

"That's wonderful news." Her eyes brightened all the more. "Now you can search for him there."

"But that's not the story she told me about him. I worked to verify what my acquaintance told me, going so far as to write several letters to your sister. She never answered. That's why I'm here." All the while, he had itched to follow up on the lead he had, torn in two by his responsibilities. If only he could be in two places at once.

"I have to confront your sister. I was hoping you would come with me to pave the way."

"I'm as unwelcome as you are these days."

"Please? If nothing else, perhaps you'll catch a glimpse of the children. Or we can drive Myrtle and Lucy home from school. What do you say?" He lifted a quick prayer that she would accept.

"It would be nice to see them. Belle can't get any angrier with me than she already is."

"Then let's go. School will dismiss in a few minutes."

"Why don't you fetch the girls while I clean up? By the time you return, I should be ready."

He collected two very excited young ladies from the school and picked up a much more subdued Ingrid from the shop.

A gleam did touch her eyes when she climbed in and hugged her nieces. "How I've missed you."

"Auntie Ingrid, I have so much to tell you." Lucy bounced on the seat, and not from the bumpy road.

"I want to hear it all. And what about you, Myrtle?"

"I don't understand why Mama won't let us see you and why you don't come over on Thursdays anymore."

"Sometimes sisters don't see eye to eye on things. We'll smooth it over, you'll see. Soon, life will be set to rights, and everything will go back to the way it was." Her voice was flat, like she didn't believe her own words.

The countryside flew by, and before Nils knew it, he was pulling into the Gunness farmyard. The odor of manure, the oinking of the hogs, the unevenness of the now-frozen mud beneath his feet, greeted him. He glanced from the brick house to the hogpen. Funny. Holes littered the pen. "What are those for?"

Ingrid gazed at where he was pointing. "Belle digs them every year before the freeze so she can dump her garbage. It would be impossible to do so in the depths of winter."

The girls hopped from the auto and skipped to the house. Nils helped

Ingrid down. Her hand was so small and delicate in his. He didn't dislike the feel of it. Not by a long shot. In fact, he hated to release his hold on her.

Belle didn't give them a chance to get in the house, meeting them on the porch, a large apron covering her bulk. "I thought I told both of you never to show your faces here again. You don't listen well."

Nils stepped between the sisters. "I had an interesting conversation with Mr. Gillespie while I was in Detroit. He mentioned writing to you in search of Sven. You told me that you had no idea where my brother had gone, but you told him that Sven moved west to strike it rich in California."

"I don't even know a Mr. Gillespie."

Nils bit the inside of his cheek until the metallic taste of blood filled his mouth. "He wrote to you."

"Mr. Lindherud, I receive so many letters on any given day, I cannot keep straight all of their names or what it is they are writing to me about."

"But you must remember Sven telling you where he was going." Nils fisted his hands. Not that he would ever strike a woman. He had learned long ago that violence never solved anything but only made more trouble.

"It might have been California. These men come and go all the time. How am I to remember all they say?"

He stepped toward her. "A town. I need the name of the town. Now. Think hard and fast."

Belle made a show of tapping her chin. "I can't remember. I barely recall your brother. Not to mention it was months ago he showed up here."

Ingrid slid to Nils's side. "What about his coat? Why would he leave it behind?"

"If he did travel to California, he would have no need of it. Lots of men leave plenty of articles of clothing behind when they hightail it from here."

"Then why did you get so angry with me when I found it in your wardrobe?"

Nils touched her arm. No need to get Mrs. Gunness riled up, at least not until he gleaned the information he needed. "Where did he go? The name of a town, please." Nils held himself back from shouting at the woman. "That's what I need. Jog your memory. Tell me where I can find my brother."

"High Point, California. That's where he went."

"I've never heard of it."

"There are plenty of towns no one has heard of in that big state. Now, I must insist that you remove yourselves from my property before I press trespassing charges against you. Good day." She waddled to the door, slamming it behind her.

He stood gaping at the red door.

Ingrid touched his shoulder. "Do you believe her?"

He rubbed his aching temples. "I don't know what to believe anymore."

Ingrid clipped the photographs she had just developed to the wire line strung across the stone-walled basement, the vinegary odor of the chemicals stinging her nose and eyes. This was film she'd been meaning to develop for a while, since the fall when she had first taken the pictures. Because they were personal snapshots and she'd been busy over the holidays, she hadn't gotten around to it.

She pinned the last image to the line then stepped back and scanned the photographs. There was one of the three younger kids playing in the yard, one of Phillip on the tree swing, and one of Jennie and Belle. Ingrid furrowed her brow as she studied the photo harder. What a strange expression on Jennie's face. Almost like she was grimacing. When had Ingrid snapped this photo?

That's right. It was the day before Jennie left for California. The evening they all had dinner together. Jennie hadn't been happy that night, had been in such a state, begging to see Ingrid the following day. Such a scowl on her face. Peering at the photograph, Ingrid could see without a doubt that something was troubling the girl. Something big. Dark, heavy bags hung under her eyes.

The poor dear. Ingrid had been too preoccupied with Nils's arrival and with getting supper that she hadn't truly paid attention to Jennie's condition. If only she had. If only she could go back and relive that night, how differently she would do it. She'd make sure to speak to her niece right away.

Perhaps she could still be of help to Jennie. She could write another letter and get up the gumption to ask Belle to mail it. Maybe Jennie still had something to share with her. She could discover what was bothering the girl before she left.

Ingrid had no idea if they had ever received a reply from their Christmas letter to Jennie.

With her stomach unsettled, Ingrid moved to study the first photograph again. This one was of the farmyard. In the back, behind the house, was the hogpen. What was that in the pen? No pig, that's for sure. Ingrid squinted to make out the small object. Why, it appeared to be a shovel handle stuck into the ground, jutting from the earth. Almost like Belle was marking a spot so she would be able to find it later.

Goodness, why would she do that? How very odd. Did it mean anything?

Ingrid shook her head. Probably nothing more meaningful than that Belle had finished burying the garbage and had stuck the spade there instead of returning it to the shed. All of this talk of missing people and the trouble with Ray had Ingrid reading too much into everything.

Still, she might ask Nils about the photograph. He might be able to put the situation into some perspective.

After allowing the photograph to finish drying, she unpinned it from the line, careful not to touch the image imprinted there. She glanced at the watch pinned to her shirtwaist. Good. It was dinnertime. She might be able to catch Nils when he came into the hotel to eat.

Once she had slipped the photograph into her purse, she hurried down the street to the hotel bustling with guests checking in and others entering the dining room for their evening meal. Taking a deep breath to steady her quaking hands, she plunged into the crowd in the dining room. The sweet, meaty odor of roast beef churned her already upset stomach. She scoured the room, searching as fast as possible to find Nils. They would have to speak outside. She couldn't stay in here a moment longer.

Just when she had decided he wasn't there, she spied him lounging at a table in the corner. As she made her way to him, threading around tables and patrons, she trembled, her heart pounding. He turned toward her and a smile crossed his face, though little lines around his eyes and mouth betrayed his fatigue. They all needed answers.

"Hi."

He stood and pulled out a chair for her. "I wasn't expecting the pleasure of your company this evening. You were so busy earlier."

"I need to speak to you about something. You have to tell me I'm seeing things."

"Have a seat."

"Not here. It's too stuffy. Can we go somewhere a little more private?"

"Sure. How about our quiet corner in the lobby?" He laid a couple of bills on the table.

"Oh. I didn't mean to interrupt your dinner. Were you done?"

"Just finishing my coffee. I always have time for you. Always."

At his words, she softened. "Thank you. That means so much."

He led her to the spot in the lobby where they had met before, the place almost hidden by a large green plant. She blew out a breath and relaxed her shoulders as she settled into a chair.

"So, what is this you want to share with me?"

She pulled the photograph from her purse and handed it to him. "Do you notice anything strange about this picture?"

Like she had, he squinted and examined the photo. Silence stretched between them as he studied it. "Do you mean this shovel sticking out of the ground?"

She sucked in her breath. "You see it too."

"Did Belle leave it like that?"

"I don't know. I've never taken note of her doing such a thing, but I suppose it's possible. Don't you think it's strange, though, that it's sticking up in the middle of the hogpen?"

He shook his head. "I don't know. I'd probably brush it off, but these strange occurrences are piling up."

"What do you mean?"

"I mean that the telegraph operator contacted me. There is no such town as High Point. At least not in California."

"I'm sure Belle made a mistake or forgot or misheard. That is explained simply enough."

Nils stabbed her with such a stare it pierced her soul. She turned away so she didn't read the truth in his eyes.

She couldn't face it. Never would admit it.

Nils wanted her to say that Belle was involved in his brother's disappearance.

No. No. No. *God, it can't be true. You wouldn't allow it to be so.*

Chapter Nineteen

Friday,
March 20, 1908

A cold Norwegian winter wind blew right through Ingrid's coat as she stood at the edge of the farmyard. The deep twilight of the late afternoon laid its heavy blanket on top of the land, so thick she could hardly draw a breath.

Belle chased about the yard, her speed amazing for a woman of her bulk, a hatchet raised over her head. She squawked as much as the chicken she sought. Around and around she ran. "I'm going to get you if it's the last thing I do. You'll not get away from me. When I catch you, I'm going to chop off your head, your wings, your legs. There will be nothing left of you."

Ingrid backed away from the horrific scene. This was her least favorite part of living on a farm. Butchering animals was gory. Watching it made her tummy do funny things. Belle caught the hen and hacked it into pieces. Then she chased another bird. Did the same thing. Over and over.

Ingrid slipped behind a large tree, the bark rough under her touch and against her cheek. She dared to peek from behind it. Funny how she could see what Belle was doing, even though darkness blacked out every other image from the scene.

Feathers floated on the frigid breeze and littered the ground like fresh-fallen snow. Ingrid turned and hid her face from the hideous sight.

"There you are, you little wretch. You're going to tell Mama and Papa what I've done, aren't you?"

Ingrid peered at Belle through her lashes. She shook her head as hard as she could. "N—no, I'd never do such a thing. I—I promise, I won't tell a soul. Please, Belle, please don't hurt me."

"You'll run inside and squeal, I just know it." Belle raised the hatchet above her head. "This is what I do to people who can't keep their mouths shut."

Ingrid screamed and sprinted off, racing as fast as her little legs could carry her. Belle was so much bigger, so much faster, so much stronger. Blood whooshed through Ingrid's ears. A stitch pained her side. Though she drew in air, it wasn't enough. She couldn't breathe. Couldn't run fast enough.

There was Belle, right behind her, her old, worn face contorted into that of an enormous, hideous troll. Ingrid screamed again and again, for Mama, for Papa, for anyone. No one came. No one answered. She tripped.

Fell.

Belle towered over her. Raised her hatchet.

Swung it down.

Ingrid bolted upright in bed, sweat pouring down her face, soaking her nightgown and the bedsheets. She gasped for air. Several minutes went by before the thudding of her heart slowed. It was nothing more than a dream. A nightmare. It was over. She was awake. No light filtered through the windows, so it must still be deep in the night.

What an awful scare. Why did she dream what she did about her own sister? She had to stop entertaining the thought, even for a second, that Belle had committed a crime. Because she hadn't. And never would. Not her beloved sister with the most caring heart of any woman on the planet. All the family she had now.

Ingrid's dry tongue stuck to the roof of her mouth. She sat on the edge of the bed a moment to get her bearings.

What was that awful smell? Acrid. Like the burning of a hundred wood fires combined with kerosene. The remnants of the dream, more than likely. She stepped onto the floor.

Warm.

More than that. Hot. Burning hot.

She grabbed her dressing gown from the end of the bed and raced to the bedroom door. She grasped the knob for a mere second before jerking away. That too was as hot as metal from a forge.

The crackling now drowned out every other noise.

The place was on fire.

God, help me.

How was she supposed to get out of here? The window. While the drop would be far, it was her only chance to survive. She raced to it. Smoke seeped through the floorboards, choking her. Coughing, she raised the window. "Help! Help! Someone, help! Fire! I'm trapped. The place is burning. Help me! Help!"

Why did her window have to face away from the street? No one could hear her back here. The only people about this time of night were the saloon patrons. And they were too inebriated to be of any assistance.

"Help! Help!"

Was there no one out there?

She peered at the distance from the window to the hard-packed ground below. For sure, she'd break at least one leg, if not both of them. There had to be another way.

The smoke thickened. As she scurried to the bed, she bumped into the end of it, unable now to see much in front of her. She pulled off the pillows and stuffed them against the bottom of the door to keep the worst of the smoke out.

For a moment, she spun in circles, her heart tripping over itself, her breathing labored. What should she do? How would she get out? She was going to die in here. This was the end of her.

God, help me. No one else can.

No one else could.

She worked to inhale but ended up coughing all the harder. Flames now snaked up the far wall behind her wardrobe. They did nothing to light the black room.

Wait. The blanket and quilt and sheets. She should be able to tie them into a rope, one she could climb down. She'd have to knot it securely to the bedpost. And pray harder than she ever had that it would hold her weight.

She yanked the covers from the bed and got to work, tying knots, tugging on them to be sure they would hold. If only she knew better how to do this. With the way her hands trembled, she fumbled until she had the rope made. The floor was hotter than ever. More flames licked the wall. The bureau smoked, then caught.

She had no time to waste. She had to get out of here.

With every last ounce of her strength, she secured the rope to the bedpost. Covering her mouth, she carried her makeshift rope to the window and flung it out.

Lord, save me. I commit myself to You.

An untouched glass of water sat on the nightstand beside Nils's hotel bed. He perched on the edge of the mattress and stared into the depths of the clear liquid. He mussed his hair. What was he going to do? Every lead he'd gotten on Sven's whereabouts was nothing more than a dead end.

He'd been back and forth to LaPorte almost every weekend. The trips were exhausting. Weeks had passed since he had slept more than a few hours a night. He was an insomniac to begin with, but it was getting ridiculous.

The pace was bending him to the breaking point. Sooner or later, he would have to give up something, either the search for Sven or the dealership. How could he choose, though? To keep body and soul together, and to keep Gillespie from coming after him, he had to keep the dealership in the black. For Mama's health, they needed to find Sven.

Here he was again, then. The answers lay in this town. Specifically, they had to lie at the Gunness farm.

The trouble was, he couldn't prove there had been any foul play. And Belle was under no compunction, either by her own conscience or by the authorities, to share with him or anyone else just where his brother had gone. If he had gone anywhere.

God, is he even alive?

Nils couldn't imagine his life without his little brother. Sure, Sven had been a thorn in his side from time to time. What little brother wasn't? Like the time Sven spilled popcorn on the floor and blamed Nils for it. Or the time when Nils was talking to a girl he liked at school and Sven had wriggled between them and made smooching sounds.

Despite that, they'd had many good times together. Sneaking downstairs on Christmas morning to peek at how many gifts Father Christmas had left them. Or catching toads in the pond on a hot summer day. Or jumping together into a leaf pile.

Too bad Sven's heart wasn't really invested in the business. They had made a good team at the dealership. Sven could sweet-talk just about anyone who came through the door to buy a motorcar. He had a special way about him, so charming and suave. Very sophisticated for a young man.

Except when it came to Mrs. Gunness. That woman had held some sort of sway over him. Persuaded him to give up everything they had worked so hard for and come here to live on a hog farm. None of it made sense. Why couldn't Nils put the puzzle pieces together?

Maybe Ingrid was correct and Ray was the one to blame for Sven's disappearance. Perhaps Nils had been digging in the wrong hole this entire time.

He rubbed his aching shoulders and stood to stretch them, then took a turn about the room. Princess jumped from the bed and padded to the window to peer into the darkness. When she did so, she whimpered and cried. "Princess, hush. You'll wake everyone."

The dog carried on, her cries growing louder by the moment. Nils went to her to pull her away. "Come on, there's nothing out there." He paused in front of the window and lifted the lacy curtain from over the glass pane. Though the world outside lay silent and dark, a glow lit the night sky not far away.

Blood red.

A fire.

In the direction of Ingrid's shop.

Nils pulled on a pair of pants, grabbed his coat, and slipped on his shoes. He commanded Princess to stay, then flew down the stairs to the front desk and shook the night clerk awake. "Ring for the fire department."

The man jerked from his slumber. "Here?"

"No. Near Ingrid Storset's confectionary shop on Main Street. Tell them to hurry." Maybe they were already there, but it didn't hurt to call them again. Just to be sure.

Nils raced down the middle of the street, now clear of traffic. No automobiles. No wagons. No streetcar. After a couple of blocks, his legs and lungs burned. He continued on. The closer and closer he got to Ingrid's place, the more intense the red glow, the higher the angry red flames jumped into the sky, filling the air with ash and choking smoke. Now the sweet odor of burning pine filled the air.

The clanging of the fire truck's bell was the most melodious sound Nils had ever heard. The horses pulling it raced past him, and he sprinted to keep up.

At last he rounded the corner. It was indeed Ingrid's place that was on fire. The firefighters were hooking up their hoses and preparing to pump water on the intense flames. He raced toward the closest one. "Where is she? Is she safe?"

"Who?" The muscular man had to shout for Nils to hear him above the crackling of the flames.

"Ingrid Storset. The woman who lives here."

"Can't get into the building. The fire is too hot."

"You have to."

"Let us do our job."

Nils scurried about the scene, a number of bystanders now congregating. He searched every face in the flickering firelight, praying one of them might be Ingrid.

Perhaps she had spent the night at Belle's. But what if she hadn't?

Her apartment faced the back of the building. Had they checked there? Why weren't they searching for her?

He flew around the corner. Her window was open. She threw something out. A rope made of blankets. She stepped out of the window.

"Ingrid!"

She withdrew and then poked her head out. "Nils! I'm trapped. I can't get out of my room. Please, you have to help me."

"I will. Hold on."

"Hurry. The flames are coming. They'll catch me soon."

"Don't move. I'll be right back."

Once more in front, he shouted at the same man. "She's trapped in the back. Get a ladder over there. We have to get her out before it's too late." Considering how much he had missed her when he was in Detroit, how much more would he miss her if he never saw her again? The thought ripped him in two.

The firefighter dropped his hose. With Nils's assistance, they carried the long ladder and hustled to the building's alley side and placed it against the building. Glass shattered as flames broke through a downstairs window.

"Hurry." Ingrid leaned farther out the window. "It's getting so hot. I can't stand it much longer."

"Don't worry. I'm coming."

The fireman pushed Nils out of the way. "Keep back. I don't want anything happening to you."

"But—"

"Do as I say."

Nils stepped back and craned to stare at Ingrid, who was halfway out the window now.

"I'm coming for you, ma'am." The firefighter ascended the ladder. "Just hold on. A few more steps, and I'll be there."

Nils held his breath, helpless to do anything more than pray. And pray he did, begging God to spare Ingrid's life.

The man reached the top of the ladder. He held out his hand to Ingrid. She screamed.

Then disappeared from sight.

Pain seared Ingrid's ankle. She turned away from the window. The hem of her dressing gown had caught fire. She beat it out, but it scorched in another place, ready to burst into flames.

The firefighter appeared in the window, his face ruddy. "Let's go!"

"My clothes are burning." The pain was almost unbearable.

"There's no time to waste." He yanked on her arm and pulled her halfway out the window. "Now turn around. Down you go. Nice and easy."

Once she was out, he beat the flames from her clothes. Still, every step down the ladder was torturous. About halfway, she had to stop. "I can't go any farther. The pain is too much."

A crash above startled her. Good thing the firefighter had a tight grip on her, or she would have fallen to the ground. The entire building was caving in.

"Come on, Ingrid. You can do it." Nils's voice carried from below her. Cheered her. Urged her on. "I'm going to be right here waiting for you."

She could do this. For him.

With ginger steps, she descended to the ground. No sooner had her feet touched the earth than Nils lifted her into his arms and held her close to his chest. A sensation washed over her, one she hadn't had in a long time. One of being protected, cared for, and safe. Almost like she was finally home after all these years as a stranger in a strange land.

She allowed herself to relax in the cocoon that Nils provided. He whispered into her hair. "I'm so thankful you are okay. I prayed so hard for you, and God has answered my prayers."

"And mine. He sent you to me."

"I couldn't sleep. When I saw the red in the sky, I was so afraid. I had them ring the fire department right away."

"You saved my life. No one else answered me, even though I called and called. A minute more and. . ." A shudder ran through her body.

"You're injured, and it's cold. Let me take you to the hotel and get the doctor."

Only then did she peer down. She was dressed in nothing more than her nightgown and her robe. "You can put me down. I'll be fine."

"Are you sure?"

"Yes."

When he did as she bid, she wrapped the robe tighter around herself to protect her modesty. She took a single step into the snow in her bare feet. "Ah!" The cold on her burns sent pain shooting through her heels and the backs of her legs.

"I have to carry you." Before she could protest, Nils swept her into his arms once more and started for the street.

As he did so, a glint in the dim light caught her eye. "Stop. What is that?"

Still cradling her, Nils bent down and retrieved the object from the snowbank. He handed it to her. A silver matchbox.

Her breath hitched.

"You know who this belongs to?"

"I'm not sure. There are two like this that I know of." She inspected the filigree engraved into the silver casing, scrolling in an intricate pattern. One she was very familiar with. One she had stared at and admired many evenings.

"What do you mean you're not sure exactly who it belongs to?" His breath whispered across her cheek as he spoke, driving away a bit of the chill on both the outside and the inside.

"There is a pair of them. One belongs to Ray Lamphere. The other"—she swallowed hard—"belongs to Belle."

Chapter Twenty

Flickering firelight danced across the silver matchbox as Ingrid held it in her trembling hand, the engraved pattern on it so familiar to her. But whose was it? Ray's? Belle's? Despite the heat from the burning building, Ingrid shivered.

Nils bent to examine it, his head now blocking her view. "There's no way to tell them apart?"

"Not that I know of. Belle bought one for herself and one for Ray. While he worked for her, the boxes often sat side by side on the shelf above the stove in the kitchen. I've spent many hours in that spot, stirring sauces or frying meat, staring at this. I never saw initials or a scratch on either one. In every way, they were identical."

"We have to let Sheriff Smutzer know. It's a clue to whoever started the fire."

Again Belle's name was associated with a nefarious activity. "Wait. Think about this for a minute. We don't know that anyone started this fire. The chemicals I work with in the darkroom are flammable. They could have ignited. I thought I turned out all the lamps before I came upstairs, but perhaps I didn't. You're jumping to conclusions."

"Can't you smell the kerosene?"

"I have kerosene lamps in the basement. That proves nothing."

"What if the investigators discover it's arson?" His voice was low and husky.

"Then I will hand the case over to them." Perhaps. Belle was innocent. Why, she'd been here the other day while she was in town running errands, trying to make amends. Before she left the farm, she might have stuck the matchbox in her apron pocket without thinking, and it could have dropped out when she was here.

"Do you promise?"

"Don't you trust me? Besides, it's likely Ray's and not Belle's. I'm sure the next time I go to her house, I'll see it sitting in its usual spot on the shelf above the stove. Just because your brother's trail goes cold at my sister's farm doesn't mean she had anything to do with his disappearance, and it doesn't mean that she's a bad person." Ingrid's voice rose in pitch with each word.

"Of course. I'm sorry. I didn't mean to imply anything by it. You're right. I'm jumpy and jittery and desperate for answers. Clutching at straws now."

"It's understandable. Truly. I can't imagine being in your situation."

Still, as she lay in bed in the hotel room Nils had arranged for her after the doctor bandaged her, dawn streaking the fleur-de-lis patterned gold wallpaper, the idea that it might be Belle's matchbox they had found plagued her. If the fire was set deliberately, it had to be Ray.

It had to be.

She rolled over and covered her head with the pillow in a vain attempt to block out the screams from her earlier dream that echoed in her head.

Saturday, March 21, 1908

The bitter coffee slid down Ray's throat, burning his tongue along the way. He had overslept this morning and was getting a late start. Mr. Wheatbrook would be upset if the chores didn't get done on time. He couldn't lose this job. Though Belle's actions were spiraling out of control, he still loved her. Nothing she did would change that. He had to stay close to her.

He threw on his coat and headed for the barn, carrying the slop bucket with him. The morning had warmed, and the snow on the ground, a few inches of it, was soft and mushy. His boots left deep prints as he trudged toward the pen.

About halfway there, the sheriff's red Ford Runabout swung into the yard, skidding to a stop in front of him.

He smoothed his mustache. Great. What was Belle up to now? It could only be her making trouble for him. He'd been keeping his nose clean since the incident with Ingrid. Well, there was that little tryst with Old Liz, but no one knew about that. People may not like her race, but as long as no one discovered it, they couldn't do anything about it.

Smutzer stepped from the car. "Morning, Lamphere."

"Morning, Sheriff. Anything I can help you with? A cup of coffee maybe?"

"Hello, there." Mr. Wheatbrook stepped from the porch and headed in their direction.

This morning just got better and better.

"No to the coffee, Ray. This isn't a social visit."

"I supposed it wasn't." He set down the metal pail and stuffed his hands in his pockets.

"What's this all about?" Mr. Wheatbrook scowled. "You in more trouble again, Ray?"

The sheriff didn't take his focus from Ray. "There was a fire in town last night. In fact, it was at Miss Storset's building, which burned to the ground."

Ray leaned forward. "Miss Storset? Is she injured?"

"Some burns on her legs, but she'll be fine. Are you disappointed to hear that?"

"What are you insinuating, Sheriff?" Ray shifted his feet.

Mr. Wheatbrook held his hand up. "I'd like to know the answer myself."

"You set that fire, didn't you, Lamphere?"

"I had nothing to do with it, sir." He shrugged to highlight his nonchalance.

"Didn't you threaten Miss Storset a while back? The only reason you got off was because of Lindherud."

"What is this about, Lamphere?" Wheatbrook stood with his arms akimbo.

"Can we go inside and talk?" Ray turned toward the house. The men had no choice but to follow him.

With shaking hands, Ray poured three cups of coffee and set them on the oversized farmhouse table.

"Tell me how you set fire to the building last night." The sheriff sipped from his cup.

"I did no such thing." Ray's stomach tumbled as he lifted his own mug to his mouth.

"The fire chief says it was deliberately set."

Ray shrugged in an attempt to appear unconcerned. "I don't see how that has anything to do with me."

"Where were you last night between two and three?"

"Asleep."

"Where?"

"Here." The lie rolled off his tongue.

Mr. Wheatbrook shook his head. "I was up for a glass of water about midnight and saw you sneaking away. You weren't here last night. Tell the sheriff the truth now."

Did he have to?

"Off to set fire to Miss Storset's place?"

"No."

"Then where? If you can't produce an alibi, I will arrest you for arson and attempted murder."

What did he say to that? He couldn't go to jail, but he didn't want anyone to know who he'd been with. Least of all, Belle. It might well ruin any chance he had with her.

The sheriff drummed the table. "I'm not going to wait much longer while you invent a story."

Ray swallowed hard. "I was at Old Liz's place."

"The woman who lives in the shack at the edge of town?" Wheatbrook's eyes were wide.

"Yes, that's the place."

Ray's boss shook his head. "I can't believe you would associate with someone like her."

"We're going to check out your alibi. You'd better hope she corroborates your story. Let's get going."

Much too soon, Ray and Sheriff Smutzer were standing in front of Old Liz's shack. The shutters hung at varying angles. Several windows were broken. A number of shingles were missing from the roof. After he'd gone out on a limb, she'd better tell the sheriff he was here.

They climbed the rickety steps, and the sheriff knocked on the door.

The aging black woman, a bright red bandanna over her head, opened it. "What you doing here? Ray, you in some kind of trouble again?"

Why did everyone have to ask him that?

Smutzer stepped forward. "Was Mr. Lamphere here with you last night?"

"Well now, let me see."

From behind the sheriff, Ray nodded, willing Old Liz to answer in the affirmative.

"Yes, sir, he shore was."

Ray blew out a breath.

"What time?"

"I couldn't rightly say."

Ray slapped his forehead. It wasn't enough that he was here. He had to be here at the right time, which, judging by what the sheriff said earlier, was between two and three in the morning.

"I got no clock, sir."

Smutzer nodded. "I understand. Can you give me some idea of the time? Your best guess."

"I dunno."

"Near dawn?"

"No, sir. More closer to the dead of night would be my guess. He was here a long while before the sun come up. Sneaked out before daylight."

"And you would swear to it in a court of law?"

"Yes, sir, though not a soul on the jury would believe me."

She did have a point. Would that change the sheriff's mind?

"Thank you." The sheriff spun around and marched down the steps.

Ray leaned close enough to whisper to her. "Thanks for getting me out of a jam. I owe you."

"And you better believe I'm gonna cash in on that." She cackled, revealing empty spaces where teeth had once been.

"Let's get going, Lamphere," the sheriff called from inside his car. "And don't think this investigation is over."

Chapter Twenty-One

Nils peeked into the hotel dining room where a number of patrons were consuming their bacon and eggs and downing the last drops of their coffee. Though he scanned the crowd, he didn't spy Ingrid. Not that she would fancy eating in the dining room.

The front desk clerk approached him and clapped him on the shoulder. "I haven't seen her yet this morning, nor have I received an order for room service. I imagine she's getting some well-deserved rest."

Was it that obvious Nils was searching for Ingrid? "I hope that's what she's doing. If so, that's good. I need to go take care of a few things. Let her know I'll be back soon."

"You like that girl, don't you?"

Nils shrugged. "I suppose I do." Yes, he really did. More than he was ready to admit to anyone, Ingrid had grown to be very special to him. The fire last night, the chance that she could have died, drove that point home.

But he couldn't pursue a romance with her right now. Sven had to be his priority. If there was anything he could have done to help his brother and he didn't do it because a woman distracted him, he would never forgive himself. He couldn't live his life until he knew what had happened to his brother.

The trouble was, how did he go about finding Sven? So far, every lead had turned out to be a dead end.

His gut told him Belle knew more than she was saying. Each time he spoke with her, her story changed. Her only motivation would be that she was hiding information. Information that would lead him to his brother's whereabouts.

He quivered like a bowl of Mama's lingonberry jelly.

Today, he had an excuse for going to the farm to see what information he could glean. No one, as far as he knew, had informed Belle of her sister's misfortune. While he was there, he might be able to determine if she still possessed the silver matchbox. If so, it would clear her and shine the spotlight on Ray.

That would make Ingrid happy.

And making Ingrid happy would make him happy.

He motored to the farm, pulling to a halt in front of the brick house. Steeling himself, he marched to the front door and rapped on it.

Mrs. Gunness opened the door, thunder in her face, her eyes stormy, her lips pursed. "It's you. I told you to stay far away. Would you like to be charged with trespassing? You and Mr. Lamphere could share a cell."

Nils raised his hands. "Stop right there. I'm not here to harass you. I'm bringing some news from town."

She narrowed her eyes. "What news?"

He stared at her, ready to gauge her reaction to what he had to say. It could be very telling. "There was a fire last night at Ingrid's. Her place burned to the ground."

"Do they know how it started?"

"No mention of that at this point. It's early in the investigation."

"I'll be interested to see what they have to say. Hmm, I wonder why they didn't contact me immediately. Ingrid doesn't own the building. I do."

"Yes, I knew that. The blaze happened very late, so I'm sure they didn't want to bother you. There was nothing you could do at that point."

"Yes, but I need to contact my insurance agency right away."

Phillip ran up to Belle and tugged on her skirts. "I want some milk."

"Don't interrupt me when I'm talking." Belle pried his hands from the material.

Wriggling by Belle, Nils slipped inside. "Give the boy his drink. I don't mind."

"You have told me all I need to know."

"I have more to say. Take care of Phillip. I'm happy to wait."

Belle huffed but turned toward the kitchen. Nils followed. He gave the room a cursory glance. No silver matchbox on the shelf above the stove. Then again, she could have moved it. Perhaps it was somewhere else in the room or the house.

She withdrew the milk bottle from the icebox and poured Phillip a glass.

"Aren't you concerned for your sister's well-being?"

Belle stopped with the glass midair. "Of course. How is she faring? Was she injured?"

"She was. She barely escaped with her life. If I hadn't happened to wake up in the middle of the night and notice the glow in the sky, she would probably be dead."

The glass slipped from Belle's hand and crashed to the floor. "Oh my. Oh my. Is she in a bad way?"

"Thankfully, just some burns on her legs from her clothing catching on fire."

She covered her face. "My love, my love. My beautiful, beautiful sister. How could this have happened?" She dropped to her knees.

Phillip hugged his mother's neck. "Don't cry, Mama. Please don't cry."

Time for Nils to make his escape. "I'm sorry to have caused you distress, but I thought you should know about your sister."

She stared at him. "I think it's time for you to leave. You have upset me and my son enough for one day. I will be in town shortly to make an insurance claim and to check on Ingrid. Do you know where she is?"

"She's at the Teegarden Hotel. The doctor has already tended to her."

"Thank you. Now please, go and leave us in peace."

He'd go, but he was going to speak with Ingrid as soon as she was up to it. The time for talking was over. The time for waiting for Belle to tell the truth was over. The time for action had come.

He had a plan.

As he made his way to his motorcar, he glanced toward the hogpen. There, in much the same place as in the photograph, was the shovel sticking out of the dirt. Several other holes littered the property.

What was going on?

The red-velvet chairs in the corner of the lobby, the same corner where she and Nils had spoken before, were the perfect place for Ingrid to finish her meal and rest her legs while not being exposed to the public. She didn't need the added stress of dealing with well-meaning people asking about the fire and if she would rebuild.

Questions she didn't have the answers to. She swallowed to ease the burning of tears at the back of her throat.

Not because of the loss of the confectionary. No, it was almost a relief to have that burden lifted. No more speaking with customers.

The loss of her photography equipment and her darkroom was more distressing. Everything she had worked for, everything she had dreamed of having, gone. In a matter of minutes. All it did was lead to more questions in her life.

What was she going to do? Where was she going to live?

She could stay at Belle's. Her sister would welcome her, there was no doubt about it. Getting to see the children every day would be another perk.

She reached into her skirt's pocket and fingered the silver matchbox. The reason she hesitated to go to Belle for help. Whose was this?

Why did everything have to point to Belle? The two buildings in Chicago she had owned that had both burned to the ground. Peter's death. Now this. The cloud of suspicion over Belle's head grew ever darker.

Ingrid coughed, her throat scratchy from the smoke. Then again, there was Ray. He had already tried to harm her once. He very well could have set the fire, though how that would ingratiate him to Belle, she couldn't figure. Perhaps he was upset with her, believing she was standing between him and Belle, discouraging Belle from welcoming his advances.

Nothing made sense. Not a single thing.

Even Nils. God had brought him to her at the perfect time. Almost too perfect. What were the chances he would wake up and see the fire and arrive at the building just in time to rescue her? That it would be him and not someone else? Perhaps this was his way of threatening Belle to get the information he desired about his brother.

The pain behind her left eye matched the throbbing of her calves. Who knew which way was up anymore? When would these misfortunes end?

The words of scripture she had memorized whispered in her heart. *"In this world, you will have trouble. Take heart, I have overcome the world."*

Lord, I don't see You overcoming anything. The world is still as crazy as ever. When will there be peace? When will all this misfortune and evil end? Will I have anything left when it is over?

Perhaps she should return to Norway, to the arms of her family. There, though, she wouldn't have her own business. She wouldn't be her own woman. Despite all of the misfortunes, America was better than the old country. Besides that, she didn't have the money for the passage.

How would she recover from this turn of events?

The potted palm to her left rustled, and then Nils stood in front of her. "It's good to see you up and about. How are you feeling?"

"Not too bad, all things considered."

"I was at the farm this morning to tell your sister about the fire."

Ingrid sat up straighter. "What did she have to say?"

He fidgeted with the end of his tie.

"What?"

"To me, she didn't seem surprised. She also didn't ask about you. I had to bring up your condition."

"That doesn't mean she wasn't concerned. Shocking news affects people in different ways. I'm sure that's what it was." But was it?

Nils touched her hand. "Maybe. Now, though, it's time to find out once and for all what your sister has been up to, if anything, and what it has to do with my brother's disappearance."

"Knowing would be good." Perhaps that was the key to closing this chapter and moving on to a better part of life. One that held more happiness. "What do you propose?"

"When I was there this morning, I was in the kitchen. I glanced where you said the matchbox should have been."

"And?" Ingrid held her breath and slid to the edge of the chair.

He stared at his hands. "I didn't see it."

She clenched her fists. "That doesn't make her guilty."

"I know, I know." Nils's words were quiet. "You have to turn in the matchbox to the sheriff. You know that, don't you?"

She shook her head, her pulse throbbing in her wrists. "No. Not yet. Please. Not until we have more information."

"The authorities might be able to trace it to Ray."

Her breathing steadied. "I'm glad you understand it might not be Belle's. That it probably isn't Belle's. She could have put hers somewhere else. First, though, we have to search her house. Perhaps we'll find the matchbox."

"No, first you're going to surrender the matchbox to the authorities. Then I will go to your sister's house. The risk to you is too great. Besides, you've been through a terrible trial."

"Please, let's look at Belle's house first. Just to prove to you that she didn't have anything to do with the fire. My sister is innocent. She wouldn't do anything that would put me in harm's way. We're all we have. There's no other family in this country. We have to go. I must clear Belle's name and prove her innocence."

Nils sighed. "This isn't a good idea, you know. The sheriff will accuse you of withholding evidence. You could wind up in a heap of trouble."

She drew in a deep breath to steady her nerves. Nils was right. This was crazy. But look at all Belle had done for her. This time, Ingrid could do something for Belle. "I'm willing to take that chance."

"You're willing to sit in a jail cell?"

Goose bumps raced up and down Ingrid's arms. To tell the truth, it took all of her willpower not to run in the other direction. "Yes, I am. I'm asking you to trust me. Can you do that?" She cared about Nils, a great deal. He had become very important to her. If he couldn't trust her, though, the slim possibility that they would have a future together, one she wanted more and more, would vanish like the morning's fog.

Nils sighed. "What if she catches you?"

"If I'm there and she does, I provide a good excuse for your presence." She rose to her feet, pain shooting through her calves. "I'm going with you to the farm before we take the matchbox to the sheriff, and that's the end of that."

"You are determined, aren't you?"

"I can be when I want to be."

He cupped her cheek, and she shivered. "Are you sure about this? We don't know what we might find there."

"I'm positive. No matter what, I want the truth. It's about time we have it. With it, maybe people will leave Belle alone and stop treating her as the town villain."

"For your sake, I hope you're right and that we don't find a single piece of incriminating evidence."

They spent a while in the lobby's corner putting together a plan, a time when they could be in the house when Belle wasn't there and there was little chance of her returning early.

When they finished, Nils brushed a kiss across her forehead. For a long time after he left, she sat staring at the hotel's door where he had exited.

They were taking a risk. They both wanted answers, but different ones. No matter what happened, one of them would be disappointed. More than that. Likely devastated.

Was she doing the right thing?

How could she even know?

Weary and aching, she climbed the stairs to her room. The maid had fixed the bed. If Ingrid could sleep for a little while, perhaps the world wouldn't look so bleak when she awoke.

She crawled under the quilts and pulled the covers over her head.

Then she gave in to the tears and allowed herself a good, long cry, mourning a world that would never be the same again.

Chapter Twenty-Two

Monday,
March 23, 1908

A chill wind whistled overhead, rattling the still-bare tree branches that hung low over the edge of the road out of LaPorte. The thick, dark clouds all but obscured the sun, so the light was more like dusk than midday.

Nils rode in the passenger seat of Ingrid's hired buggy from town. With her burned legs, she couldn't walk. And when Belle left the house, she shouldn't spy his automobile parked alongside the road. That would blow their cover. For that reason, he had left Princess at the hotel today.

"How providential that your sister herself provided the perfect reason for you to be at the farm."

Ingrid kept tight hold of the reins. "When she visited me earlier today, she told me I could take whatever I wanted of Jennie's clothes, because she wouldn't need them anymore."

"Was that how she phrased it?"

"Exactly."

"You don't think—"

"Of course not." Ingrid glared at him for a long moment before returning her attention to the street. "No matter what people say about her, no matter what rumors float on the air about what she might have done, she loves her children with the fiercest devotion I've ever seen in a mother. We didn't have much growing up. Barely enough to keep body and soul together. Belle only sent Jennie away because she wants more for her children than we ever had."

Ingrid had blinders on when it came to her sister. Then again, he wasn't one to talk. He hadn't seen the trouble Sven was getting himself into. If he had pressed him harder, Sven might have stayed. Might have never disappeared into thin air. "I understand."

Again she glanced in his direction.

He fiddled with the buttons on his coat. The time had come to share his secret with her. When she heard, she might not want anything to do with him. But if he hoped for any kind of future with her, whatever it might hold, he had to be honest and up front with her. "We had some money growing up. We lived comfortably. The only thing was that we were living off ill-gotten gains."

To her credit, Ingrid focused her attention in front of her and didn't comment on his proclamation.

"My father borrowed a great deal of money and dug himself a deep hole of debt. When he couldn't repay it, he borrowed more from a shady man at a high interest rate. Papa couldn't repay that either. The lender came after him, and Papa beat the man to a pulp.

"The police arrested Papa, and he's serving a long prison sentence. I am determined to show him that I can make a decent living by hard work. I can take care of Mama and Sven by earning an honest living." If only he weren't so deep in debt himself. He had borrowed time, but that would run out. Soon. Would his story end the way Papa's had?

"I'm sorry about your father. That must be so hard."

"Coming to terms with the fact that he wasn't the man I believed him to be was difficult, but it forged me into the man I am. Independent. Determined. Resourceful."

"This topic isn't something you like to speak about." Her words were soft and gentle, like a stream over rocks. Not harsh and condemning.

He loosened the fists he didn't know he'd been clenching. A sudden gust of wind almost blew his fedora from his head. He clung to it. "I only told you because I can trust you. You would never betray my confidence. We haven't always seen eye to eye on my theories about my brother, but you have never been unkind to me. You have never judged me but always sought to understand me. I appreciate that about you." In fact, it was one of her most attractive qualities. One among many.

Just before they turned the bend in the road and Belle's farm came into view, Ingrid stopped the buggy, and Nils jumped down.

"Are you sure you won't get too cold hiding in that ditch?" She peered down. "It looks wet and muddy. I don't want you to get sick."

"I'll be fine. Just help your sister get moving as soon as possible. I'll wait until she's well out of sight before coming to the house."

Ingrid pulled away, and he hunkered in the depression, crouching so he could just see the road but low enough that he could duck at a moment's notice.

He had told her part of his story but not all of it. She hadn't minded about his father, but what would she think when he told her how deep in debt he was and that he couldn't take care of his family after all?

Ingrid must have been quite efficient, because in no time, Belle's buggy, carrying her and Phillip, jangled down the road, headed toward town. He crouched low, held his breath, and didn't move. The creak of the buggy wheels grew softer and softer until they faded on the wind. He blew the air from his lungs and clambered up the ditch.

Who knew how long the search would take? They had to be fast but thorough. He sprinted toward the house and banged inside, where Ingrid waited for him in the kitchen. Her green eyes held a sheen of tears. "It's not here. The matchbox is gone."

He approached her and took her by the upper arms. "Listen, that doesn't mean that she set the fire. Perhaps she placed it elsewhere. Used the matches to light another stove and left it there." Though he didn't believe it himself, for her sake, he gave her this ray of hope.

"You might be right. I'll check."

He moved to the parlor. No matchbox by this stove. The desk in the corner caught his eye. Papers littered it, piled on top of each other, all rather precarious. One gust from an open window, and they would scatter.

He flipped through them. Bills. Notices of area auctions. Then a stack of letters tied with a ribbon.

Nils gasped. That was Sven's handwriting on the envelope. Sorting through them, Nils discovered that all the letters came from Sven. There must be three dozen. How long had Sven been corresponding with Belle?

There were other stacks of letters, each from a different man. Henry Gurholdt. Olaf Lindbloom. Where had these men gone? Did their families even realize they had come here?

He picked up a nearby pencil and wrote the names and addresses on one of Sven's letters. He'd only take Sven's so Belle wouldn't notice her desk had been disturbed.

Nothing else of interest struck him in here. As he left the parlor, Ingrid trounced downstairs.

"Did you have any luck?"

She shook her head. "I was so positive I would find that matchbox. It has to be here somewhere."

"We both need answers, remember? I'm in this with you. I'll help you every step of the way." He moved to the next room, tried the doorknob, and found it locked. "What's in here?"

"I don't know. Belle never allowed me in there. She said it was her private space."

"Give me a hairpin."

"You're going to pick the lock?"

"Unless you know where the key is?"

"I don't. I think she keeps it with her."

"Then we won't know what's behind this door until we open it."

"I'm not sure." She chewed on her lower lip, her gaze darting from Nils to the door and to him again.

"Don't back out on me now. One way or another, I'm going to open this door."

"Fine. I'm sure there's nothing in there. Except maybe Belle's matchbox." Her hand trembled as she pulled a pin from her updo and handed it to him.

"Thank you." Not more than two minutes later, he had the door unlocked. "Are you ready?"

Her eyes were wide, but she gave a slow nod.

He pushed the door open.

Ingrid squealed and fell to her knees.

His stomach somersaulted to his toes.

The room was piled with trunks and the floor covered with clothes.

Men's clothes.

Ingrid shook like a poplar leaf in a hurricane as she sat on the cold, hard floor, attempting to make sense of the scene in front of her. At least a dozen or more trunks were crammed into the tiny room. Not only trunks but also piles of men's clothes. Shirts folded and stacked in one corner, pants in another. Several fur coats had been piled on a chair. "What is this?"

Nils helped her to her feet then stepped into the room. There wasn't much space to maneuver. He spun in a circle as he scanned the area. "This isn't good."

No. No. She refused to believe her sister had done anything wrong. Not her beloved sister. They shared the same parents. The same blood flowed through their veins. Her sister, who loved her children more than her own life, would never harm another human. "There has to be a rational explanation for this."

"You imagine a rational person could do this?"

"All the men who answered her advertisements snuck away in the night. Or most of them, anyway. Perhaps they really wanted to get away."

A tree branch scraped the window, the sound sending a chill up and down Ingrid's spine. The house creaked in the gale. Nils sent a glare her way. "Think about it. Why would they want to get away? Why would they want to get away so much that they left behind their trunks full of their clothes? No one would do that."

"The coats. Many of them were heading to Texas or California where they wouldn't need them. It makes sense they would leave those behind, perhaps as a form of payment to Belle for putting them up for a few days. You know, the life of a hog farmer isn't glamorous. It's hard work, work that some men aren't willing to commit to."

He held out the stack of letters in his hand. "Look at how many times she and my brother corresponded. He knew full well what he was getting into here. Because of our circumstances, he understands hard work. He isn't afraid of it."

He wanted to pin all the blame on Belle. He could see no other reason for this other than that Belle had done something wrong. Ingrid knew it wasn't like that. "Maybe he wanted to get rich quick," she said. "To make his fortune an easier way. Mr. Botchkiss, the stationmaster, may have told him about California. His grandfather went there in '49."

"Take a look around. All of these men did the same thing? All of them? You're telling me they all moved to California within days of arriving here?"

"I—I—I don't know what I'm telling you. I'm scared." Try as she might, she couldn't keep the warble from her voice.

He wrapped her in an embrace, much as he had done the night of the fire. "I know. I am too."

She melted in his warmth. Together, they trembled. "Why?"

"Because I'm afraid I'll find the answer I've been dreading." After holding her a few more minutes, he released her, and right away, the chill returned. "We don't have time to stand around. Start sifting through what's here for any clues about these men. I'll search for my brother's belongings."

Ingrid inhaled, long and slow, in an attempt to still the riotous beating of her heart. The attempt proved vain. Nils was correct. Who would leave without their belongings? Even if you didn't need a coat when you arrived in California, you would need it for the journey along the way. Some of these men had arrived in the spring and summer. Why would they have brought their heavy coats with them if they weren't planning on staying?

The wind howled, rattling the windows. Her muddled brain couldn't make sense of it all. Did Belle steal from these men? Was that why they left in such a hurry? Were they afraid of her? She was a rather intimidating woman. Had she threatened them?

Ingrid refused to allow her brain to think of the other possibility.

Because it was impossible.

She couldn't move. Didn't have the heart to wade through clothing that belonged to other people. Their personal effects. That would be a violation of their privacy.

"No. No, no." Nils's cry came from the other side of the room by the trunks. "Ingrid, come here. I need your help."

On legs that must have weighed a ton each, her heart racing, she picked her way through the well-organized mess to Nils. "What?" The word squeaked from her throat.

"This is Sven's trunk. I recognize it, because he bought it just before he left. He had his initials engraved on it. He liked having his initials etched onto his belongings." Nils traced them, his touch reverent. "Help me move the ones on top of it so I can open it."

The trunks, probably still full, were heavy and awkward. Ingrid was warm by the time they reached Sven's trunk at the bottom of the stack.

"I need that hairpin again."

She handed it to him and stepped back as far as she could, which wasn't far enough in the crowded room. As he picked the lock, she hugged herself, squeezing ever harder.

Nils swung the lid open, kneeled beside the trunk, and pulled out several items, including a razor, a comb, several shirts, and a couple pairs of shoes. "These are all his. I recognize everything. If he left here of his own accord, he didn't leave with anything other than the clothes on his back."

After several more minutes of digging through the trunk's contents, Nils shut the top. He backed up and stroked his pointed beard, his attention on the trunk. He squinted and moved closer, his gaze zeroing in on one spot. "What is this?"

Hands sweating, Ingrid came to his side. A dark stain marred the golden wood. "I don't know."

"It's blood."

Dear God, it can't be.

Chapter Twenty-Three

Belle's chest heaved as she stood in the secret room's doorway staring at Ingrid and Mr. Lindherud. "How, how, how dare you?!" She had returned from her errand to discover the two of them in her private room.

Ingrid swung around, the color of her face matching that of a newly fallen Norwegian snow. "Belle."

"What are you doing in here?" Belle pushed through the mess until she stood in front of the two culprits. "These are my personal belongings."

Mr. Lindherud had the audacity to lift a shirt from one of the trunks. "This belongs to my brother. Why did he leave it here?"

"That is none of your concern. Hundreds of men have such shirts."

"This is his trunk." The man closed the lid and traced the initials on it. "You can't deny this belongs to him."

"I can't help it if he ran off and left it here."

"Why would he go to California without his clothes? Everything he brought?" Mr. Lindherud stepped closer to her, close enough to send prickles over her skin.

She backed away. "How should I know? One morning he was gone, but his possessions remained here. He didn't discuss anything with me."

"I thought you said he told you he was going to California."

"He mentioned that someday he would like to go there, that's all. I didn't know he was serious about leaving for there the next day." Heat rose in her face. If only they would stop questioning her. She hated it. Hated having the town, even her own family, making these accusations. Why couldn't people leave her alone?

"Belle." Ingrid's voice was soft and tinged with sadness. "What's going on? You can tell me anything. You know that. Why is this trunk here? Why are all these trunks here?"

Belle covered her ears. "Stop! Stop! I can't listen to any more. Get out of my house. Now. Both of you. Before you regret it. And don't breathe a word about this to anyone. This is my private business. You had no right to snoop. I could have you arrested for trespassing." She glared at both Ingrid and her companion.

"You told me I could take some of Jennie's things. It's not trespassing to be invited into your sister's home."

"Jennie's room is upstairs. Unlocked. That is where I gave you permission to be. Not down here, snooping through personal possessions."

"These aren't your personal possessions." Mr. Lindherud narrowed his blue eyes.

Belle liked him less and less by the second. "I said get out. I'm done talking. If I have to, I'll take the meat cleaver to you."

Mr. Lindherud leaned toward her, his nose almost touching hers. "Is that what you did to my brother?"

She swung around, prepared to do what she had to in order to protect herself and her property. She would get that cleaver. She would use it against him.

Just three steps into the hall, Mr. Lindherud pushed by her and out the front door. Ingrid paused next to her. "Belle, please, tell me what is going on."

"I can't believe you would bring him into my home. You know how I feel about him." She drew in a ragged breath. "You went behind my back. What kind of sister are you?"

"I'm the kind of sister who loves you very much and doesn't want to see you come to harm. I was looking for that blue dress Jennie loved so much, and couldn't find it. But I'm confused, and I don't understand what is happening here. These things don't make sense to me." Ingrid spoke almost as if she were a little child.

Belle softened her tone. There was so much of the world that Ingrid didn't comprehend. "Of course not, little sister. You are still young and naive. Men are mysterious creatures. Who knows why they do what they do? I'm confused, and I have many more years behind me. It's natural that you wouldn't understand. Don't worry, though. Nothing bad will happen to me. Only to your Mr. Lindherud, if he continues to sneak around behind my back. He was the one who put you up to it, wasn't he?"

Ingrid studied the toes of her shoes.

"That's what I thought." The man was the devil in disguise. "For my sake, for your sake, stay away from him. He's not the kind of person you want to associate with. Look at his brother for an example. A man who promised to come here and work with me and take care of me. A handful of hours after he arrived, he bolted, leaving behind everything."

"You're right, of course. I knew there was a logical explanation to all these strange events."

"There always is. Trust me. Can you do that?"

Ingrid pecked her on the cheek. "I do. I'll try harder. Just one more question."

Questions, questions, questions. What was this, the Spanish Inquisition? "Just one more."

"What is the stain on Sven's trunk?"

"Stain?" Belle furrowed her forehead.

"There's a mark on it, right in front. Nils, well, he thought it might be blood." Ingrid bowed her head again.

Belle fisted her hands then forced herself to relax them. He would have to be dealt with. "Trunks get dirty. Porters aren't the neatest people, and the way the luggage is slung around on a train, it's amazing it's as clean as it is. I didn't even notice a spot, but I'm sure that's what it is."

Ingrid peered up and sighed. "Oh yes, that must be it. I'm so relieved. Do you know where Jennie's blue dress is, and then I'll be off?"

"You might want to check her wardrobe again. I can't imagine where else it might be."

Ingrid darted upstairs. Good, now Belle had an opportunity to speak to Mr. Lindherud. She strode out the door and toward the waiting buggy where he stood. "I would thank you not to be filling my sister's head with crazy notions. What game are you trying to play?"

"Game?" The cocky gentleman tipped his head. "I assure you, this is no game. Sven's disappearance is very, very serious. And so is the evidence you have locked away in your house."

"Pft. Evidence? You are out of your mind. Now stay off my property and away from my sister. I wasn't joking about the meat cleaver."

Mr. Lindherud was getting to be a problem. A big problem.

Tuesday, March 24, 1908

"Mr. Lindherud, I cannot arrest Mrs. Gunness for writing letters to your brother. If I did that, I'd have to arrest everyone in this town for posting mail on an almost-daily basis."

Nils huffed and stilled his foot to keep from tapping it. He and Ingrid stood in the doorway at the sheriff's residence. Smutzer was dressed in a sweater and a corduroy jacket, a fishing pole in his hand. After several warm days in a row, the lakes had cleared of ice and the town's top lawman was on his way to do some angling.

But not the right kind.

Ingrid twisted her handkerchief in her hands until it was almost in a knot. Her eyes were wide, like those of a frightened puppy. He brushed against her, only for a second, just to reassure her of his presence. She glanced his way, her lips drawn in a firm line.

"What about the trunks we discovered? The ones filled with men's clothes?"

Smutzer shook his head, almost knocking his cap from on top of it. "If the men wanted to go west to seek their fortunes and chose to travel lightly, I cannot argue with that. If I didn't have a wife and a family, I would be sorely tempted to do the same."

Any moment, steam would pour from Nils's ears. "You don't find it the least bit strange?"

"Plenty of strange things happen all the time. Look at the woman." Smutzer nodded to Ingrid. "No offense, miss. She's not the greatest prize. She's had a string of bad luck. Some people attract it more than others. Who can say why? Not to mention that she's rather an odd duck—no offense again, miss."

Ingrid backed up two steps. Nils grabbed her by the elbow to keep her from fleeing. Smutzer possessed little tact, especially when he was eager to get to one of the many lakes surrounding LaPorte. "Please, the subject is difficult enough for Miss Storset. Treat her with a modicum of compassion."

Smutzer grimaced. "My apologies, Miss Storset. I'm sure it must have been unsettling to discover what was in that room. I assure you, however, that you have nothing to be concerned about. There have been no reports of missing men, so their families must be aware of where they went. Your brother, Mr. Lindherud, is not as considerate of his as these others have been."

There was the case of Ole Budsburg, though Nils hadn't received a reply to his letter to his family. Perhaps they had located him.

If the sheriff didn't have any intention of following up on the names and addresses Nils had gleaned, he most certainly did. He'd write those letters tonight. "Miss Storset has something she would like to share with you."

Again she shrank back, but Nils held her firm. Little by little, she opened her fingers to reveal the matchbox lying in her palm.

"We found this on the ground outside of Miss Storset's place the night it burned. It is my understanding that both Mr. Lamphere and Mrs. Gunness possess matchboxes just like this one."

Smutzer reached into his pocket and drew out an identical one. "Many people have them. A popular catalog item, if I'm correct."

"Th–th–that's right." Ingrid came to life. "Ray and Belle looked in the Sears and Roebuck catalog for them." She turned to Nils. "So there is an explanation for everything."

Smutzer held out his hand. "I will take the matchbox, as it was found at the scene of what we believe to be an arson. However, it doesn't bring us much closer to knowing who started that fire. Your sister, Miss Storset, says she was at home with her children. She said Phillip crawled into bed with her, which he says he did. Mr. Lamphere was"—Smutzer cleared his throat—"otherwise engaged."

Ingrid handed the matchbox to him, hesitating just a bit.

"Now, if there is nothing further, I believe I will be on my way. And from now on, both of you keep your noses out of other people's business. Am I making myself clear?"

Nils escorted Ingrid back to the hotel. For the first time in a while, she smiled. "The sheriff isn't concerned, so neither should you be. And he's right. We have to stop snooping. It only leads us to jumping to conclusions."

He nodded. "I suppose you're right."

They enjoyed the stroll the rest of the way in the pleasant weather, speaking about mundane matters. The coming of spring. What might be on the menu at the hotel tonight. Whether dogs or cats were the best companions. Fortunately, she agreed that dogs, particularly Princess, were her preference.

Nils, however, listened to her with half an ear. Because despite what Smutzer had warned them about, he planned to continue to investigate his brother's disappearance. Once he had those letters written, he had a course of action in mind.

Monday, April 27, 1908

Clouds scuttled over the half moon, hiding Nils in shadow. Perfect for what he needed to do.

Ever since the day he and Ingrid had searched her sister's house, he had become more and more convinced that Belle Gunness was responsible for Sven's disappearance, despite what Smutzer had to say. And though his gut twisted at the thought, he was more and more convinced that Sven had met a dreadful end at her hands.

Why else would she keep his trunk, still full of his clothes? Plus, you couldn't ignore the bloodstain on it. The one there no doubt belonged to Sven.

And the letters. Though he had written to the addresses on the envelopes, he had yet to receive any replies.

Then there was Ingrid. No matter the overwhelming evidence pointing toward her sister, she refused to believe Belle could harm another human being. How could she be so naive? Then again, it must be difficult to believe something so terrible about your sibling.

Was he being just as blind, not wanting to accept that Sven would run off without informing either him or Mama?

Impossible.

That's what Ingrid believed about her sister, though.

No more dwelling on that. He crept from the stand of pines on the edge of the Gunness property along Fish Trap Lake. His shoes oozed in the mud, the snow now melted into a sludgy mess. While he would leave traces that he'd been here, he couldn't wait any longer to get to the truth. Yes, it was risky, especially after Belle's threats, but it was a risk well worth taking. He'd be alert and keep his wits about him.

The truth lay in the hogpen. He'd stake his life on it.

The hogs were shut up for the night, tucked away from foxes and coyotes that might want a tasty treat, especially with the piglets that had just arrived. Tiny squeals came from the barn.

The shovel handle he and Ingrid had seen in the photograph was gone. He glanced around. No other markers stood in the pen. The darkness was good in that it hid him but bad in that it kept him from seeing well. He stepped around the yard. Some of the spots were softer than others, like they had been recently dug. That's right. They had seen holes in various places.

There were no holes now. Belle had filled them in.

Though the light wasn't good, he pressed on. There had to be a shovel in the barn. The building was big enough to make out in the dark.

The place reeked of pig manure and dirty hogs. If these men did all scuttle away because they didn't like the work, that would be no surprise. His eyes adjusted to the darkness. The moon pierced through the clouds and into the window long enough for him to catch a glimpse of tools hanging on the far wall.

He started toward the farm implements. Behind him, the straw rustled. He halted. Held his breath. Dared to glance over his shoulder.

The rustling came again. Nils almost laughed. Nothing more than the hogs moving about. Probably the suckling pigs searching for a midnight snack.

He grabbed the shovel from the hook on the wall and proceeded to the pen once more. Now no light emanated from the moon. The clouds must have thickened. He grabbed on to the wooden fence and walked along the pen's edge, searching for those soft spots he had come across before.

Of course, now that he was on the hunt for them, he couldn't find one. He completed a circuit and came up empty. He shook his head. Had he been imagining them earlier, believing he'd discovered things that weren't really there? Wanting so much to find what he was searching for that his mind played tricks on him?

No. No. He had come across soft dirt. Just not on the edge of the pen. To find those spots again, he would have to move closer to the inside.

While not a methodical or scientific way of going about it, he set out across the enclosure. After several minutes, he came across a patch of dirt that was softer than where he'd been walking. Even though the entire pen was one giant mud puddle, this place was springier than other spots. The perfect place to begin digging. For what?

For whatever answers might lie here.

He stuck the shovel into the earth and threw the scoop to the side. Several more times, he repeated the process. The early-spring night was balmy. Soon he shed his coat and rolled up his sleeves.

A creak coming from near the house stopped him. Whether his heart pounded from exertion or fear, he couldn't tell. For a long while, he remained statue still. In the deep of the night like this, no one would see him unless he moved.

No more sounds, other than from the hogs and the hooting of the owl overhead. Even that ceased as the great bird took to flight, the beating of his wings silent.

Nils waited several more minutes, his ears attuned to every sound. Nothing out of the ordinary. Maybe his imagination again.

At last, he resumed digging. It wasn't long before he struck something hard. Solid. He was right. Something was buried here. He set the shovel aside and pulled on his work gloves. Then he knelt in the mud and excavated by hand.

Little by little, he was making headway. Soon he would know what this hole held. Perhaps he'd have the answers he'd been seeking for months.

Then the world went black.

Chapter Twenty-Four

Ray stood over the cock-cold body of Nils Lindherud, who was face-down in the mud of the hogpen. What was he doing here? With a shovel in his hand, no less. Not a place he needed to be. Should Ray do something? If so, what?

For a moment, he contemplated this predicament, his arms crossed over his chest. Siree, he didn't want to get in trouble for this, that much was for sure. He was in enough hot water with the sheriff. The last thing he wanted was to have the law badgering him.

"Nils." Ray kicked his side with the toe of his boot. "Nils, wake up."

The man didn't move. Was he dead? No, no, he couldn't be dead. Impossible. Or was he?

Ray knelt in the mud. With a great deal of effort, he flipped Nils over and felt his neck for a pulse. Whew, there was one. Good and strong and steady. He was just knocked out was all. He'd wake up soon enough.

Should he move him? Ray smoothed down his mustache. If he moved Lindherud, he couldn't claim that he'd caught him trespassing on Gunness property. Then again, *he* was trespassing on Gunness property. So maybe the best course of action was to leave the man where he was. Just watch from the shed to make sure he eventually woke up and was okay.

Then again, if he moved him, then he could say that he found Lindherud in the woods in this condition. If he was questioned, he could say that Lindherud was likely out drinking and had gotten into a fight with a bar mate. That was plausible.

So which one was the right course of action? The one that would keep Ray out of trouble, for sure. Maybe the best thing to do was to hightail it out of here before anyone discovered him standing over

Lindherud. They might get the wrong idea.

Yeah, that was what he should do. Dawn wasn't too far off now. Just an hour or so. He was making for the pen's gate when Lindherud groaned. That solidified his decision. He raced toward the barn and hid behind the door. Good thing the earlier clouds had cleared. Now the moonlight was just enough for Ray to watch what happened.

Lindherud moaned and groaned some more. He clutched his skull. The chap must have an awful headache, hit on the noggin the way he was.

Lindherud felt his head then studied his hand. Figuring out he was bleeding, he was. He sat up, just for a second, before flopping to the ground again. Bet he was dizzy and queasy too. Well, he shouldn't be digging up trouble, that's for sure. Exactly what was he doing? Ray didn't hold much sympathy for him.

The man sat up again, this time remaining in a sitting position. He glanced around the farmyard. Ray huddled closer to the door, just daring to peek around the edge so he still had a view. Lindherud continued to clutch his head. A minute or two passed.

With a great moan, he slid to his hands and knees. He attempted to stand but splatted face-first into the mud. Ray held his breath, now peeking between the slats in the door.

Lindherud pulled himself up again and this time managed to crawl several feet in the direction of the gate before he fell. Over and over he continued this process. What was taking him so long? Ray had to get out of this barn before sunrise when Belle and the children would come to do the morning chores. If she caught him here, she'd have his neck. No telling what she'd do to Lindherud.

Not that Ray cared one way or the other.

A light flickered on in the upstairs bedroom window. Belle's window. She'd be out here soon. He had to get away, back to the Wheatbrook farm. He had his own chores to take care of. Didn't need his employer to get sore at him.

Splat. There went Lindherud into the mud again. Here was Ray's chance, while Nils couldn't see anything. He sprinted from the barn and around the back, racing into the woods and away from the Gunness farm.

He'd been crazy to go there in the first place. Then to discover Lindherud there? That ruined all his plans. Probably got him into a boatload of hot water too.

No, he was fine now. No one would know he'd been there. No one would connect him to what had happened to Lindherud.

Once he made it to the road, Ray slowed to a trot, clutching his chest to still the wild thumping of his heart. He made it to the Wheatbrook farm just as the rooster crowed. At the cock-a-doodle-doo, several lights flickered on, brightening the windows. The Wheatbrook family was waking. They'd expect him to be in the barn hard at work. He'd better get to it.

Ray had the stalls mucked and was moving to feed and water the horses when Wheatbrook entered the barn.

"Morning, Ray."

"Morning, Boss." Ray yawned, big and loud.

"Sounds like you had a long night." Wheatbrook chuckled.

"Naw, just didn't sleep well. Tossed and turned most of the night." Ray exited the room where they kept the feed and almost ran headlong into Wheatbrook. "Sorry about that. Didn't see you there."

Wheatbrook stepped back. He furrowed his brow. "Why are you all dirty?"

Ray glanced at his overalls. He was covered in mud. How had that happened? Oh, right, probably when he turned Lindherud over to feel for his pulse. How did he explain this? "Um, I, um, slipped in the mud and fell. All the rain we've had has made a mess of things."

With an eagle eye, Wheatbrook studied Ray for a moment more. He tipped his head and kept his gaze on Ray. "You sure about that?"

"Absolutely."

Wheatbrook sniffed. "You smell like hogs."

"With all due respect, sir, this is a hog farm. That's bound to happen."

"Make sure you wash your clothes. And take a bath. You reek."

"Will do, as soon as I finish up." He had to bathe before his court date later today anyway.

Wheatbrook trotted toward the cow, picking up a milk pail along the way.

That was too close.

How long before the sheriff came knocking and connected the dots between him and Lindherud?

Monday, April 27, 1908

Dawn was just brightening the horizon when Ingrid set off in the direction of the train station. Though Belle was working with the insurance company to get enough money for Ingrid to rebuild the confectionary, it would be a while before they could even start. So Ingrid had time to take photographs for the *Herald*. Perhaps by the time the insurance was settled, the paper would hire her on and she wouldn't need to stand behind a counter and speak to people all day.

Today was promising to be a good day. The spring sunshine warmed the earth. Winter was over. Her new camera was due to arrive on the overnight train from South Bend. She had dipped quite a way into her savings and purchased a new one.

The biggest obstacle was that she didn't have a darkroom. Perhaps Belle would allow her to use a room in the house or perhaps the barn. Then again, they hadn't been on friendly terms the past few weeks because of the incident with Nils.

Though Belle's explanations had made sense at the time, Ingrid couldn't reconcile them. They didn't truly make sense. Why keep the trunks? Why not send them back to the men's families? Nightmares plagued Ingrid. All day, she was unsettled. That's why getting back to work would be the best medicine. She would have an activity to focus on instead of what Belle might or might not be involved in.

She was so deep in thought she didn't see where she was going until she bumped into someone. A large someone who grabbed her by the shoulders to steady her.

"I'm so sorry."

The deep, rich voice was familiar. She gazed into Nils's blue eyes. "Oh, it's you. I didn't expect you up so early. You usually sleep later."

"Well. . ." His voice wasn't as strong as usual.

She stepped from his grasp and studied him. His clothes, his face, his hair, were covered in thick, dark mud. His hair was matted, and was that dried blood caked in it? "What happened to you?"

"We need to talk. In private."

"What you need, first of all, is a good bath and some medical attention for your wound."

He shook his head, wincing with the movement. "I need to go to the sheriff, and I want him to see me in this condition."

"And smell you. The odor reminds me of the hogs. Were you at the farm? What went on there?" For once, she couldn't cease the flow of questions from her mouth.

"It's a long story that I only have the energy to tell once. I do want you to hear it, though, so please come with me."

The camera could wait. She strolled beside him as they changed direction and headed toward the sheriff's office. Nils weaved and staggered down the street, almost as if he'd had too much liquor. Had he been drinking? Was that what propelled him to go to the farm?

They arrived at the sheriff's office only to discover that he wasn't in yet. The deputy on duty directed them to a bench and brought them each a cup of much-welcomed coffee. They sipped in silence.

By the time Ingrid had drained her cup to the dregs, she couldn't hold the questions in any longer. "Won't you please tell me what happened?"

He moaned as he shook his head, leaning over his knees.

"Perhaps this could wait. You should be at the doctor getting checked out instead of wasting time here."

"I'll be fine."

"You don't look it." She reached over and rubbed his shoulder, his muscles taut beneath her fingers.

At last, the sheriff arrived. He spotted them as he walked in the door and motioned them to follow him. Once at his desk, Nils and Ingrid seated themselves. The sheriff cleared his throat. "Looks like you had a rough night, Mr. Lindherud."

"True. But I have some information." His words were halting.

"Take all the time you need."

As he described going to the farm and digging, finding something buried in the mud, then getting hit over the head so hard he fell unconscious, Ingrid's mouth fell open a little more with each word he uttered.

"What do you think was in the hole?" Sheriff Smutzer made the inquiry that tingled on the tip of her tongue.

"I don't know. All I know is that there is something buried on the property. Or multiple things buried in multiple spots. Someone didn't want me to find out."

Sheriff Smutzer took furious notes as Nils spoke. "But you don't know who hit you over the head?"

"It was dark and whoever it was came up behind me. I didn't catch even a glimpse of him or her."

"This is what you get for snooping, Mr. Lindherud. I warned you not to go over there again. You only send trouble raining on yourself. You could have been killed." Sheriff Smutzer rubbed his clean-shaven cheek. "Despite that, I'll bring Lamphere in for questioning. Whether you should have been out there or not, he had no right to do this to you."

Ingrid nodded. "Good. Ray has been nothing but trouble from the first day."

Nils straightened, and his eyes took on a fire and intensity Ingrid had never witnessed in them before. "Don't either one of you see? This isn't Lamphere's doing. It's Belle's. Why else would she have trunks full of clothes locked away and parts of her hogpen excavated if she wasn't killing and burying the men who came on the pretense of marrying her?"

Ingrid sucked in a breath. "No. No, no, no. I refuse to believe such lies about my sister. She's a God-fearing woman with a deep capacity to love. She couldn't hurt another human being. She can't even kill a spider."

Nils turned to her and clasped her hands between his. "Wake up. See the truth, hard as it may be to bear. Your sister killed my brother and buried him in her hogpen. There's no doubt in my mind."

Ingrid squeezed her eyes shut. He was rushing ahead of the evidence, just like the sheriff had warned them.

Because if what Nils said was what happened, her heart would break into a million pieces.

He had to be wrong.

Chapter Twenty-Five

Why wouldn't Ingrid listen to him? Nils struggled to understand. Well, he did, in a way, know why she resisted. Now the truth stared her in the face, though. How much longer could she deny it?

The sheriff was no better. It wasn't Lamphere they needed to bring in. Not that he was the most savory character, but he wasn't the culprit. Of that, Nils was positive. Just because Belle was a churchgoer didn't make her a good person.

How could he convince them that they should be paying attention to Mrs. Gunness? He glanced between Ingrid and the sheriff, his head pounding like a hammer on a rail line. "Belle is the one hiding evidence. The property belongs to her."

The sheriff sent him a glare that would have withered the Amazon rain forest. "I've told you before that I'm the law enforcement in these parts, and it's best you leave my job to me. Look." He made a wide gesture in Nils's direction. "Your meddling has almost gotten you killed. The best thing for you to do is to go to the hotel and get some rest. Have a doctor look at that gash."

"Isn't it similar to the gash Mr. Gunness suffered? The one that ended his life? Who is responsible for his death?"

Sheriff Smutzer stood, towering over Nils. "You listen here. She was never charged in that case. In this country, you are innocent until you're proven guilty."

Nils came to his feet, the world spinning like a Ferris wheel, and stared down the sheriff. "You aren't doing anything to prove anyone guilty. The woman is getting away with murder." His voice rose so the entire room fell silent.

Except for Ingrid's gasp. Covering her mouth, she scraped her chair back and fled.

Smutzer motioned in the direction she had disappeared. "Now look what you've gone and done. You'd better start thinking before you open your mouth and spew nonsense. I have your statement. You are free to leave. I'll do my job." With that, Smutzer zipped his jacket and strode from the room.

Nils thumped to the chair and clutched his pounding head. What more could he do? Nothing. Not a blessed thing. He had done all in his power, to the point of almost getting himself killed. Now he'd alienated Ingrid. Perhaps he should return to Detroit. Break the news to his mother that he had failed her, just as he had in the past. The dealership was going under.

The deadline had long since expired. The biggest surprise was that Gillespie hadn't tracked Nils here yet.

He would. Any minute now.

That wasn't the worst part. With some hard work and a bit of God's help, he could weather this financial storm. Though it might take a while, he could and would recover and come out on top again. There were even job opportunities here in LaPorte. But if Sven was lost to them forever, there would be no replacing him. No more brothers for Nils. No more sons for Mama.

Telling her about her younger son would be the hardest thing he ever had to do.

Slowly, he rose and wormed his way around the desks in the station until he exited into the bright spring sunshine. He forced himself down the stairs and in the direction of the hotel. The blood on his head had dried. No need for a doctor to stitch him. He'd take a bath, a couple of aspirins, and have a good, long nap.

Then he'd drive home and smash Mama's heart to pieces.

Before Ray had finished slopping the hogs, the sheriff pulled into the Wheatbrook farm in his red Runabout, braking to a halt not far from where Ray lugged the slop pail. They must have figured it out. Must have somehow connected him to Nils Lindherud. Not what he needed. Not today.

He was already in enough hot water. Now it looked like he was about to get into a whole bunch more. He swallowed hard, though his mouth was as dry as August.

"Morning, Lamphere." Smutzer stepped from the automobile.

"Morning, Sheriff. Aren't you up and about awfully early?"

Smutzer eyed him. Him and his mud-stained clothes. He should have changed right away, before chores. Here he was, wearing all the evidence the sheriff needed.

"You're mighty dirty there."

"That happens when you work on a hog farm, especially in spring. Don't worry. I'll spiff up before going to court." Ray chuckled a little, but Smutzer didn't.

"I'm not here about your court date, though it's interesting that this all happened the night before you are to stand in front of a judge."

"All what?" Ray made sure to crinkle his forehead, like he didn't know what Smutzer was talking about.

"You know exactly what I'm referring to."

"Afraid I don't."

"The attack on Nils Lindherud at the Gunness farm last night. Someone bashed him over the head pretty good. Funny thing is, he was covered in mud, just like you are."

"As I said, you can hardly work on a hog farm without getting muddy. Pretty near impossible."

Smutzer crossed his arms. "Change your clothes. Then I'll personally escort you to court. Afterward, you and I are going to have a bit of a chat."

Ray set the slop pail on the ground. "I'd better tell Mr. Wheatbrook what's going on. He's going to be none too happy."

"You change. I'll take care of your employer. If you'd quit getting into trouble, this wouldn't be a problem."

Ray trudged off. Great, just great. He should have left Lindherud lying facedown in the mud. Let him die. He'd caused nothing but trouble since he'd arrived. Whatever he got, he deserved.

Fifteen minutes later, Ray sat in the motorcar beside Smutzer, heading into town. Ray hardened himself, refusing to allow his stomach to keep flipping around like it was a spring foal. They pulled to a stop in front of the red sandstone courthouse. Arched windows graced each of the four sides of the square building, a steeple-like projection shooting into the air from the middle of it.

Walking toward the courthouse just in front of him was Belle, her wide hips swinging with the motion. She should be his. By all rights, she should be his. Why did she keep rebuffing him? This ploy, taking him to court on trespassing charges, was nothing more than a game she was playing with his heart.

He scurried until he came even with her. "Good morning, Belle."

She glared at him, staring hard.

"You know, someone's been digging around your property."

"So I saw."

He glanced at her hands, dirt underneath her short, cracked fingernails. "Do you know who it was?"

"Of course not. Happened during the night while I was sleeping. Just yards from where my children and I were in our beds, someone came snooping. The thought of it alone makes me shiver."

"Well, I can tell you who it was. It was Nils Lindherud. That's what the sheriff said. Lindherud admitted to being there and everything. He was covered in mud and had a gash on his head."

"I knew it. I knew it." She turned to him, her eyes flashing. "He refuses to give up the search for his brother and insists on pinning the blame for it on me. He can't accept that his brother ran away from him, as far as he could get."

"He believes he's found the truth."

"Truth? There's no truth to be found. Let him dig in my yard all he wants. He'll find nothing." Yet Belle's voice held a quiver, as if she wasn't quite convinced of the words she spoke.

"I think you have bigger fish to fry than me." Ray winked at her. Perhaps with this trouble with Lindherud, she would drop the case against him.

"You're full of it. I don't want you or Nils Lindherud or anyone at all on my property."

"You just said he could dig all he wants."

She harrumphed. "Nothing more than a figure of speech. I have nothing to hide. That doesn't mean I want him sneaking onto my land in the middle of the night. Who knows when he's going to come into the house and kill all of us in our beds?"

Smutzer nudged Ray. "Let's move along. I can't believe you're standing here having a conversation with the woman who brought trespassing charges against you."

Ray trudged toward the door beside the sheriff. "Just a friendly chat. Trying to get her to drop the case."

"Good luck."

"Tell me about it. That woman is as hard-nosed as they come."

They proceeded into the courtroom, the judge's bench on a platform above them, the seats in the room filled with the accused and the accusers. Soon the judge called Ray's case. The older, slight man with round glasses peered at Ray. "What do you have to say for yourself in response to these charges?"

"What's the harm in coming to call on someone? I didn't know you needed special permission to do that. I didn't mean her or her kids any harm. I wouldn't hurt a fly, and that's the truth."

From behind him, Belle snickered. Let her laugh all she wanted. She was about to get her comeuppance.

The judge eyed her then returned his attention to Ray. "She claims you were in her house, rummaging through her wardrobe. Is that what happened?"

"I just wanted to get back some clothes I had left behind when she fired me. That's my stuff in there, and I have every right to get it if she won't give it to me."

"Why were you going through her belongings?" The judge narrowed his eyes, his bushy gray brows almost obscuring them.

" 'Cause I couldn't find everything. How am I to know where she's hiding it all? It's only right that I get my clothes returned to me. If she won't let me in and won't give them to me, what other choice do I have?"

The judge dismissed Ray and called Belle to the stand. With a beefy hand on the Bible, she swore to tell the truth. "He has been bothering me and pestering me constantly. This isn't the first time I've caught him trespassing. The thought of him rummaging through my most personal belongings sends a shudder through me."

"Is it true that you are in possession of some of Mr. Lamphere's belongings?"

"Why would I want to hang on to his filthy clothes? The only male in my household is but five years old. I have no use for them. I have severed ties with Mr. Lamphere, but he refuses to leave me alone. Please, make sure it will be the last time he sets foot on my property without my permission." She spoke the words with a trace of tears in her voice.

"Let justice do its job, Mrs. Gunness. You may step down." The judge removed his glasses, pinched the bridge of his nose, and returned his spectacles to their rightful place. "I find you guilty, Mr. Lamphere, and order you to pay a one-dollar fine. That is all." He pounded his gavel and left the bench.

"One dollar," Belle hollered from her seat in the back of the room. "That's all this snooping pest gets is a one-dollar fine? That doesn't hurt him any."

Ray turned toward her, his breaths coming in rapid succession. He couldn't hold his tongue. "It hurts me plenty. You're a spiteful woman who will do anything to make yourself look good and others fear me. Trust me when I say this—someday sooner rather than later, you're going to get your due. I hope your house burns down around your ears."

Smutzer grabbed Ray by the shoulders and steered him from the courtroom. "Watch your mouth. If you keep flapping your lips, you're going to find yourself in a whole heap of trouble. Speaking of which, you and I need to have a little chat. I haven't forgotten about that."

Once Ray had paid his fine, he and Smutzer moseyed to the station, where the sheriff held him in an interrogation room. "Now, Lamphere, you're going to tell me the truth about what happened to Mr. Lindherud last night."

"There's nothin' to tell. I don't know anything about it."

The sheriff leaned on the table, his eyes cold and hard. "Why were you muddy?"

"That's like asking why the pope is Catholic. That's the way it is for my job. By the time you got there, I'd been hard at work for a while. Already dirty. It happens."

"Interesting, but while we were at the courthouse, my deputy took a phone call from Mr. Wheatbrook. Seems he saw you first thing this morning, at dawn's first light, and you were already caked in mud and smelled like the hogs. How do you explain that?"

"Same way I explained it before."

"You are lying." Sheriff Smutzer spit the words.

"No, I'm not."

"Tell me the truth."

"Truth, truth. That's all anyone wants these days." Ray stood and slapped the desk. "Fine. You want it. Here it is." Ray stared the sheriff in the eye. "Sure, I was at the Gunness farm overnight. But I didn't do a thing to hurt Mr. Lindherud. When I found him, he was already lying on his stomach in the mud with a huge gash on the back of his head. I tried to help him. That's how I got all muddy. When he started to wake up, I skedaddled. That's the truth. The true truth."

"And I believe him."

Ray startled and spun around.

Nils Lindherud stood in the doorway.

Chapter Twenty-Six

Since Ingrid's camera hadn't arrived until the noon train, she made arrangements with Mr. Botchkiss to have it dropped off at the hotel. Now she was headed to secure new living arrangements. She had spent enough time in the hotel, draining her savings. What she needed was a place of her own where she could work on her photographs.

With the strain between her and Belle, she wasn't even going to ask to live with her sister and her family. It would be best for the both of them if she found another residence. Besides, perhaps she could find a place to have her darkroom.

As she passed the courthouse, she glanced up. There came her sister down the walk, her strident voice carrying on the warm spring breeze. "A dollar. Can you believe it? A lousy dollar. That judge is out of his mind. Out of his mind." No one else was around.

"Belle?" Ingrid stopped in front of her sister.

Belle startled and halted.

"What's wrong?" Ingrid asked.

Her sister's countenance brightened. "Oh, just the same old story with Ray. We settled that trespassing citation this morning. Though now I need to file one against your friend, Mr. Lindherud."

"I know about that. I was with him at the police station."

"Well, he believed he could come onto my property while my children and I were sleeping and start digging around. That is inexcusable behavior."

"But—"

Belle held up her hand. "Never mind about that. I'm going to put all this ugliness behind me for now. I don't want to think about Ray Lamphere or Nils Lindherud today. Or even about how you stabbed me in the

189

back. Nothing is more important to me than family. In fact, I'm going to cook a big dinner tonight. And we'll play games. Say you'll come. Please. The children miss you."

The complete change in Belle's attitude left Ingrid dizzy. Still, she did miss the girls and Phillip, having not seen them in weeks. Besides that, who knew what information she might find to clear Belle of Nils's crazy charges? Belle was correct. Nothing was more important than family. "Sure. That would be wonderful. Thank you. This means so much to me."

"Other than the children, you are all I have in America. As long as you keep that man off my farm, we won't have any more problems. It's time to put matters to rights. Before it's too late."

"We have plenty of years in front of us to be together."

"None of us knows the number of our days."

Ingrid rubbed her arms so the little hairs on them would lie down. Time to change the direction of the conversation. "When would you like me there?"

"I just have some shopping to finish. Why don't you bring the girls home from school?"

"That sounds wonderful."

"Plan to spend the night too."

"Let me see how my day goes. I've been terribly busy."

"Then you need a rest. I insist."

"We'll see."

A few hours later, Ingrid and the girls ambled up the lane toward the brick farmhouse, the children giggling and chattering and running ahead of her.

"Hurry up, Auntie Ingrid." Lucy skipped toward the porch. "As soon as we finish our chores, I want to play hide-and-seek with you."

"No." Myrtle shook her head so hard the bow in her hair slid. So reminiscent of Jennie. "Aunt Ingrid is going to help me finish my new puzzle."

"Girls, girls. I can play with both of you."

The two of them laughed and hugged her before racing into the house.

Ingrid followed at a more sedate pace. Two huge trunks sat on the front porch. More trunks? What did they contain this time? As far as she knew, no other marriage prospects had shown up at Belle's place in the past several weeks. Though Ingrid attempted to slide the trunks inside, they were both too heavy to budge a single inch.

When she opened the door, a heavenly aroma greeted her. She popped into the kitchen to find Belle slaving over the stove, several pots bubbling and pans frying. "What's all this?"

Belle turned toward her, face flushed. "Dinner."

"So much just for us?"

"We're celebrating."

"Celebrating what? It's not anyone's birthday, and you were upset about the judge's fine for Ray."

"Celebrating family, my dear sister." With a spoon in her hand, Belle leaned over and pecked Ingrid on the cheek. "There is nothing more important in the world."

"On that point, we agree." Though she might not approve of everything Belle did, her sister was her own flesh and blood. "Let me grab an apron, and I'll help you."

"Nonsense. I have everything under control. You spend time with the children. They've missed you so."

As if to emphasize her point, Phillip trotted in from the other room and latched onto Ingrid's leg. "I can't believe you're here. Mama bought me a new wooden train. It will go with the engine that Santa gave me for Christmas. Come see it."

"Before I do that, I have to help your mama move those two trunks inside from the porch."

Belle wiped her hands on her dirty apron. "Finally. I didn't think they would ever arrive. I must have been so busy in the kitchen I didn't hear the deliverymen. Yes, please help me carry them to the basement."

"We can't lift them. They're much too heavy. I can't even push them."

"Nonsense. I'm strong, and you're stronger than you look. I'll bear the brunt of the weight."

Ten minutes later, sweating and panting from exertion, Ingrid stood in the dark, dank cellar having helped Belle carry the trunks downstairs. Even though Belle did the majority of the work, Ingrid's arms burned.

"Thank you, dear." Not a single bead of sweat dotted Belle's forehead. "What's in them?"

"Oh, just some supplies I need. Now, I must get back to my dinner, or we'll have scorched beefsteak."

"Auntie Ingrid, are you coming?" Phillip stood at the top of the steps and hollered down.

Belle waved her away, and Ingrid climbed the stairs then followed Phillip, who scampered off.

She doted on the children until dinner when they feasted on beefsteak, salmon, potatoes, and plenty of cookies and jam. It was better than Christmas dinner. After dessert, Ingrid pushed away from the table. "That was delicious, Belle. Thank you so much. I truly enjoyed it. I'm not going to have to eat for a week."

"I'm so glad. Now, why don't we clear the table, and then we all can play Little Red Riding Hood and the Fox."

The family hadn't indulged in that game in quite a while. "Don't the dishes need to be washed first?"

"They'll still be here tomorrow. Tonight is a night for fun."

They left the plates and cups stacked beside the sink and retired to the parlor. They got out the board game and sat, laughing and joking, though a sheen of melancholy overshadowed Ingrid when the fox caught Little Red Riding Hood. The clock ticked away the hours, and Belle still didn't put the children to bed. Phillip yawned and lay down on the davenport, his eyelids flickering shut.

Breathless with laughter, Ingrid leaned over her knees and turned to Belle. "Do you want me to put him down for the night?"

"We're having too much fun."

"But it's getting late, and the girls have school in the morning."

"We're having fun, Auntie Ingrid." Lucy bounced up and down.

"Another half hour." Belle resumed the game.

Finally, about eleven, Ingrid put another stop to the game. "I have to get going. It's late."

Belle shooed the children off to bed. "Please say you'll stay."

"I'm paying for a room at the hotel."

"I'll cover that. Just stay. You can sleep in your old room in the frame part of the house. I insist."

Ingrid peered out the window into the inky darkness. No moon, no stars broke the black night. She shivered and tugged her sweater about her shoulders. "I don't fancy walking home when it's so hard to see."

"And with Ray on the loose, who knows what he might do if he discovers you out and about by yourself? I would feel so much better and will be able to get a good night's rest if I know you're tucked safely upstairs in your old room."

It wasn't like Ingrid would be moving in. Not to mention that Belle had shown once again tonight that she was a wonderful and caring mother and a good sister. What harm would spending one night do? "Yes, I think I'll stay. Thank you."

"Wonderful." Belle clapped her hands as if she were one of the children. "I know you took Jennie's nightgown, but you're so slight, I believe you might fit into one of Myrtle's. Let me go see."

Ingrid waved her off. "That's not necessary. I can ask her. I'll make sure they're all under their covers and not still goofing around."

"Thank you." Belle lumbered toward the kitchen while Ingrid headed for the stairs.

She found Lucy and Myrtle climbing into the bed they shared. Jennie's bed remained empty, the quilt pulled over the pillow, like she was due back any moment. Perhaps she was. Maybe Belle had changed her mind about sending her daughter so far away. Ingrid would ask in the morning. How good it would be to see Jennie's smile, hear her laughter, watch the blue bow in her hair bounce as she danced.

With a sigh, Ingrid secured a nightgown that might be a little short but would do for one night. She bent to kiss Lucy. "Good night, sweetie."

"Auntie Ingrid?"

"Hmm?"

"You're my favorite aunt. I love you." Lucy gave Ingrid's neck a tight squeeze.

Tears rose in Ingrid's throat. "I love you too." She swung around to Myrtle's side of the bed.

The girl latched onto her arm and refused to let go. "I have to tell you something." Her whispered words held a sense of urgency. Maybe it was being back in Jennie's old room, but the words were so much like hers, Ingrid felt her stomach clench.

"You can tell me anything."

"I'm scared." Though the darkened room hid Myrtle's features, there was no mistaking the fear in her voice.

"You have nothing to be afraid of. Your mama and I are here, and we're going to make sure you're taken care of. More importantly, God is here watching over you. Mama and I may go to sleep, but the Bible tells us that God never does. He always has His eye on His little sparrows."

Myrtle squeezed Ingrid's hand even harder. "What if I told you the person I'm afraid of is Mama?"

From some unknown source, a chill wind blew across Ingrid's cheek. "Why would you say that?"

Lucy piped up from the other side of the bed. "'Cause sometimes, like tonight, Mama acts funny. She's all mad one minute and happy the next and the next she's crying. She doesn't make sense when she talks to us about stuff. She makes it sound like we're going on a trip or something."

"She hasn't mentioned anything to me." Although Belle's behavior had always been erratic, it was true that in the past several months, it had grown worse.

"Did she mention to you about Jennie going away?" Myrtle rustled in her bed.

"No." Ingrid drew out the word.

"You see? She doesn't tell you everything. But she has me and Lucy awfully scared. Even Phillip runs away from her and hides in his room. This morning, she spanked us for going near the basement stairs."

That didn't sound like the loving mother Ingrid knew Belle to be. "Do you want to go on a trip?"

"No."

"Unh-uh."

Ingrid kissed Myrtle's forehead and pried her hand from the girl's grasp. "I'll talk to your mama and see what I can find out. I can't imagine that she would want to send you away. She loves you very much. So very, very much. But if she does, I'll try to convince her to let you stay. How does that sound?"

"Thank you, Auntie Ingrid." Myrtle was much calmer now. Good, she could sleep.

Ingrid tiptoed from the room and shut the door behind her. The rest of the house was dark and quiet. Belle must have already gone to bed. Ingrid would have to speak to her tomorrow about the girls. She climbed the stairs to her old room, the place she had stayed when the family had first arrived in LaPorte. Spacious and cool, it had its own private stairway outside, so Ingrid could come and go as she pleased. It also had a door between that part of the house and the main living quarters, one that could be locked for privacy and security.

She changed into Myrtle's borrowed nightgown, the girls' words hanging in the air as she undressed. Why would Belle be thinking about sending them away? It was one thing to ship Jennie to a finishing school. She was almost a woman. Myrtle and Lucy were still young.

Was that why Belle had the party tonight? Was she planning to send the girls away tomorrow?

Though she had been so sleepy before, now Ingrid tossed and turned. When she did fall into a fitful sleep, her slumber was filled with screams and smoke and flames.

Chapter Twenty-Seven

Long after most of the hotel patrons had retired to their beds and fallen under slumber's spell, Nils sat in the now-closed dining room nursing a cup of coffee so cold it should have been filled with ice. He was close, closer than he had ever been, to uncovering the mystery of Sven's disappearance. Literally uncovering it. There was no doubt in his mind. Whatever Belle had buried in her yard held the answers.

Why wouldn't anyone listen to him? Was it because he was an outsider? Perhaps. This city, though swelling in population, was more like a small town. Tight. Close knit. Wary of strangers. He'd been here long enough, though, to convince them he wasn't someone to be feared. Hadn't they learned that about him?

Maybe it was because he was rocking the boat. He blew into town and accused a supposedly God-fearing woman of a crime. But couldn't they see that the puzzle pieces fit? Belle Gunness had been the last person to see Sven. Whatever she hid on her property would give Nils the answers he sought not only for himself but for his mother.

He had received one reply, from the Gurholdt family. Henry's poor parents had been frantic about their son since he disappeared in 1905. Three years. Imagine waiting three years to hear news of your missing child. Unfortunately, they had no more information to give. He hadn't told them where he was headed when he left them in Wisconsin.

Even Ingrid was blind to the signs that pointed to her sister. Though he had waited for her to return to the hotel so he could speak to her, she never came. She must have decided to spend the night at Belle's. That's where the clerk had informed Nils she was headed.

He rubbed his unkempt beard. After his expenses both here and at home and at the business, there wasn't a penny left over. He only had this cup of coffee because it was the dregs left before the cook dumped the pot for the night. The truth was that finding Sven consumed him both day and night to the point where he almost didn't think about the dealership.

Out of habit, he blew on his coffee. He peered at the night clerk to see if he had noticed. The man was deep in discussion with a burly fellow, his curly hair tousled. He pounded his fist on the desk. Princess, who had been curled up at Nils's feet, let out a low growl.

Nils studied the man harder. Oh no. What was Gillespie doing here? Nils wouldn't be able to hightail it away from him. To get to the stairs to his room, he would have to pass Gillespie. There was no way he could do it without being noticed.

The kitchen door. There had to be one there. He could slip out the back and enjoy a nice, long midnight stroll about town until Gillespie decided to haul himself back to Detroit.

Even that was delaying the inevitable. Gillespie wasn't going to leave LaPorte without having it out with Nils.

Mama had warned him not to get too caught up in work. She'd told him there were more important things in life. Family. God. That's what she had meant. Without them, nothing else mattered. He'd lost sight of that until recently. Now, instead of the dealership being first and foremost in life, his search for Sven was.

That wasn't right either. God should be first. Had to be first.

But Nils would give every last penny to get the answers he needed regarding Sven's disappearance. He was so close now, so very, very close. He couldn't give up on his brother. If they had each other, they had everything.

For so long, he'd worn blinders. Since Papa had gone to prison, Nils had carried the heavy mantle of family caregiver. He'd tried to keep his family afloat in his own strength. That, however, was impossible. When he tried to rely on himself, he was a miserable failure. He needed God's strength. Every good gift came from above.

Lord, forgive me for putting money before my family and before You. I am weak and helpless. You are strong, the Giver of all good gifts. Help me to rely on

You. Grant me wisdom in this situation. Bless what I'm about to do.

There was only one remaining course of action. He had to confront Gillespie. Here and now. If Gillespie harmed him, at least Nils had the night clerk for a witness. Maybe the clerk would phone for the police and stop the altercation before Nils wound up in the hospital.

Or worse.

He scraped back his chair and came to his feet. Stiffening his shoulders, he marched toward Gillespie, Princess nipping at his feet. "I believe you're looking for me."

Gillespie spun on his heel and came face-to-face with Nils. "What a stroke of luck. I just rolled into town after driving almost all night, and when I walk in to get a room, I discover where you've been hiding, you lily-livered coward."

"Now see here." Nils worked to keep his voice low and avoid disturbing the other guests. "You know why I'm here. You know why I'm behind on my payments. And you know what? At this point, finding my brother is more important to me than anything. My dealership is nothing compared to justice for my family. If it takes every last cent I have, I will gladly give it."

"You are more of a fool than your father."

"My father is sitting in prison because money was more important to him than his wife and two boys. I'm not going to make that same mistake. The dealership is yours. I'll telephone in the morning and have the transfer papers drawn up. My debt to you will be paid. In full. I never want to see your face again." For the first time since he'd taken Gillespie's money, he managed to draw a deep breath, the weight on his chest now lifted.

He should have done this months ago.

Gillespie turned to the clerk. "You are a witness to this, understand? You heard him agree to hand his dealership over to me."

The clerk, his face the color of paste, nodded once.

Nils flashed the poor man a smile. "And you are also a witness that Gillespie agreed that my debt to him was paid in full."

Again the clerk nodded.

Nils didn't relax his tense muscles, not even for a second. "I believe our business here is finished. From my understanding, the hotel is full tonight, so you can get in the fancy automobile I gave you and head to Detroit right now. My lawyer will be in touch with yours as soon as he gets to the office."

With a huff, Gillespie strode from the room. Only then did Nils slump against the desk. "What a relief. That man is gone from my life forever."

"I can't believe you gave up your dealership. What are you going to do now?" The clerk was bug-eyed.

"I'm going to find my brother. First thing in the morning, I'm going to the sheriff, and I'm going to demand that he do a little digging at the Gunness property. He might be surprised at what he discovers."

"Mrs. Gunness isn't going to like that one bit."

"I'm beyond caring about what Mrs. Gunness will or will not like. Finding my brother is my top priority."

"If you haven't gotten any answers from her in all these months, what makes you think she's going to tell you something new now?"

"I don't know. I just have this feeling that I'm close to solving the mystery of my brother's disappearance. I can feel it deep in my soul."

The clanging of the fire bell broke off their conversation. Nils raced outside, only the gas streetlamps breaking through the darkness of the night.

The fire engine raced by, the driver slapping the reins on the horses' rumps.

"What's going on?" Nils yelled over the clanging of the bell.

"Fire." The driver kept his focus forward. "At the Gunness place."

Nils fell to his knees. *Dear God, not again.*

Tuesday, April 28, 1908

Ingrid fought her way up from a dream in which she was drowning in the ocean. She couldn't breathe. Though she struggled against the blanket and pillow over her head, she couldn't free herself. If she couldn't draw in fresh air soon, she was going to suffocate.

She flicked her eyes open. An acrid, sickeningly sweet odor invaded the room along with thick black smoke. No, this couldn't be happening again. Only a few short weeks ago, she had awakened to this same nightmare. This time, as before, it was no horrible dream but a horrible reality.

Her heart banged against her ribs in an irregular rhythm. She had to get out of here. Had to warn the rest of the family. She sprang from the bed and threw her dressing gown over her shoulders as she sprinted for the door. The knob was hot, so hot she flinched. Once she had wrapped the bottom of her nightgown around the knob, she tried again. This time, she managed to open it.

A wall of flames greeted her, eating through the floor, licking up the wall, devouring the house in front of her. "Belle! Myrtle! Lucy! Phillip!" Though she screamed their names, no answer came.

The searing heat ate at her lungs.

She slammed the door shut.

The stairway. She could get out that way. But what about the rest of the family? What if they weren't out? The fire was so intense. So hot. The flesh on her legs was still tender from the burns she'd suffered a few weeks ago. But the children. And her sister. She couldn't allow them to burn alive.

Her breath coming in ragged gasps, she flew out the door and down the steps, all the while screaming her family members' names. Fire shot through every one of the first-story windows, casting an orange-yellow glow over the hogpen, the shed, and the trees around the property.

Her eyes adjusted to the weird light. All this time, she screamed for the girls. For Phillip. For Belle. Over and over the shouts tore from her throat, her scorched lungs crying in agony. Only the crackling of the flames as the fire consumed the house answered her.

No, no, no. Where were they? Her heart hammered against her chest hard enough to break her ribs. "God, help me!"

She had to wake them before it was too late. Smash their windows so they would be able to get out. Bricks. Bricks. There was a pile of them in the shed. With her chest heaving, she ran there, grabbed an armload, and sprinted to the house. She heaved one as hard as she could. It fell well short of the mark. Once more, she tossed a brick. Same result.

This wasn't working. She wasn't strong enough. She dropped the bricks to the ground. Wait a minute. There was a ladder. Maybe in the barn. She'd seen it not long ago. Yes, right inside the barn door. Again she raced off and located it. The ladder, however, was at least three times as long as she was tall. She'd never get it to the windows to alert the family.

A violent shudder jolted through her body. "God, what can I do? Help me. Help me. Please, please, please." Great sobs wracked her, dropping her to her knees.

She couldn't do this on her own. Wait. Mr. Wheatbrook. He could telephone for the fire department. He could throw a brick or lift the ladder. "Father, keep them safe." With one backward glance at the inferno, she shot off toward the neighboring farm. Her feet sank into the mud, and once she cleared the yard, into the trees, twigs dug into her soft soles. Despite the pain, she raced as fast as possible, her legs churning, her arms pumping, her lungs crying for air.

By the time she reached the Wheatbrook place, sweat rolled down her face and her back. She banged at the door. "Fire. Fire! Fire!"

A soft light flicked on. A shadow passed in front of the window, and the door swung open. "Miss Storset." Mr. Wheatbrook's hair stood up at crazy angles.

"My sister's house. On fire. Call fire department. Come with me. Get them out." She was barely able to utter the words between heaving breaths.

"They're still in the house?"

"Call, call." Didn't he realize how critical time was? "Hurry."

He disappeared for a minute then returned shrugging into his jacket. "Let's go." He pulled his unsaddled horse from the barn, hoisted Ingrid up, and the two of them galloped away.

By the time they returned to Belle's farm, angry red flames engulfed the entire house, including the second story. Where Belle and the children slept.

Ingrid couldn't stop the cry that burst from her lips. She slipped from the horse's back, stumbling as she hit the ground, her feet in agony, her heart aching more.

Mr. Wheatbrook swung the ladder over his shoulder, hoisted it to the house, and leaned it against the structure, even though flames burst through places other than the windows. Ingrid screamed for her family. Prayed for them. Hoped with all she had.

Mr. Wheatbrook peered inside then moved to the next bedroom. Then the last. He scrambled down the ladder and toward her. "I don't see anyone."

"No one?" Her breath hitched.

"I don't see them."

"But they aren't out here. Where are they?"

"I don't know. Perhaps they woke up and were trying to make their way out. . ."

He didn't have to finish his sentence. He meant they were trying to escape but didn't make it.

"There has to be a way inside. A way to get to them. A way to help them. Please. Please don't give up."

He went to the front door. She raced to the back. Locked tight.

That's right. With Ray bothering Belle, she felt safer with the house shut up. Before all this happened with him, she never locked her door. If only they could get through it. "There's an ax in the shed." She raced for it and returned in just a minute, handing it to Mr. Wheatbrook. He chopped at the door.

Flames whooshed from the opening, scorching hot against Ingrid's face, sending them both reeling.

The clanging of a bell announced the arrival of the fire department. Thank goodness. Perhaps now they would be able to rescue her family.

They hooked up their hoses and pumped water from the engine, all the while keeping their distance from the dwelling.

Ingrid resisted shaking one of the firemen. "Why aren't you going inside? Why aren't you trying to get to my family?"

He didn't take his focus from the water he was spraying on the house. "Ma'am, it's too hot. We can't get close. The structure isn't stable."

As if he were a prophet, one wall collapsed, folding in.

"No!" The guttural scream ripped from Ingrid's throat.

Chapter Twenty-Eight

The flames that sucked the life from her sister, nieces, and nephew sucked the breath from Ingrid's singed lungs. In a shower of sparks and ash, another wall collapsed. This had to be a bad dream. Couldn't be real. Couldn't be happening.

Someone came to her and enfolded her in an embrace, his arms strong, his body warm. Though he didn't speak a word, his presence alone was enough to still her body's quaking. Nils held her close as she stared at the unbelievable scene unfolding in front of her. Flames devouring, the sky glowing, the scene like a moving picture.

Belle, hardworking, caring, loving. Gone.

Myrtle, sweet, funny, personable. Gone.

Lucy, silly, goofy, energetic. Gone.

Phillip, playful, smiley, friendly. Gone.

"Maybe they weren't in there." Nils's voice was soft, almost difficult to hear above the roar of the fire and the shouts of the firefighters.

"They were. We had such a wonderful night. So much fun, so much laughter. All the bad blood between us was forgiven and forgotten. The best evening I'd had in a very long time. My precious family was reunited and loving each other the way a family should. Just hours later, this. It's unbelievable. Unthinkable."

She turned to him and studied him, the strange light casting shadows across his face. "Please, tell me this is a nightmare I'm going to wake up from any second now. That the fire isn't real. That my family isn't dead."

"Oh, sweetheart, how I wish I could. More than anything in the world. I'm afraid it's all too real. Are you all right? Were you injured?"

She shook her head. *Why, Lord? Why would I come out of this without a scratch, without a blister, without a singed hair, and they're gone? Why spare me?*

None of this made sense.

"How did you get out?" Nils's question brought her back to the scene.

"I was in my old room, the one with the outside steps. I simply walked outside. But I tried, I really, really tried to get to their bedrooms. To warn them. Get them out of that inferno. But the flames and smoke were too much. Maybe I should have tried harder. If only I could have gotten the brick through the window. Or lifted the ladder. If I didn't have to run to the Wheatbrooks' farm, maybe it wouldn't have been too late." Tears coursed down her cheeks. If only she were built more like her sister.

Oh, oh, her beloved sister.

"Mr. Wheatbrook told me he didn't see any of them in their bedrooms."

"They must have awakened and tried to get out." Her heart flip-flopped. "How horrible, how horrible. The children must have been so frightened. Dear God, the little ones, so scared. They must have been crying and screaming. What if Belle wasn't even with them?"

"Don't think about it. Don't allow your mind to go there. They love Jesus. He was in there with them, holding their hands. There still is the possibility they got out."

"If they did, where are they?" She raised her voice to be heard above the commotion. "Why aren't they here? No, Belle wouldn't allow me to worry. She would make sure I knew they escaped."

Dawn streaked the eastern sky, the red of the early morning mixing with the red of the fire. As the sun rose, so did wisps of smoke from the house's rubble. By the time the flames had burned themselves out, only part of one wall of the house remained, stark against the lightening sky.

Nils led her to a stump in the yard and wrapped his jacket around her. She didn't fight him, her legs, her entire body wooden and numb. Her burned and bloodied feet didn't even hurt. She sat but couldn't rip her gaze from the devastation. The ruins once were a house that fostered love and laughter.

Sheriff Smutzer came to her, brushing her shoulder with a fatherly touch. Oh, Mama and Papa. How would she ever tell them?

The sheriff knelt beside her, his face darkened by smoke. He must have been helping the firefighters. She hadn't been conscious of who was on the scene doing what.

"Were you inside the house when the fire started?"

She nodded.

"How did you get out?"

She answered him the way she did Nils.

"Were your sister and her family inside?"

Again she nodded.

"Do you have any idea how the fire started?"

"None. I'm sure we turned the lamps out. The stove was cold."

"Did you see anyone?"

"I was asleep."

"Did you know that yesterday, Ray Lamphere threatened to burn down the house?"

"He did this?" Her words came out on a raspy breath.

"I'm so sorry for your loss, Miss Storset. So far, we haven't recovered their bodies. Why don't you go to the hotel and get some rest? We'll notify you when we know anything else or contact you if we have any other questions."

"Are you going to arrest him?"

"Ray?"

"The scum of the earth. To do this to a helpless woman and little children. Almost to me. All over a one-dollar fine."

"Let us continue our investigation. We'll know more in a few hours. Clean up and rest some. Perhaps the doctor can prescribe a sleeping powder for you." He peered down. "And care for your feet."

Nils, who had never left her side, squeezed her shoulders. "That's a good idea. I'll drive you into town then come back and keep an eye on things here. Once you've gotten some sleep, I'll bring you back if you want."

"How can I ever sleep again, especially with Ray still on the loose? What's going to stop him from coming after me?"

Sheriff Smutzer reached out to help her stand. "We'll post a guard outside of the hotel. If he is the one who started this fire, we're going to make sure he doesn't hurt another human being."

Nils guided her away from what little was left of the house.

As one in a trance, she moved alongside him.

Then she gazed over her shoulder.

A beam of sunshine cut a path through the lingering smoke into the basement.

Nils's heart lurched as he pulled his car away from the hotel. A uniformed officer stood guard in front of the building. Another one was stationed around the back. Nothing would happen to Ingrid. *Please, Lord, don't let anything happen to her.* All she had been through. It was too much to bear in one lifetime.

Nothing short of a miracle had saved her life. Between the intensity of the fire and the speed with which it ate through the Gunness house, she shouldn't be alive today. Especially without a burn or a scorch anywhere on her body.

A fire. Another fire. Suspicious, just like the first one, the one that had destroyed Ingrid's home. Who had it out for this family?

All this time, Nils must have been wrong about Belle. He owed Ingrid an apology. She wouldn't have intentionally set her house on fire, killing herself and her children.

Would she?

Then again, who knew what evil lurked in men's—or women's—minds? Ray had possibly set the first fire. It made sense that he would set the second one.

But what if he hadn't set the first fire?

All of this thinking and contemplating did nothing but set off a raging headache. Then again, that knock on his head from the other day wasn't helping.

He stared at the road ahead, forcing himself to focus on returning to the Gunness farm. Perhaps by the time he arrived, the authorities would have more answers. Would have a solution to this mystery.

Wagons and automobiles littered the property when he pulled up, curiosity seekers come to gawk at the devastation. Smoke leaked in wisps from the pile of bricks that had once been home to a woman and her three children. Was it now their tomb?

Though he had tried to reassure Ingrid that the possibility remained that her sister and nieces and nephew were alive, that possibility was slim.

Jennie. The child who had been shipped to California. She would need to be notified. Likely she was the beneficiary of Belle's estate. When Nils returned to town for Ingrid, he would remind her to cable her niece.

At least she had the consolation that she had one remaining family member.

He parked his motorcar and made his way toward the scene. The one remaining wall, the only part of the house still standing, was a grim reminder of the ferocity of the fire.

He approached the sheriff. "Anything new since I left?"

"Nothing. The firefighters are working to put out the hot spots. The investigators have begun to search for the fire's ignition point and for bodies, but it will take time. Perhaps days. The press is already here." He nodded in the direction of the shed. "Hound dogs, each and every one of them."

"In the meantime, what can I do?"

"You've done a great deal already by taking care of Miss Storset. Thank you for getting her to agree to go to town. She needs some rest."

"Thank you for making sure she's protected. Do you believe Ray Lamphere is the culprit?"

"I've sent one of my men to the Wheatbrook farm to arrest him. Yesterday, after his court hearing, he was spitting mad. So angry that he threatened to burn Mrs. Gunness's place down around her ears. Everyone heard. That's enough proof for me that he was involved. That and the previous fire at Miss Storset's shop."

Nils agreed. What more could he do? His brains were scrambled from lack of sleep and a gash on his head.

For the rest of the morning, he wandered the grounds. With everything inside of him, he longed to pick up the shovel and dig in the hogpen, but he held himself back. There would be time. Time to convince the sheriff to do it the right way. Now the authorities needed to focus on finding out what happened to Belle and the children and to make sure that whoever was responsible for this crime, whether Ray or someone else, was brought to justice.

The trouble was, he couldn't shake the feeling that Belle herself had ignited the fire for some reason. Perhaps because he was getting too close to the truth. To save herself the trouble of having charges brought against her. Why, though, take the children with her?

He wandered toward the barn where the sheriff was. All appeared as it should be. Belle's buggy and her horses were all there. So was the cow. The sheriff was searching the shelves in the tack room. "Ah, Mr. Lindherud. I didn't realize you were still here."

"I can't stay and not do anything. Put me to work. Let me help."

"Fine. You can assist the recovery crew. Be sure to follow their instructions so evidence isn't lost or disturbed."

"Thank you." Once he had his directions, he pulled on a pair of heavy-duty gloves one of the firefighters loaned him and got to work. Of course, there was debris to sift through, but not too much left that was recognizable. The cookstove was partially melted. Forks, knives, and spoons had fused together. The wooden furniture was mostly reduced to ashes.

The day dragged on. Nils's shoulders and back ached. His parched throat burned from the lingering smoke. He coughed from the vast amount of dust and ash in the air.

At last, all that remained to excavate was the basement. The day was wearing on. Buckets and wheelbarrows full of debris had been removed. Among the items discovered were two kerosene cans. Had they been used to ignite the fire? The marshal had stated at one point that the blaze began beneath the stairwell where Belle kept the kerosene.

Along with the other searchers, Nils methodically made his way through the basement until he at last reached the far southwest corner. There was the spinet piano that had fallen to the basement when the floor above collapsed, the keys blackened, the wood charred, the pedals melted. He hollered for a few others to help him move it.

Once they did, the sounds of voices around him disappeared.

Everything in his peripheral vision dimmed. He forgot to breathe. There were three skeletons, the flesh burned off them. The largest of them was missing the skull. Though he glanced around, he couldn't locate it. He turned around and retched, emptying his stomach of its few contents.

He wiped his mouth with his filthy sleeve. Turned back toward the task.

The largest skeleton lay on top of a scorched patchwork quilt. Nils lifted the quilt.

Underneath, clutching a little toy engine, was Phillip's body.

Chapter Twenty-Nine

At the banging on the door, Ingrid bolted upright in bed. Where was she? What was going on? Then the hotel room with its cherry bureau, its violet-sprigged wash pitcher and bowl, its gauzy curtains came into focus. Not much light filtered through the curtains anymore. How late was it? She hadn't intended to rest for so long. The sleeping powders the doctor prescribed must have done a better job than she anticipated.

The banging continued. With a glance in the mirror and a quick smoothing of her disheveled hair and dressing gown, she went to open it. Nils stood on the threshold, clean though the odor of smoke emanated from him. His mouth was turned down, his eyes dull.

They must have found something. And it wasn't good.

"I trust you got some sleep?"

She swallowed against the rising lump in her throat. "Please, don't pussyfoot around the subject. Just give me the news."

"I wish there was a private place we could go, but we don't have a chaperone."

She grasped the doorjamb and leaned against it, as if that would brace her for whatever was to come. "I'm ready for whatever you have to say."

"After you left, it took the firefighters some time to extinguish the flames. Most of the day, there were hot spots they had to contend with. All but one wall of the house collapsed. As soon as was possible, they began their recovery efforts. There was a great deal of brick and debris to sift through. Nothing of any consequence was found until we reached the basement. I searched the last corner of it."

"And?" The word stuck in her vocal cords, the clamoring of her heart so loud it almost drowned out his words. Her palms dampened.

"In that corner, I discovered the children's bodies and that of a woman. I'm so sorry."

Though she had been prepared, though she relied on the doorway to hold her up, the words hit her with an almost physical force. Unable to draw breath into her lungs, she staggered backward until she knocked into the bed and fell upon it. She curled into a ball and released her pent-up sobs.

Her family, wiped out by the unconscionable actions of one man. Why did he have to do it? Was one dollar worth it? Was revenge on Belle for rejecting Ray worth it? Surely the police would arrest him now. He would hang for his crimes.

Those poor, poor children, their lives cut short. None of them would ever finish school. None of them would ever marry or have children. None of them would ever grow old.

Could it be just last night they were laughing and playing and enjoying each other's company? How fast life changed. The biggest concern for the girls was going away to school. Never did any of them imagine what fate lay mere hours away.

Other than Jennie, Ingrid was utterly alone in America, nowhere to live, no money to her name, no one to love.

And then Nils touched her back and rubbed it in small circles. He didn't stop until her weeping had run its course and she couldn't squeeze another tear from her eyes. Once her crying quieted, he handed her a snowy-white handkerchief.

When she sat up, a single tear trickled down her cheek. Nils wiped it away, his touch soft and gentle and soothing, like a warm cup of tea on a cold winter's day. She glanced over his shoulder. The door to her room stood open. How like him to always be a gentleman.

He stroked her cheek. "I'm so sorry. I wish I didn't have to bring you this news."

"I knew it. In my heart, from the very first minute, I knew they were gone. My consolation is that they are in heaven with Jesus. They are happy and whole. Right now, glory is ringing with their laughter."

"But that doesn't ease the ache in your heart."

"I suppose that will always be there. I don't know. All I'm trying to do is hang on to that thin strand of hope. Remind myself that they are free from pain and worry." She clung to it with her entire being. If she let go, she would tumble into an abyss so deep, she would never climb out.

"You have a beautiful way of putting it. God is our only anchor in a time of storm."

"Tell me."

He leaned backward, his eyes large. "Tell you what?"

"How you, you found them." Right now, pictures flashed in front of her eyes of the children screaming, Belle in a panic, their lives ending.

"Are you sure you want to hear this? It's not pleasant."

"What is going through my mind isn't pleasant. Perhaps you can grant me a measure of peace if you tell me about them. You said they were in the basement?" Though she could now speak, her tears continued to flow. Would they ever cease?

"Yes, in the far corner."

"Why were they there?"

"From the looks of it, they must have fled there to escape the flames. All of them were badly burned, but little Phillip was wrapped in a blanket. I discovered them huddled there together."

"She was trying to protect them." Her sister, loving her children to the bitter end. The waterfall of tears cascading down her cheeks intensified.

She had to go. Had to be near them. Though their connection in this life was severed, she might find a measure of comfort by being in their presence. "Take me to them." She wiped the moisture from her face with the borrowed handkerchief.

"I don't think you want to go."

"Why not?"

"You don't want to see them." He shuddered.

"I won't. I don't want to. I'll remember them as they were last night—full of life and laughter. But I need to be at the place where they died. Just to be near my family one last time."

"Mr. Cutler was to arrive soon after I left. They are probably at the morgue. The farm is crawling with reporters from LaPorte, South Bend, and Michigan City, among others. At least half a dozen by my accounting. You don't want to be in the middle of their circus. If they find out you are Belle's sister, they will hound you." He sighed and finger-combed his light brown hair. "There is more."

His words were heavy and ominous. She hugged herself, as if that could ward off everything horrific. "What?"

"Belle's skull hasn't been found."

Ray sat at the dining room table in the Wheatbrook farmhouse. Everyone else was gone. Had been all morning. Though he didn't know for sure where they were, he had a pretty good hunch. Since no one was around, he afforded himself the luxury of eating at the large walnut table with its high-shine polish.

He shoved the chicken sandwich into his mouth, watching through Mrs. Wheatbrook's lace curtains out the window. Just beyond the stand of trees that shaded the yard in the summer's heat, the road snaked by, connecting the Wheatbrooks with the outside world.

Siree, it wouldn't be long now. Not long at all. Soon the sheriff and probably a couple of his deputies would drive up the lane and knock on the door. He knew it as sure as he knew his own name. Good thing he'd had the sense all those months ago to shove that bone he'd found down the outhouse. He'd wrapped it in so much burlap, it had been hard to fit. With all the talk about men missing, he did what he had to do. At least the sheriff wouldn't find it in his possession. Or Belle's.

He heaped a pile of potato salad on his plate and gobbled down four or five bites, chasing it with a cup of hot coffee loaded with cream and sugar. He needed to enjoy such delights as much as he could. Soon they would disappear. Would he ever be served such a meal again?

Just as he munched on his third chocolate chip cookie, a car puttered down the road. They were here.

Ray steeled himself, placed his dishes in the sink, and marched to the front door. The sheriff wasn't one of the men. Just two deputies. Marr and Antiss. He'd had enough run-ins with the law to know their names.

Before they could knock, Ray flung open the door. He didn't wait for them to open their mouths before expressing the question burning on his tongue since the wee hours of the morning. "Did that woman and those children get out?"

Marr tugged on the bill of his hat. "How did you know about the fire?"

"Why don't you come in?" He held the door open and stepped out of the way. Marr and Antiss entered. He led them to the parlor where they all settled. "You see, it's like this. I wasn't at home last night. Spent it elsewhere, you might say. Got up about three in the morning to make a six-mile hike back here in time for chores. Had to take the road by the Gunness farm. As I went by, I noticed smoke coming out of the windows and around the roof."

Marr sat up straighter. "Why didn't you yell? Telephone the fire department? Try to help?"

Ray leaned forward and sniffed. Why hadn't he helped? Belle Gunness got what she deserved. Too bad about them kids, though. He shrugged. "I didn't think it was any of my business."

Marr shot to his feet, along with Antiss. Marr grabbed Ray by the arms and twisted them behind his back, clicking handcuffs around his wrists.

Antiss read him his rights. "Ray Lamphere, you are under arrest for arson and for the murders of Belle Gunness, Myrtle Sorenson, Lucy Sorenson, and Phillip Gunness. You have the right to remain silent." Antiss droned on and on, but Ray quit listening.

He had to pretend like the words didn't affect him, but they stabbed him in the middle of his chest. Belle was gone. His love and his enemy. And those little kids. They deserved better than they got. Especially with such a mother. He would swing for their murders. The sheriff, probably the entire town, had already decided his fate. No matter what he said, they believed him to be guilty.

Marr and Antiss shoved him into the sheriff's Runabout. With tires churning up dirt and flinging mud, they sped from the farm. Not long after, they screeched to a halt in front of the sheriff's office. Ray wasn't stupid. A good sweating awaited him. With little fanfare, the deputies ushered him into the interrogation room where Sheriff Smutzer and another man stood.

The sheriff eyed Ray, then gestured toward the stranger. "This is State's Attorney Smith. He'll be questioning you along with the rest of us."

Four to one. The odds were stacked against him. Well, he would stand his ground. Act casual. Not give them what they wanted.

Marr pushed him into a chair and moseyed to the other side of the table. "You want to tell the sheriff and the state's attorney what you told us?"

Almost word for word, he recounted the story he'd told the deputies.

Smutzer sat back in his chair. "And where were you coming from that you had to make a six-mile trek in the middle of the night?"

"I stayed the night with Old Liz."

Four mouths gaped open at his confession. So what if she was in her seventies and as wrinkled as a prune? She gave him a room and some food. A place to stay warm. And an alibi.

"She woke me at about three, and I set off for the Wheatbrook place. Saw the smoke when I went by."

The state's attorney shook his head. "Why didn't you do anything at that point? You could have tried to help them. You could have called for the fire department."

" 'Cause of exactly this. I was afraid I'd be blamed for the fire. You'd drag me in here and sweat me out until I made some kind of confession so you could wipe your hands and be done with me. Well, you can question me all you want, hound me and badger me, but you're never gonna get me to confess."

"Oh, we have our ways, Lamphere." A small smile lifted one side of Smutzer's mouth. "You'll sing before you swing."

Ray sprang to his feet, but Marr pushed him down. "You won't ever have a confession from me, because I have nothing to confess."

He may have been half in love and half in hate with Belle Gunness, and he was certainly glad she was gone, but he hadn't started the fire.

He did have a pretty good idea who had, though.

Chapter Thirty

Wednesday,
April 29, 1908

A thick fog hung heavy over the Gunness farm, cloaking the burned-out house in its mist. The morning sun had yet to rise high enough to melt it away.

Even though the cock had just crowed, already the farm teemed with reporters from as far away as Chicago, Indianapolis, and Detroit, men Nils had met at the hotel the night before. Word had made it out that Belle's skull was missing. The sensational headline sent the media flocking to this quiet piece of the Midwest.

Nils held Ingrid by the hand, giving it a light squeeze. "Are you sure you want to be here?"

Though dark circles rimmed her eyes and her face was gray, she nodded. "I need to be. No one has to know who I am."

"This has to be immensely difficult." She shouldn't be here. Especially with what he had in mind to accomplish today.

"How could he do it?" Her voice was hoarse from smoke inhalation.

"You've asked that before."

"And I still don't have an answer."

"Sometimes when you're dealing with people who are insane, you might never get an answer."

She turned to him and shook her head, her hair tucked under a black straw hat with a wide black ribbon and a black feather. "You're supposed to be comforting me, remember?"

He gave a half smile. "Sorry." Then he sobered. "I can't tell you what you want to hear, because I don't know. I wish I could say something that would bring relief from your sorrow." How well he knew that sometimes you couldn't stop the pain. You simply had to walk through it.

Today was going to be a difficult day. For both of them.

"I'm sure you don't want to be in the barn with the media."

"No. Absolutely not. This is not an event I want to photograph for the paper." She hugged the blanket she was carrying to her chest. "There's a stump over there in the trees." She pointed to the other side of the hole in the ground that used to be a home. "I'll plant myself there. That way, I'm close enough to the goings-on to stay informed but far enough away that no one will bother me. I hope."

Together, hand in hand, they strolled there. He helped her get settled then kissed her on the forehead. "Are you sure you're going to be all right?"

She nodded. "I'm just not sure what all right is going to look like."

"I understand. If I hear anything, I'll let you know. Come find me if you need anything."

She gazed at him with a stare that penetrated to his very soul. Vulnerable. Open. Loving. Could it be that she reciprocated his feelings? That she loved him as much as he loved her?

"Thank you, Nils, for everything. I couldn't do this without you."

Though she sat on the stump, small and frail against the backdrop of the tall pine trees, and he longed to gather her close and take away her pain, he left her there. He had a very unpleasant job to do.

The sheriff's office was already on scene, combing the property for clues as to who started the fire and what had happened to Belle. They scurried to and fro, busy with their investigation, mobbed by the reporters, not paying much attention to the handful of curiosity seekers who were trickling onto the farm.

Nils's perfect opportunity.

He slunk to the barn. In the far, cobweb-laced corner, covered in mud halfway up the handle, was a shovel. His hands shook just a little bit as he took hold of it. He tried without success to swallow.

Someone had used this shovel to bury something. Now to find out what it was.

He exited to the hogpen. Despite all the commotion surrounding them, the hogs rooted in the mud. A couple of the piglets chased each other, squealing. The large mother lay on her side, snoozing. He'd have to be sure to stay far away from her and her babies. He'd heard that sows could be very protective of their young.

Princess trotted to his side. He'd have to keep an eye on her too.

Someone had filled in the place where he'd dug before, but he hadn't forgotten where it was. He located the spot without trouble, the dirt and mud still soft. Despite the early-morning chill, he slipped off his jacket and rolled up his sleeves.

Locking his jaw, he set to work. One, two, three shovelfuls. He lost count. When he rested, Princess kept up with the digging. Finally, the edge of his shovel hit something. Not anything hard. Soft. His breath whooshed from his lungs.

Princess whimpered and whined. She jumped around and circled the hole.

Nils snapped his fingers. "Stop it. That's enough." He rarely had to scold her, but she wouldn't settle down.

He willed his weak knees to hold him upright. Not wanting to draw attention to what he was doing by calling for the sheriff, he instead carried his shovel to where Smutzer spoke with a deputy.

"Excuse me."

"Lindherud. What is it you want?" The sheriff scowled.

"You need to see this. I think I've found something."

Smutzer peered at the shovel in Nils's hands. "Have you been digging again?"

"Sir, I'm convinced that Mrs. Gunness was up to no good in the hogpen. And now I've discovered the evidence. With or without you, I'm going to continue digging. It's your choice whether or not you want to be there."

Smutzer huffed. "Fine. But I have another investigation I'm conducting."

"I believe the two are connected."

Smutzer and his deputy followed Nils to the hogpen. He pointed out the hole he had dug. "I've hit something. Let's see what it is." He gripped the shovel so hard, he thought his hands might fuse to it. He might never be able to let go. What would he find in the hole? Would what was in here provide the answers he'd been searching for since December?

He continued digging, enlarging the hole until it exposed a burlap bag.

Together, Nils, Smutzer, and Marr hefted the bag from the ground. The burlap had partially rotted. Princess tore at the sack until Nils pulled her away.

He stepped back, trembling from head to toe, his stomach flipping in his belly. He forced himself to breathe.

Smutzer ripped away the burlap.

Inside were a man's mummified remains.

The facial features left no doubt.

This was Sven's body.

From her perch atop the tree stump, Ingrid observed the activity taking place around Belle's farm. Photographers swarmed the place like ants at a picnic. All around the property, they had set up their cameras and were busy taking shots of the basement where the bodies of her loved ones had been found. Others snapped photos of the barn and the shed, even the trees where she sat.

When they did that, she hunched down so her face didn't show. So far, no one had bothered her.

Where had Nils gone? Since this torturous affair had begun, he'd been her rock. The only one she had to turn to. And someday soon, he would return to Detroit. Her windpipe narrowed. She drew in a ragged breath.

No, Lord, that's not true. I have You. What was that verse I read months ago about being a father to the fatherless? That's what I need You to be for me now. Other than Jennie, I have no one. No one but You. You are sufficient. I'm going to lean on You, Father, and trust that You will uphold me in Your everlasting arms. Help me to remember I'm not truly alone. Be ever near me. Be my guide and stay.

Her breathing eased. No matter what, no matter who died or who forsook her, God never would. Though by outward appearances she was alone, that wasn't true. God was holding her hand. Very much like Nils had before. When he went home, she would still have Jesus. That was enough.

Even so, her heart had been shattered into a thousand shards, each one stabbing her chest with white-hot pain. She had to remember Belle, Myrtle, Lucy, and Phillip were in heaven. They would never feel a pain like hers again. Over and over, she had to bring this truth to mind. If she didn't, she would go crazy.

The fog had cleared but the overcast hadn't. A deep gloom covered the scene, heavy, low-hanging clouds that refused to unleash their load.

She scanned the farmyard once more. There was Nils, in the hogpen with Sheriff Smutzer and his deputy. They pulled something from a hole. If it took three of them to lift the item, it must be heavy. Was it a bag? Perhaps a burlap bag? Belle had buried her garbage in bags like that.

The sheriff ripped it open.

Nils stumbled backward. Nodded. Dropped to his hands and knees.

He needed her. At this point, it didn't matter if the media found out who she was. He needed her. She rose from the stump, gathered up her skirts, and on painful feet raced across the farm to the hogpen.

She caught a glimpse of what was in the bag.

A body.

A man's dismembered body.

Unable to bear the sight a moment longer, she turned away, gagging. Crouching beside Nils, she tried to focus on him. Whispered in his ear. "Who is it?"

"Sven."

His pronouncement robbed her of all speech. She wrapped him in an awkward embrace, holding him fast, supporting his trembling body, hers quivering in time with his.

Several tears fell from his face and dampened her own cheeks. "I thought I was prepared. All this time, I knew he was here, but I didn't know where. I believed that knowing would set me free of this burden I've been carrying. That knowing would ease my grief over the loss of my brother."

"But it hasn't."

"No, no. It has made it worse. Did you see him? Did you see what condition he was in?" Nils half shouted the words.

"Yes." She allowed her tears to flow.

"How could she? She not only killed him and buried him, she also butchered him just like her hogs."

Ingrid's stomach churned. Though the admittance cost her everything, she could no longer deny the fact that her sister was a monster. The woman she had loved her entire life was evil personified.

Like Nils, she could only question why Belle would commit such a despicable act. "Was he a believer?"

He turned to her, his eyes watering, shimmering blue. "Yes. From the time he was little, he loved Jesus."

"Then right now, he's walking the streets of gold with Myrtle and Lucy and Phillip." She could no longer imagine that Belle was with the Lord. "That's all that's been keeping me upright the past thirty-six hours."

"There's another soft spot over here," Sheriff Smutzer called from a place a short distance away. By this time, a light drizzle added to the misery. Faces of those fascinated by the macabre pressed against the hastily erected wire fence.

The sheriff and his deputies dug in that location. Not three feet down, they ceased their digging. Yanked another gunnysack from the ground. When they opened it, the sight sent Ingrid's stomach whirling. She released her hold on Nils and raced to the far corner of the hogpen, where she was sick.

Would she ever be able to erase the horror she had just witnessed? Body parts. That was all that was in there. Just parts. She couldn't even think about the rest. Would never allow her mind to go there again.

By now, the discovery had caused quite a commotion. The deputies struggled to push back the press. To keep them from the grisly scene. Nils staggered to his feet and stumbled toward the new hole. Moments later, he found Ingrid where she sat in the mud and muck, the rain dampening her clothes until she was soaked through and shivering.

She stared at him. "When is this horror going to end?"

Several times, he opened and closed his mouth. Like her, he had no words. "I'm afraid it's just beginning."

"What do you mean?" How could it get worse?

"There are several bodies in there. Impossible to say exactly how many. At least one woman. And one adolescent girl."

"Adolescent?" What was he talking about? Not only his brother and others, but a woman and a child? What had Belle been up to?

"She had long blond hair. With a blue bow."

She covered her mouth with her mud-caked hand. It couldn't be. She hyperventilated. Not Jennie. Please, not Jennie.

Chapter Thirty-One

Not Jennie. Not Sven. Not all the others.

Ingrid's stomach churned. How could Belle have done it? How could she have killed her own daughter? What kind of monster was she?

Bile rose in her throat. Nils held her as she emptied her stomach yet again, offering his handkerchief for her to wipe her face. She gazed at him, his wide eyes wild, almost seeing right through her. "You were right. All this time you tried to tell me, tried to warn me about my sister. But you were right. I should have believed you. If I had, maybe Jennie wouldn't be. . ." She couldn't bring herself to finish the sentence.

Was that what Jennie had wanted to speak to her about that day so long ago? No, not all that long ago. If only Ingrid had listened. Had insisted that Jennie tell her right there and then. The poor child was frightened. Perhaps she had even stumbled upon what her mother was doing. "That was it."

"What was?" Nils's voice was soft against her ear.

"Jennie. She tried to tell me what she'd found out about Belle. She knew what her mother was up to. Why didn't I push her harder? Why didn't I make sure she told me that very night? Belle knew Jennie wanted to speak to me and probably had a pretty good idea of what she wanted to say."

Ingrid sat up and wiped away a strand of hair with her muddy hand. "After I left, my sister killed her daughter. If I had listened, all of them might be alive today."

Nils pulled her close, so close he must be able to feel the pounding of her heart. "You can't blame yourself. You had no idea what Jennie wanted to tell you. You still don't. She might have wanted to tell you about that young man she was sweet on. Perhaps they had made plans. Or maybe he was about to break her heart. Or the other way around. You don't know."

"I'll never know." The sobs welled from deep inside her, spilling over into a primal cry, refusing to stop. From time to time in the background, shouts permeated her haze. Shouts that more bodies had been exhumed. She shivered, unable to control her entire body's twitching. Cold. So cold.

As gentle as any father, Nils lifted her from the ground. She snuggled close to him, like a babe in arms. He rubbed her arm, warming her. Jostling her very little, he carried her away from the hogpen, now littered with open gashes, past the burned-out home, to his waiting automobile. He wrapped her in a blanket, set her on the seat, and after cranking the motor car to a start, climbed in. Princess snuggled on her lap.

"Where are we going?" Not that she cared. She just had to get away, as far away from this place as possible. Even as they turned onto McClung Road and threaded through traffic on their way toward LaPorte, she didn't gaze back. That was too much like Lot's wife. She would never return to Sodom and Gomorrah, a place of such evil and a place now destroyed.

While Nils held to the steering wheel with one hand, he drew her close with the other, tucking her in beside him. "I'm taking you to town. I'll have the maid draw you a warm bath and then assist you."

She peered at him, lines etching his face around his mouth and eyes. She had been so wrapped up in her problems, but he was mourning too. Their grief fresh and raw and unbearable. "How are you holding up? To find your brother the way you did. . ." Again her windpipe threatened to close.

"Belle stole so much from both of us." His voice cracked. He swallowed hard. How was he managing to keep his composure? "I need to tell my mother, but I don't want to do it over the telephone, where she has to go someplace public to speak to me. And I don't want to do it in a letter, when she's reading it alone with no one there to support her. With all the goings-on, I hadn't given it much thought, but I suppose I need to return to Detroit right away and break the news to her."

"Will she be all right? What about her heart condition?"

"Pray that she'll be able to handle it."

"Take me with you. Away from this madness, this insanity." She grasped his upper arm and squeezed. At last, a course of action. A way to escape this misery. "Please, don't leave me here for the media circus to consume me. I have to get away to mourn in private. There is nothing left for me here."

For the longest while, he didn't answer. Had she been too forward? Perhaps he had wanted to leave alone. To forget about everything and everyone here. Including her.

If possible, her heart broke even more at the thought. She had no one left in the world. She could return to the rest of her family in Norway, the brothers and sisters she had remaining, but she had no money to cross the Atlantic once more. Truth be told, she loved Nils and couldn't imagine her life without him. For a while now, she had wanted nothing more than to build a life with him.

He remained in stony silence. That was not how he felt. She withdrew from his embrace, drawing the blanket closer around herself, the chill wind blowing straight through her. The shivering returned. Though he reached for her, she backed away, swiping at fresh tears that streamed down her wind-burned cheeks. Princess licked her face.

The trees whirred by, blurred by the speed of the automobile and by her tears. When she had first arrived here with Belle and her family, she had loved this place. The vastness of the land, the greenness of it, the promise of it.

Now it was nothing more than a place of terror and tragedy. A land of desolation.

A place she desperately had to escape. If not with Nils, then another way.

When Ingrid slid away from Nils on the seat, a knife-like pain stabbed him in the heart. What he had to say to her couldn't be said while they bumped down the rutted lane toward LaPorte. At last, as tears cascaded down her cheeks, he located a farm lane where he could pull off. He prayed they wouldn't get stuck in the mud.

"Ingrid, look at me."

She shook her head and swiped at the moisture on her cheeks.

"Ingrid, please." He scooted closer to her, little by little, until their shoulders brushed. "I can't say what I need to say when you won't look at me."

"I know what you're going to tell me, and I don't want to hear it. Please, take me back to the hotel and let me figure out my life."

"No, I don't think you know what I'm about to declare."

"Declare?" At last, she gazed at him with her tear-glazed eyes shimmering green in the fading daylight.

"Yes, declare. This may not be the time. In fact, I know it's not the time. We're both reeling from unimaginable losses, you even more than me. A muddy farm lane on the edge of LaPorte is really not the place. But I understand what you're feeling. Alone."

She gave an almost imperceptible nod of her head. Good. He had read her right.

"Though I still have my mother, and I thank God for her, she's all I have."

"All of my memories of my sister are ruined."

"I'm sure." How horrific for her. How could she remember the good times now that she knew what had been going on underneath her nose? At least his memories of his brother brought him a measure of relief and comfort.

"I have no one to share what I'm going through, to walk this road with me. Just me and the Lord."

"That's where you're wrong. You aren't alone."

"Who is there? For a moment, I dared to believe that I still had Jennie, that she and I could sustain each other. But she's gone too. Belle stole everyone from me. Everyone." She sucked in an unsteady breath. "In a way, because she insisted so strongly and sent the money for me to come to America, she also stole my Norwegian family."

"What she did was unspeakable. Unfathomable. But she didn't take everyone. I'm still here."

"You're going to Detroit, back to your mother. There is nothing left for you in LaPorte. You may never return. I've valued our friendship more than you can know, but it seems that it has come to an end. I always knew it would." Her last words faltered.

Emotion welled in him also. "There is something, someone, left for me here."

She raised a blond eyebrow in question.

"You. Haven't you been able to see it? Have I been that opaque? You have become quite dear to me."

"That's what makes parting all the more difficult."

Oh, he was going about this all wrong. "What I meant to say was—"

What if she didn't feel the same way about him? What if she didn't share his sentiments? How humiliating. She had labeled their relationship as friendship. Then again, to not say anything, to go home to Detroit and wonder for the rest of his life what might have been, would be worse than any humiliation he could suffer. He cleared his throat. "You have me, Ingrid. You have me. My heart, my soul, my all. Just like God, I will never leave you nor forsake you. I want, for as long as God gives me strength and breath, to be your family."

Her weeping ceased. She hiccupped a few times, all the while staring at him. She pulled out his borrowed handkerchief and wiped her nose. "Your family?" Her voice was deep and husky.

"Yes, your family."

"Because you feel sorry for me?"

"No, absolutely not. This has nothing to do with our shared grief or with what has happened to you, though those events have brought me to see the kind of woman you are. Strong. Able to withstand whatever life brings. Caring. Thoughtful. In the middle of your terrible suffering, you thought of me. You are the kind of woman I want by my side for the rest of my life."

"Are you proposing?"

"Maybe not formally, not right now. I don't have a job or any means to provide for myself and my mother, much less a, well. . ." Heat bloomed in his face. He had no way to support a family and didn't know when or how he would be able to. Right now, he had to trust the Lord to provide. A calm filled him.

"When I propose, I want it to be at the right time and in the right place. For now, I need you to know that you aren't going to endure your suffering alone." He reached out and grasped her hand, clinging to her as if clinging to life itself. "We're in this together. The two of us and God. Is that a deal you can accept?"

Though no smile crossed her lips, she nodded with more vigor this time. "Yes, Nils, yes. Not because you are all I have left, though I love you for wanting to be with me during this trial, but because you are a man of integrity. You don't give up and you don't give in. I'm a better person because you walked into my life. I thank God every day for you driving into our town. Your coming here and being so persistent with your beliefs, so persistent in your dealings with the sheriff, may have saved more lives. Who knows what else Belle had planned?"

"Thank you for that. I had been feeling helpless, like I hadn't done enough to discourage my brother from coming here. If I had pushed my case harder, perhaps the other men who showed up at the house after Sven might have lived."

"What's important is that she's been stopped. For once and for all. My sister will never hurt another living soul." Again she broke down. This time, she allowed him to embrace her, to hold her. She burrowed into the crook of his neck, her tears dampening his shirt collar.

The road ahead of them would be long and bumpy. There was no doubt about that. Having her to ride along with him, though, would make it all bearable. "We'll come out on the other side. You'll see. God will heal us. It will just take time. Together, we are stronger than we are when we are separate. I love you, Ingrid Storset."

Chapter Thirty-Two

Detroit, Michigan
Saturday, May 9, 1908

A light spring rain pattered the roof above the bedroom. Ingrid shifted in the rocking chair that she had pulled up to Mrs. Lindherud's bed. "I'm glad to see you sitting up today."

The older woman, her gray hair in a neat, long braid, gave a wan smile. "I cannot thank you enough, my dear, for your tender care these past few days. Even with all that is happening in your life, that you would take time for me speaks volumes about your character. I believe my son has picked a fine young woman."

"Though I wish it were under better circumstances, I've enjoyed getting to know you." And Ingrid had. Nils's mother was a kind, gentle woman, much like her son. The news of Sven's death had hit her hard and sent her to her bed, but the doctor Nils had called said she would recover.

They all would, in time, though the scars Belle left would linger forever.

"You are a resilient young woman."

The all-too-familiar sting of tears burned the back of Ingrid's throat. She fought against them. "I don't feel strong. Anything but. If not for Nils, if not for you. . ."

Mrs. Lindherud patted Ingrid's hand. "Tears don't make you weak. God gave us tears to cleanse us and to heal us. I've done enough crying of my own in the months since my dear Sven left. And in the past few days, since I've learned of his death." Her own eyes, the same shade of blue as her son's, filled with moisture. "What makes us strong is our faith. Paul says that we can do all things through Christ who gives us strength. That's who we must cling to in such trying circumstances. All other ground is sinking sand."

Nils's mother's words brought to mind the hymn. Ingrid hummed the tune, trying to remember the words. They came at her in a rush.

"Sing it, dear. Please sing it."

Ingrid studied her hands and picked at a hangnail. "I don't like to sing in front of people."

"No need to be shy around me. Remember, Christ gives you the strength. I can tell from your humming that you have a beautiful voice."

"Only if you sing with me."

Mrs. Lindherud nodded. Together, they sang the words, such a balm to the soul.

My hope is built on nothing less
Than Jesus' blood and righteousness.
I dare not trust the sweetest frame,
But wholly lean on Jesus' name.

On Christ the solid rock I stand,
All other ground is sinking sand,
All other ground is sinking sand.

When darkness veils His lovely face,
I rest on His unchanging grace.
In every high and stormy gale
My anchor holds within the veil.

On Christ the solid rock I stand,
All other ground is sinking sand,
All other ground is sinking sand.

His oath, His covenant, His blood
Support me in the whelming flood.
When all around my soul gives way
He then is all my hope and stay.

On Christ the solid rock I stand,

All other ground is sinking sand,
All other ground is sinking sand.

Tears streamed down both women's faces as the last echoes of the hymn filled the room. *When all around my soul gives way, He then is all my hope and stay.* Ingrid had an anchor. She had a Father. The best, most faithful, most unchangeable Father there ever was. Belle failed Ingrid, many times over. But her Father never would. If she placed her hope in Him, not a wishful hope but a sure hope, she would never be alone.

Mrs. Lindherud squeezed Ingrid's hand. "Thank you, my dear. I needed that reminder."

"No, I must thank you. I see your courage and strength in this unthinkable time, and knowing where that courage comes from gives me hope that someday I can have that too."

"This has not been the first difficult or trying time in my life. Perhaps, if the Lord calls me home soon, it will be my last. So don't wait to draw on that courage. We aren't promised tomorrow. Think of those whose lives have been cut short, who thought they had another day and perhaps another one after that. We all must cling to God's promises today."

Today. Yes. She had hidden in the shadows too long, afraid of everything. But she didn't have to be. Not with a God who was all her hope and stay. *Lord, please grant me the courage and strength I need so much right now. Support me in this whelming flood, in this stormy gale. I'm trusting, trusting, trusting in You and in You alone. Be near to me and uphold me. Grant me the strength and courage I need to face whatever lies ahead.*

"That was beautiful, Mama."

Ingrid gazed upward. Nils approached his mother's bedside and took hold of her other hand. "How long have you been there?" Had he heard her sing?

"When I heard the music, I couldn't resist. Your voices were beautiful, but the words were even more stirring. I've trusted in many things over the years. Sven's death and the manner of it have ripped the foundation from underneath me. My family is everything. And that starts with God, my Father." He leaned over and kissed his mother's forehead.

Such a peace flooded Ingrid's soul. Her tears dried. Yes, there would be difficult days, times of weeping, moments of heartache ahead, but she had so much. So, so much.

She nodded at the newspaper in Nils's hand. "What's that?"

He hid it behind his back. "Nothing. I forgot I was even holding it."

She stood, her mouth going dry. "If it's nothing, you won't mind my reading it."

"It's nothing you need to see, Ingrid. Really. I don't want you to suffer any more."

"Please. I promise, I'm going to be fine." She made sure her words were strong and confident.

Nils hemmed and hawed for a while longer but finally handed the paper to her. The *New York Times*, dated May 7, just two days earlier. Belle's story was splashed across the front page, along with four theories about the fire and the woman's headless body. A shiver raced along Ingrid's spine.

The four hypotheses included one that Belle killed her children and herself by setting fire to the house to conceal the crimes. The second stated that she was afraid of being exposed, so she killed her children, put the headless corpse of another woman in the house, and set the house on fire while she fled. Another was that Ray killed them all and set the fire. The last was that a gang from Chicago that Belle may have been involved with came and committed the heinous deeds.

Ingrid dropped the paper. Belle might still be alive? How could that be? If she killed all those people they were digging up in the hogpen, including Jennie, and had likely smashed Nils over the head, perhaps even set fire to Ingrid's place, who knew what she might have done?

Nils crossed to her side of the bed and touched her shoulder. "Are you all right?"

"Yes." Her voice croaked, and she cleared her throat. "Yes. All that matters to me is that the children are dead. There is no doubt about that. As far as my sister is concerned, if she is alive, I pray God will touch her heart and she will turn herself in to pay for her crimes."

As she said the words, she straightened in her chair. She had never been so strong in her entire life.

Sunday, May 10, 1908

Nils and Ingrid strolled hand in hand through the streets of Detroit. Tucked inside of his, her hand was small and soft, even with the chemicals she used to develop her pictures. Not an unpleasant sensation at all.

The May sunshine warmed their backs, and they spoke of a number of topics, anything and everything that came into their minds. In all the time he'd known her, Ingrid had never been so relaxed. Perhaps her relationship with Belle had been more of a strain on her than she had realized. Out from under Belle's tyranny, Ingrid was free to truly be herself.

Ole Budsburg's sons had identified his body. One of the searchers had discovered Henry Gurholdt's watch in the rubble, along with Olaf Lindbloom's. Those families now knew what had happened to their loved ones. How many others would never know?

In Sven's personal belongings, Nils had discovered a letter. Even now, in his mind's eye, he could see the words on the page.

Dear Nils,

As we go our separate ways, please don't be upset with me. This is my choice for my life. I hope you can accept it as such. I'm going of my own free will and my own accord. I'm not leaving to get away from you. Just the opposite. Leaving you and Mama is the hardest part of this affair. I have enjoyed working for you and learning from you. You are the best brother any man could ask for. Perhaps you and Mama will consider coming to LaPorte to open a dealership there. I can only hope. I will miss you tremendously. Please come visit soon.

Your devoted brother,
Sven

Just knowing that Sven didn't leave because Nils drove him away was a relief. He could rest easy knowing they had parted on good terms, that

Sven had loved him. He held tight to the peace that letter afforded him.

Together Nils and Ingrid turned the corner from the quiet, tree-lined residential area to a busy road where both automobiles and horses and buggies jockeyed for position. Pedestrians crowded the sidewalks, while boys on bicycles wove in and out among the shoppers and businessmen.

Up ahead came a familiar sight. A low-slung brick building with large plate-glass windows overlooking the street. The dealership. He hadn't been back since he'd turned it over to Gillespie.

"Hey, don't squeeze so hard." Ingrid batted at his arm, a grin across her face.

He released his grasp. "Sorry. I didn't realize I was hurting you."

"You didn't. Just cut off the circulation to my fingers." Again her words were light and playful.

"It's just that. . ."

She nodded ahead. "Is that the dealership? Your mother told me it was nearby."

"Yes, that's it."

"Can we look? Or would you rather not go anywhere near it?"

He sighed. "I suppose we can peek in the window. You can get a glimpse of what my life used to be like."

"Belle stole that from you too, didn't she?"

"No. It was my own foolishness that caused me to lose the business. If I had saved more money before buying it, had worked a little longer learning the business, I could have made a go of it, I'm sure."

"That's the answer."

"What?" He scrunched his eyebrows as he stared through the window, automobiles shining in the showroom.

"I'm Belle's only surviving relative." She swallowed hard. "That money she had from all those men is mine, but I don't want it. You should take it. Buy the business back. With the incredible suffering you have endured, it should go to you. Some I will give to the families of the people the authorities can identify. The rest is yours."

He stiffened. He couldn't take her money. Didn't want to have anything to do with cash so tainted with blood. "Why don't you want it?"

She turned her attention to a shop farther down the street, away from him. "Because of how she got it."

"That's exactly why I can't take it. I won't have anything to do with money that cost people their lives. Pay the other families, the ones the authorities can identify. I'll take what my brother brought. Beyond that, if you truly don't want it, donate it to a charity."

She turned toward him. "You're right. Yes, that is a wonderful idea. Good can come from the evil Belle did. But what will you do?"

"You had a good thought. I can get a job with another dealer. I know most of them in the city. I'm sure one of them will hire me. When the time is right, when I'm more financially stable, I'll purchase my own dealership once more. I may not be able to provide the lifestyle we had before, but that was unsustainable."

"None of that matters, you know."

"I know." He rubbed the top of her hand. "What matters is that I have Mama and I have you." He winked, and her fair cheeks pinked. My, she was beautiful.

"Let's keep walking." She tugged him along. They came to a park and found a bench where they could sit and watch the children play in the soft grass.

"I do need to speak to you about a more serious matter." If only he didn't have to go and ruin what so far had been a perfectly wonderful day.

She pulled away a little.

"I've been contacted by several news outlets wanting an interview with me. They've been inquiring about you too, wondering if you would speak with them. I think I know what your answer is going to be, but I wanted to ask you about it first."

"Yes."

He leaned away and stared at her. "Did I hear right?"

"You did." A little of the color drained from her face, but she lifted her chin. "I will speak to the reporters. There may be questions I won't care to answer, but I will give them enough to satiate them."

"You do know that the farm has become like a circus. Thousands of people take picnic lunches out there daily, waiting to see what the authorities will dig up that day. I'm sorry for being crass, but that's what's going on there."

"I don't want to return to LaPorte. Ever. That place holds too many awful memories for me. Perhaps all I'll have to do is give an interview to the paper here in Detroit. The other papers can reprint the article."

"Are you sure about this?" What a completely different woman from the retiring little thing he'd first encountered. Ingrid was still shy but exuded so much more confidence.

"I'm sure. I can do this. I know I can. It may not be my favorite activity, but I will get through it. Especially if you're there with me."

"I wouldn't be anywhere else. What did I do to deserve you?"

Her smile faltered. "Your mother has been sharing with me how good can come out of evil situations. What my sister did to your family and countless others like yours is unspeakable. The most horrible crime in the world. But there is good. Some good. The children are at peace in heaven. And I met you. If not for her, if not for your brother, we wouldn't have each other. While it's terrible to contemplate, it's true."

"Sven would be happy for us."

"I wish I could have gotten to know him."

"At least you got to meet him."

"He seemed like he was a wonderful person."

"That he was. He'll be greatly missed. When we get married, and if God blesses us with children, would you mind naming a son Sven?"

Her eyes glistened in the dying daylight. "Only if we can name the girls Lucy and Myrtle."

"It's a deal." The best deal of his life.

Chapter Thirty-Three

Upstairs, in the bedroom Mrs. Lindherud had fixed for Ingrid, she fussed with her hair and straightened her pink-striped day gown about a thousand times. Peering into the mirror over the dresser, she pinched her pale cheeks to bring some color into them. A little bit better, but not much.

Murmurs from downstairs floated up and sent shivers through Ingrid's midsection. A pool of reporters waited for her in the Lindherud parlor. Men from Detroit, LaPorte, South Bend, even Chicago and New York. Though she steeled her spine, she could do nothing to halt the quivering of her hands.

A tap on the door. "Can I come in?"

Nils. Her trembling lessened. "Yes."

"Are you ready?" He had trimmed his beard into a neat point and slicked back his hair. The handsomest man in the world.

"I think so."

"I know you are." He crossed the room and planted a kiss on her cheek. "You're going to be just fine. Remember, God will be on one side of you, and I'll be on the other."

"I couldn't do this without the two of you."

"Then it's a good thing you have us."

"Will you pray with me before I go down?"

He nodded. "That's an excellent idea." They bowed their heads. "Dear Father, we ask that You be with Ingrid now as she speaks to these reporters. Give her a calm and a peace that come only from You. Hold her fast. Grant her the words to speak. Be ever near her. We ask this in Your name. Amen."

"Amen." Ingrid straightened, drew in a deep breath, and nodded. "I'm ready."

Together, they proceeded down the steps to the neat little room decorated with wallpaper bursting with flowers, a simple red settee, and a polished coffee table bearing a vase with three red roses. Ingrid had bought them, one for each of the children. Nils had pushed a few kitchen chairs into a semicircle on the edges of the room. In the middle of that circle were two chairs. One for her. The other must be for Nils.

They took their places. Before Ingrid could open her mouth, the reporters, dressed in suit coats and ties, fired questions at her so fast, she didn't even catch most of them.

Nils motioned for the newspapermen to stop. They quieted.

One reporter with a handlebar mustache shouted from the back. "Did you help your sister plan her getaway?"

Ingrid swallowed her gasp. Was this what their questions would be like? If so, she had to leave. Now.

As if sensing her desire to flee, Nils touched her knee. "Gentlemen, please. One question at a time. And please be respectful of Miss Storset and the ordeal she has been through. You may ask a question, but she is under no obligation to answer it."

Thank You, Lord, for Nils. "I'll answer that question, Mr. Lindherud." She turned her attention from the man beside her to the men gathered in front of her. "I am not sure if my sister is alive or not. From what the coroner told me, the size of the woman's body found at the home is too small to be my sister. If she is alive, I had nothing to do with her escape, and I have no idea where she is."

"But you escaped that house when no one else did."

"That is true, but only by the grace of God." Ingrid explained the night of the fire, step by step, in detail, pulling out every English word she knew. Everything she knew, everything she had told the sheriff. By the time she finished, she could no longer sit ramrod straight but slumped in her chair. "That is it, all I can tell you."

"Did you see any warning signs? Know that anything suspicious was going on in the house?"

"Looking back, knowing what I know now, maybe there were clues. At the time, I never thought my own sister could do such horrible things."

The questions continued to flow. Inquiries about Belle's childhood in Norway and her life in the States, about her children, about her husbands, about Ingrid's involvement in the crimes, about Ray Lamphere. The entire time, Nils clasped her by the hand, his strength, God's strength, flowing into her.

At last, she'd had enough. The reporters were repeating questions, just using different wording. She couldn't answer any more. Couldn't explain any better than she already had. She'd given them the information they were seeking. "Thank you, sirs, for coming today. That will be all. Please do not contact me or anyone I know."

She dared a glance at Nils, then gazed over the crowd once more. "I will have nothing to say after today. What is done is done. The sheriff will find out if my sister is alive or not and who set fire to the house. I plan to live the rest of my life in peace."

To another set of rapid-fire questions, Ingrid stood, Nils coming to his feet alongside her. He released her, and she strode toward the kitchen. While he dismissed the reporters, she slumped into a chair at the kitchen table.

Mrs. Lindherud bustled over. "Oh, my dear, you handled yourself with such grace. You were wonderful. Now, though, you look tuckered out. How about a cup of tea? When they've gone, you can go upstairs for a nap."

"Thank you. That sounds heavenly."

No sooner had Mrs. Lindherud placed the fragrant, steaming cup of tea in front of her than Nils entered the room. He came to Ingrid and hugged her shoulders, giving her a squeeze. "You were marvelous. Well done. Are you sure you don't want to make a career of this?" He pulled out the chair beside her and sat.

"Absolutely positive. Perhaps I will take photographs that will be printed in a newspaper, photographs of birthday parties and happy events, but I never want to be on the receiving end of their questions again."

"And you won't be." Nils sipped the tea his mother brought him. "That's the end of that. We can mourn our losses in private and move forward with our lives. Together."

Together. What a beautiful word. Never alone. A cord of three that could never be broken.

But not yet. "There's one more thing I have to do."

Monday, May 18, 1908

Ray pushed away the tray the jailhouse warden had brought. The Salisbury steak was cold, the gravy over it congealed. The mashed potatoes were as lumpy as the mattress on the cell's narrow bed. How long would it be before he would get out of this miserable hole and get back to his life, such as it was? Such as it would be without Belle.

He coughed, and bright red blood covered his handkerchief. That had been happening quite a bit lately. Looked like he already knew his fate.

He reclined on the hard bed and picked up the Bible the pastor had brought him when he visited the other day. He'd told Ray to start reading in the book of John, so that's what he was doing. Even with all this spare time, he was only on chapter 3. What with not being the best reader, trying to absorb all the book was saying was hard.

The passage about being born again was giving him trouble. That was strange. Like Nicodemus said, you couldn't be born twice. That wasn't possible.

Sure, Ray had heard all his life about Jesus. Knew about His miracles and how He died on the cross. Knew about Jonah and the whale and Noah and the ark. All that stuff. But this was new. Different. Unusual. This stuff didn't make sense. Well, he'd keep reading, and maybe it would come together.

Following with his finger, he read the confusing words that came after the story about Nicodemus. None of the chapter made any sense. Then he came across verse 36. *"He that believeth on the Son hath everlasting life: and he that believeth not the Son shall not see life; but the wrath of God abideth on him."*

That made a little bit of sense. According to the Bible, if you believed in Jesus, you went to heaven. If you didn't, you went to hell. That was pretty clear. But how did you get there? Whether he would hang for killing Belle and her children or this suspected tuberculosis took him first, he was going to come to the end of his life sooner rather than later.

Hell scared him. But how did you avoid it? Just by believing? That couldn't be possible.

"Lamphere, you have a couple of guests."

He stuck the ribbon in the passage and shut the Bible. "Yeah, who?"

"You'll never guess."

He wasn't up to playing games with the guards. "Guess I won't."

"Miss Storset and Mr. Lindherud."

Not them. Please, not them. They would accuse him of setting the fire. Ingrid would be furious about him killing her family. Except that he didn't do it. Would she believe him? He had to convince her of it. "I'll see them."

The deputy took him from his basement cell and led him upstairs to the dark interrogation room. If only he could gaze on the light of day. By this time in late May, the weather should be fine. Oh, for a little sunshine.

Ingrid and Nils were already seated at the table by the time he entered. They studied him as he made his way around and took the chair across from them. "What do you want?" Might as well cut to the heart of the matter.

Ingrid stared at her hands as she twisted her handkerchief between her fingers. Not Belle's work-worn hands. Soft hands. Ones that hadn't butchered pigs or mucked stalls. "I needed to talk to you in person. I never wanted to come back to LaPorte. This is the hardest thing I've ever done." Her eyes watered, but her voice was strong. Gone was the stuttering girl. "What can you tell me about the night of the fire?"

Figured she'd want to know that. He leaned across the table. "Listen, I loved your sister. Wanted to marry her, but she wouldn't have it. I wouldn't do anything to hurt her or those little ones. They were innocent. They didn't deserve to be caught up in this whole mess."

"You're telling me that when you worked for Belle, you never saw what she did?"

Ray shook his head. "When your brother disappeared—and I'm real sorry about that, Mr. Lindherud—she sent me on a wild-goose chase to South Bend. Something about getting horses, but they weren't there when I arrived. She always made sure I wasn't around when they disappeared. And I never snooped to see if I could find out anything else. Well, except for the time I found his brother's coat in her wardrobe." And that bone he'd shoved down the outhouse. He'd heard they found it, but they had no idea he was the one who had stuffed it there.

Ingrid bit her lip. "Do you think she is alive?"

"That's not for me to say. She didn't tell me anything. If you remember, I was getting fined for trespassing. I certainly wasn't in her confidence then."

Ingrid nodded. "That makes sense. I believe you. One thing bothers me, though. When you say you saw smoke at the house but kept on walking, why didn't you stop? You said it was none of your business, but you knew Belle and the children were sleeping in there. If you loved her and you didn't set it, why didn't you help?"

"Look where I am. Does this seem like fun and games? It's not. This is serious stuff. I'm going to be charged with four counts of murder. Murders I didn't commit, I swear. I was scared they would pin the fire on me, and sure enough, that's what they've done."

"Can you blame them?" The red in Nils's face deepened. "After what you did to Miss Storset, you've proven to be a violent man."

"I didn't want her hurt. Just wanted to scare her enough that Belle would pay attention to me."

"And couldn't that be why you set the Gunness house ablaze too?" Nils's voice rose in pitch.

Ingrid stepped in. "You might have stopped their deaths." For a moment, she stared at the scarred tabletop. "For whatever you've done, I forgive you. I will pray for you, Mr. Lamphere, that God will touch your soul. I will also pray for truth and justice."

Long after his two visitors left, Ray pondered Ingrid's last words to him. She was going to pray that God would touch his soul. He flipped open his Bible and went back to earlier in the chapter, starting with verse 15. *"That whosoever believeth in him should not perish, but have eternal life. For God so loved the world, that he gave his only begotten Son, that whosoever believeth in him should not perish, but have everlasting life."*

Wow, it said it twice, right in a row. All you had to do was believe. Was it too late? With all the stuff Ray had done in his life, he wasn't getting to heaven on his own. But if all he had to do was believe. . .

With a prayer to heaven for salvation, he did.

Chapter Thirty-Four

Thanksgiving Day,
November 26, 1908, 7:20 p.m.

As the jury of twelve men strode into the courtroom, Ingrid couldn't stop the jiggling of her leg. She twisted her handkerchief into a tight knot. Nils rubbed her shoulder. His ministrations did little to calm her. What had those men, over the course of twenty-six hours of deliberation, decided about Ray? Had he killed Belle and the children? Had he set fire to the house?

The trial had stretched from November 9 until this point, an agonizing three and a half weeks. At times, the prosecution was on top, befuddling the defense's witnesses, drawing strong testimony from theirs. At other times, the defense was doing a brilliant job, tearing apart the accounts of the state's witnesses and experts. She leaned to whisper in Nils's ear. "I don't know what's going to happen. I have no idea which way they're going to rule."

"We'll know in a very short time." He nodded as the jury foreman handed a slip of folded paper to the bailiff, who passed it to Judge Richter, a man who very much resembled President Roosevelt minus the mustache and the glasses.

He entered the verdict in the docket then cleared his throat. "We find the defendant guilty of arson."

Having been warned by Judge Richter that any emotional outbursts would not be tolerated, Ingrid bit back her gasp and clasped her hands tighter in her lap to keep them from shaking. Arson, but not murder. How could that be? If he set the fire, he killed them. If he didn't kill them, he didn't set the fire.

Judge Richter dismissed the jury. "Mr. Lamphere, please rise."

Ray obeyed the order. From her vantage point across the room from his lawyers, Ingrid had a clear view of their ashen faces. They had truly believed the jury would acquit Ray. Perhaps they should have.

"Do you have any reasons to state why sentence should not be pronounced upon you?" Judge Richter stared right at Ray.

He gazed at the floor. "I have nothing to say at this time."

"Then I sentence you to an indeterminate term of two to twenty-one years, fine you five thousand dollars, and disenfranchise you for five years. Officers, please escort the prisoner back to the county jail."

With a strike of Judge Richter's gavel, the trial ended.

Nils spirited Ingrid away before the press had any chance to mob her. They slid into his automobile and set off straightaway for Detroit, despite the late hour and the fact that it was a holiday. For that, she would be forever grateful to him.

She turned to Nils. "What do you think?"

In the dim light of the car's lamps, he bit his lip. "To me, the verdict makes no sense. Why guilty of arson but not murder?"

"My thoughts exactly. You know, the jury asked the judge twice for information, which he declined to give them. I wonder if they were deadlocked and this verdict was a compromise."

Nils kept his attention on the road in front of them. "You may be right about that. Just like the crimes, just like the trial, the verdict is crazy, not really a conclusion at all. A hundred years from now, my guess is that they will still be speculating about this case and what the truth really is."

"At least it's over." Ingrid sighed. "We can put this chapter of our lives behind us, though what happened in this past year will always be with us. The time has come to set our faces toward the future." Over the months since the fire, she had tried living in the past, but it didn't ease her pain or heal her wounds. Forever, she would remember Jennie, Myrtle, Lucy, and Phillip with a great deal of fondness. Jennie and Myrtle would be especially excited about her relationship with Nils, giddy over the thought that he might propose any day.

She smiled, their lilting laughter echoing in her head. Yes, there would be moments of pain for the rest of her life. There would also be moments of joy, happiness, and contentment.

God alone knew the truth of what took place at the farm on April 28.

That would have to be enough.

Friday, December 25, 1908

Nils offered Ingrid his elbow as they stepped from the house, soft snow-flakes drifting on the very slight breeze. What a perfect evening for what he had planned.

"What a perfect day." Ingrid sighed.

Almost as if she had read his mind. If it was like this now, what would it be like in twenty, thirty, forty years? Wonderful. Amazing. Beyond belief.

Who would have guessed that God would have orchestrated events this way? There was a great deal of sadness in their story, but there was also a great deal of joy.

"I believe that was the best Christmas I ever had."

"Truly? It was just the three of us, like every other day."

"Truly. Except maybe for that last night I spent with Belle and the children. I'm choosing to cherish that memory, cling to those good feelings, and forget what came afterward. I'm choosing to remember the children's excitement over their toys and the fun we had playing games. Even that last time I tucked them into bed and kissed them good night."

"I'm glad you can look back on that with fondness."

"Your mother outdid herself. The ham dinner was delicious, and I don't believe I've ever had a better cherry pie. She was so sweet too, to give me that little locket for a gift. All I need is to take a photograph of you so I can put it in there."

"You don't miss the confectionary?"

"Not at all. That was Belle's dream, not mine. Yes, I like to bake and create delicious candies, but I don't care for selling them to the public. I may not be as shy as I once was, but that doesn't mean I'm not happier in the darkroom."

"So long as you come out every now and again to spend a little time with me." He glanced at Ingrid, her cheeks glowing with the cold, a few flakes resting on her fine lashes. Not even the Christmas tree with all its candles lit was more beautiful than her.

"And thank you for the lovely pearl earrings. I shall cherish them always."

"That isn't everything I have for you in the way of a gift."

She turned to him, her mouth in a small O. Perhaps she knew it was coming. Now that he had procured a job with another Ford dealership in the city, he could do this properly. At the edge of Cadillac Square, under the dim glow of a streetlight, Nils pulled her to a stop. "Are you ready?"

She nodded, the lights dancing in her eyes.

He reached into the pocket of his wool coat and pulled out the box. Then he dropped to one knee. "Ingrid Paulsdatter Storset, you are the love of my life."

"I love you too, Nils."

"I never thought I would say this to you, but would you please not interrupt me?" He grinned, and she chuckled in return.

"Go ahead."

Okay, so this wasn't going to be a surprise for her. The least he could do was make it memorable. "As I was saying, you are the love of my life. Before you came into it, I didn't realize how much I needed you. I never want to let you go. Will you please be my wife from now until death do us part?"

"Yes." The shine of her face outdid all of the Christmas trees in all of the city. "From now until death do us part."

He rose and swooped her into his arms, kissing her all over her face. "I love you, Ingrid."

"I love you, Nils. Think of all we have to look forward to. A life full of joy and laughter and God's blessings. And children." She smiled at him and stroked his cheek. "So many riches, even in the hard times. Because you, Nils, are worth more to me than all the gold in the world."

Historical Notes

The railway station I describe as being in LaPorte burned down in 1907 and wasn't rebuilt until later in 1908. However, I really needed a train station, so I exercised creative license and had it still standing.

Edgar M. Botchkiss was the stationmaster of a now-extinct town in the LaPorte area, Alida Station, in the 1870s. Since I couldn't find the name of the stationmaster of LaPorte, and the Botchkiss name was too good to pass up, I used it.

Ray Lamphere, Sheriff Smutzer, Deputies Antiss and Marr, Belle Gunness, Jennie Olsen, Myrtle and Lucy Sorenson, Mads Sorenson, Peter Gunness, and Phillip Gunness are all historical people. Belle (born Brynhild Paulsdatter Storset on November 11, 1859, in Selbu, Norway) came to the United States in 1881. She was actually the youngest of eight children. For the purposes of this book, I thought of her more as the oldest of the children with Ingrid being the happy surprise eighth child.

Belle married Mads Sorenson in March 1884 in Chicago. She was much loved in the community and known for her care for children, often volunteering to take care of those who needed a home. Among them was Jennie Olson. She came into Belle's custody while her mother was dying and her father was unable to care for her. The dying mother bequeathed Jennie to Belle. After Jennie's father remarried, he tried to regain custody of his daughter but was denied by the courts.

Four children joined Mads and Belle between 1896 and 1898: Caroline, Myrtle, Axel, and Lucy. It is doubtful that any of them were Belle's biological children. I haven't been able to locate birth certificates for any of the children. Caroline and Axel died in infancy.

Mads died on July 30, 1900, on the only day his two life insurance policies overlapped.

Somewhere between July 1900 and April 1902, Belle moved to LaPorte, Indiana, and purchased a forty-eight-acre farm. This was enough to attract Peter Gunness, a widower, who married Belle in April 1902. Five days later, his infant daughter died. Only eight months into the marriage, Peter Gunness was dead from a blow to the head. The story I tell in the book is the one Belle gave the authorities. Everyone knew Belle had murdered him but no one could prove it. She was never charged.

Phillip Gunness came into the family a few months after Peter Gunness's death. Again, no birth certificate exists for Phillip, and it is unclear if he was Belle's biological child.

Peter had another daughter from his first marriage, Swanhild Christine. Soon after Peter died, her uncle collected her and raised her. She is the only child to survive living with Belle. She married and has surviving descendants.

Ole Budsburg, John Moe, Henry Gurholdt, and Olaf Lindbloom were among Belle's many victims.

The Lindherud family are all fictional characters, though Sven and Nils are based on Andrew and Alse Helgelien. Andrew, a Norwegian immigrant who hailed from Aberdeen, South Dakota, answered Belle's advertisement in a Scandinavian newspaper. They corresponded over the course of many months. Though only Belle's letters to Andrew survive, we can surmise the relationship through them. As the months went by and Andrew put Belle off time and time again, she became increasingly firm with him, almost ordering him to come to LaPorte. She told him not to tell anyone and to arrive with his money sewn into his coat so it wouldn't be stolen.

In January 1908, Andrew gave in and made the trip. He was last seen with Belle Gunness at a bank in LaPorte. Fortunately, he told his brother, Alse, where he was heading. As time marched on and Alse had no word from his brother, he became alarmed, finally making the trip to LaPorte.

Authorities on Belle Gunness believe that, with his impending arrival, Belle grew concerned her crimes would be discovered. This may have led her to poison her children and set fire to the house. Poison was discovered in the bodies of some of her victims. It is believed that she gave them strychnine in their dinners, then butchered them and buried them in the hogpen. One skull was found in the outhouse.

Alse dug up the first body, that of his brother, Andrew, on May 5, 1908.

Alse was married and has many living descendants.

Ray Lamphere was Belle's farmhand. He had intentions of marrying her, but when Andrew arrived, his services weren't needed. Belle fired Ray in February 1908. For purposes of the book, I have her firing him in the early fall of 1907.

Emil Greening was one of Belle's farmhands, and it is rumored that he and Jennie had eyes for each other. When Jennie disappeared in 1906, Belle told everyone who asked that her daughter had gone to a finishing school or some kind of Lutheran college in Los Angeles. No one seemed to question it. Jennie's body was one of the first pulled from the hogpen. She was identified because of her long blond hair. Emil Greening left Belle's employ soon after Jennie's disappearance. Shortly thereafter, he moved to New Mexico with his family. He married and had two children.

Belle did try, without success, to have Ray declared insane. When that failed, she began filing trespassing charges against him because he continued to snoop around the property, even after she fired him. One case was settled with a five-dollar fine. The two did go to court on the day before the fire, where Ray was again found guilty of trespassing. This time he was ordered to pay a one-dollar fine. Belle was furious. In a heated argument, Ray threatened to burn her house down around her ears.

Belle did buy the children new toys the night before the fire. Her farmhand, Joe Maxon, who escaped the blaze in much the way I describe Ingrid escaping, shared with authorities the dinner they had that night, which is as I tell it. In the days prior to the fire, she received a couple of heavy trunks from Chicago. To this day, no one knows what was inside them, though speculation runs rampant.

According to Joe, they also played Little Red Riding Hood and the Fox after dinner. He went to bed at eight o'clock, but the rest of the family stayed up much later.

The bodies were found exactly as I have described them, with the exception of Phillip clutching a toy train. The coroner's reports of them are gruesome.

When Ray was arrested by Deputies Marr and Antiss, his first question was, "Did that woman and those children get out?" He had been with Old Liz (I have called her that, though in fact she was popularly known by a racial slur) the night of the fire and had seen smoke coming from the Gunness home on his way to the Wheatbrook farm. He didn't report it for fear he would be implicated in setting it.

He was convicted of arson on Thanksgiving Day 1908, but acquitted of murder. It is believed that the jury couldn't come to a decision on his guilt or innocence, so they opted to convict him of the lesser crime. His sentence, which is what I include in the story, didn't make any difference. He died on December 30, 1908, of tuberculosis.

Belle's sister Nellie lived in Illinois. She had been estranged from Belle for about eight years prior to the fire. She and her son and daughter came to LaPorte to identify the bodies, then promptly left and never returned. All four bodies were buried in Forest Home Cemetery in Forest Park (Chicago), Illinois. Nellie was Belle's only heir, but neither she nor her five grown children wanted her money. They attempted to donate it to a Norwegian orphanage, but they too turned down the money.

What is my theory on what happened to Belle? After extensive reading and research, I believe that Belle poisoned the children and set fire to the house out of fear of her deeds being discovered. I cannot come to a conclusion as to whether Belle survived the fire or not. That is one part of the story that will be shrouded in mystery forever.

Acknowledgments

As with any book, this one was not written without the support and contribution of many. First of all, I owe a great debt to the LaPorte County Historical Society Museum in LaPorte, Indiana. Their exhibit on Belle Gunness is extensive, and I drew heavily on it. To see some of the pictures I took while there, please visit www.truecolorscrime.com and click on *The Gold Digger*. Thank you to everyone who works there, who explained Belle to me, who pulled resources for me, and who took the time to explain to me that LaPorte is a wonderful city with many citizens who have done good for the world.

Thank you to Harold Schechter, author of *Hell's Princess*, one of my primary sources for this book. Though I didn't get to meet you in person when I was in LaPorte, your exceptional research and compelling account were a great help to me.

Thank you to Steve and Muriel for putting me up for the night when I visited LaPorte. I love you both, and seeing you was a wonderful bonus to coming to Indiana to research the story.

To my crit partners, Diana, Jen, and Jenny. You all rock. Thank you for helping me to mold the story into something people will want to read. The same goes for Ellen Tarver. Without your eagle eye, poor Nils would have both blue and green eyes! I love working with you. Your kind words spur me on.

Thank you to Becky Germany, Shalyn Sattler, Liesl Davenport, and the entire Barbour Publishing team. You are the best to work with. You and all your hard work are much appreciated. Thank you for your faith in me.

My amazing agent, Tamela Hancock Murray, thank you for all you do. You knew I could write romantic suspense before I knew I could.

Thank you for believing in me and nudging me to stretch and grow. You are a gift to me.

I say this with every book I write, but my family is tops. My husband, Doug, you are the greatest. Thank you for giving me the time to write, taking care of Jonalyn, even taking parent duty alone for a weekend so I could go do some research. Without your support, this wouldn't be possible. Brian, Alyssa, and Jonalyn, my fabulous kids, thank you for being you. You have a crazy mother, but you love me anyway. What mom could ask for more? I love you all.

Above all, thank You, Lord, for the multitude of blessings in my life. Each and every one comes from You. Soli Deo Gloria.

Liz Tolsma is a popular speaker and an editor and the owner of the Write Direction Editing. An almost-native Wisconsinite, she resides in a quiet corner of the state with her husband and their two daughters. Her son proudly serves as a US Marine. They adopted all of their children internationally, and one has special needs. When Liz gets a few spare minutes, she enjoys reading, relaxing on the front porch, walking, working in her large perennial garden, and camping with her family.

True Colors. True Crime.

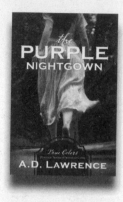

The Purple Nightgown (March 2021)
by A.D. Lawrence

Marvel at true but forgotten history when patients check into Linda Hazzard's Washington state spa in 1912 and soon become victim of her twisted greed.

Heiress Stella Burke is plagued by insincere suitors and nonstop headaches. Exhausting all other medical aides for her migraines, Stella reads *Fasting for the Cure of Disease* by Linda Hazzard and determines to go to the spa the author runs. Stella's chauffer and long-time friend, Henry Clayton, is reluctant to leave her at the spa. Something doesn't feel right to him, still Stella submits herself into Linda Hazzard's care. Stella soon learns the spa has a dark side and Linda a mean streak. But when Stella has had enough, all ways to leave are suddenly blocked. Will Stella become a walking skeleton like many of the other patients or succumb to a worse fate?

Paperback / 978-1-64352-892-2 / $12.99